TANGLE

'Perhaps father will go
other men have done,' Eleanor suggested hopefully. 'They say small shops like ours are finished now the factories have all the machinery to make men's woollen stockings in big quantities.'

'No, no,' Amy was despairingly sure this would not be so. 'He'll start in that old shop again, and I shall have to be here with him all day long. After all, he gets my labour free.' Amy covered her mouth as if to hide the expression of dread from her daughter.

Eleanor slipped her arm around her mother's waist. 'I'm older now, I'll be able to help you.' She gasped in surprise as her mother pushed her violently away.

'No, don't you interfere! Do nothing and say nothing, understand?' Amy's face was pale and almost wild-looking.

Eleanor nodded, but the rejection hurt.

'Don't you worry,' Amy's smile was rueful and her voice more normal as she went on, 'it'll just be a bootlace job, that's all.'

'A bootlace job?' Eleanor had no idea what her mother meant.

'When I'm really down, I tell myself I have to make more effort, heave myself up with my own bootlaces!'

Tangled Dynasty

Jean Chapman

Hamlyn Paperbacks

A Hamlyn Paperback
Published by Arrow Books Limited
17–21 Conway Street, London W1P 6JD

A division of the Hutchinson Publishing Group

London Melbourne Sydney Auckland
Johannesburg and agencies throughout
the world

First published 1984

Typeset in VIP Bembo by
D. P. Media Limited, Hitchin, Hertfordshire

Made and printed in Breat Britain
by Anchor Brendon Limited, Tiptree, Essex

ISBN 0 09 933830 0

For my beloved parents,
Albert and Elsie Clowes of Countesthorpe,
Leicestershire,
my own country boy and city girl.

How creeps the past upon the present,
its long dead fingers
tangling the future

1

It was the dawn of the first winter frost when Eleanor came downstairs to find her mother leaning over the shallow brownstone sink, staring out of the kitchen window. She looked over her mother's shoulder to see a great crow sitting on the nearest ice-bloomed post of the clothes-line. Amy did not turn her eyes from the black carrion, and Eleanor thought she looked pale and sickly.

'Your father will soon be home from the war,' Amy said quietly. 'It's a sign.' Then she caught her breath as a second crow came slapping its wind-tattered feathers, squabbling and cawing as it tried to land on the same post. 'Two bad omens coming to roost in the same house!'

'You surely can't believe all that superstitious old nonsense, mother. Anyway, I thought another crow meant the first didn't count!'. Then Eleanor was silent, shivering in the ice-cold kitchen, as she too fearfully anticipated the return of her father to the house. She had read of the spontaneous demonstrations of joy in the big cities when, at the eleventh hour of the eleventh month of 1918, hostilities had ceased. Many families in their small village were planning parties and hanging out red, white and blue bunting to welcome their menfolk back. Eleanor thought it would be more appropriate if they hung black crêpe outside their cottage.

She had not forgotten the nights she had crouched on her bed fearfully listening as her father threatened, and her mother pleaded to be left alone, begging him to keep his voice down. She remembered the unexplained noises, the sudden thumps and worse, the evil-feeling, near-silences, when alternately she thrust her head beneath her pillow or, holding her breath, listened until she was so chilled she had to creep beneath her blankets once more. On mornings when her mother could not hide her bruised face, she prayed harder than ever before in her young life, prayed that he would die – even though she feared holy retribution.

When conscription had finally caught her father and many other men in its net in 1916, the women and young boys of the village had stepped into their roles overnight. The work-load had been heavy before, and there had never been a village boy who declared he had nothing to do in the hearing of an adult, for he was immediately found a task – chopping wood or collecting horse manure for the garden. As the everyday tasks were taken up by this new work-force, yokes carved to fit far broader shoulders had their chains shortened, to ensure that the buckets of water cleared the ground as they were carried from the village pump.

Necessity was a rapid teacher, and women and boys quickly learned to tend the precious vegetable plots and to increase the odds of a 'hundred to one shot' of a piece of meat on their plates by snaring an occasional rabbit. They ate large suet dumplings before their dinners to stem appetites; they tied and dragged their kindling from the fields; and they harvested and gleaned every last berry, mushroom, blue-stalk, hazel-nut and grain from the fields, hills and spinneys within walking distance of their Midlands village.

Eleanor had not cared what extra work, or extra privation, she had had to undertake or suffer, if it meant her father was kept away from home.

'Perhaps your father will have changed, after all the fighting,' Amy said, breaking into her thoughts.

'Let's go, mother, before he comes, please!'

'Where?' For a moment, fleeting panic caught her unawares, then she remembered her role. 'No, I'm being silly!' She opened her arms and clasped her daughter, rocking her reassuringly, trying to laugh away their fears. 'We'll be all right. All things mellow as they get older, perhaps even your father.'

'Why did you marry him?' Eleanor asked as they stood in each other's arms. The question brought a stillness as Amy seemed to cast her mind back a long, long way.

Her arms fell from Eleanor's waist and she went over to pull out the drawer in the middle of the scrubbed pine table. From under an exercise book of recipes and household tips, she drew out an envelope in which had come a rare letter, and a snapshot, of her husband. Eleanor moved closer and saw her father in the uniform of the Durham Light Infantry, and begrudgingly she had to admit that in his cap with the bugle-shaped badge, khaki jacket, breeches and puttees, he looked smart, striking even. His skin was fine and showed his black moustache to advantage, but Eleanor hated the arrogant way he stood, with one booted foot slightly thrown forward as if demanding all the attention and, as she remembered him, he always had done just that. Her heart plummeted as her mother took the photograph and propped it before a jug on the kitchen dresser. She was already making preparations for her husband's return. He would expect his photograph to be on show.

'He was a handsome man . . . still is of course,' Amy went on as she stood looking at his picture. 'It was nice to be seen out with him. He liked his own way even then, and we had to be married. Anyway . . .' Amy went on hastily, 'his people had been blacksmiths for generations and he had this cottage with the workshop behind, as well as the knitting machines. Reuben Lewis was considered a good catch.'

Eleanor wondered whether he might have been a different man if he too had had an anvil to beat, to work at until the sweat streamed down his huge torso. Even though he had been away nearly three years, and there was an age of growing-up between fourteen and seventeen, she could remember the feeling of frustrated energy, the air of barely controlled impatience about her father, as he had worked over the loom, making the broad woollen cloth for men's underwear, or turning out men's half-hose on circular knitting machines.

The two older men who had worked for Reuben before the war had found jobs in city factories. Eleanor had felt they had been glad to get away from the Lewis yard and its morose master. She could remember her own astonishment when she had first visited another stockinger's shop in the village and found it alive with talk, leg-pulling, political haranguing, and with time to stop the clattering shuttles to praise the little girl who had come with a message from one master stockinger to another. In her father's shop there had never been more than the odd muttered comment or cursory order. Her message given, she was found an apple by one of the men, which he had polished on his shirt sleeve before handing it to her.

'Pity she's a Lewis.' She had stopped outside, the bright apple poised on her teeth ready to take the first bite, and listened. 'Old Laxton, the sexton, reckons he's seen three Lewis women buried who still had black eyes as a parting gift from their menfolk.' Suddenly she had not wanted his apple, which moments before her mouth had been watering for. She had thrown it away.

'Perhaps father will go into town to work, like the other men have done,' she suggested hopefully. 'They say small shops like ours are finished now the factories have all the machinery to make men's woollen stockings in big quantities.'

'No, no,' Amy was despairingly sure this would not be so, and continued as if talking to herself, shaking her head faster and faster. 'No, I know. He'll start in that old shop again, and I shall have to be here with him all day long, toeing the socks he makes, making up the vests and things. After all, he gets my labour free. All the time – except when he's away selling round the villages, all the time . . . he'll . . .' Amy plucked up the ends of her long white apron and covered her mouth as if to hide the expression of dread from her daughter, 'be here.'

Eleanor slipped her arm around her mother's waist. 'I'm older now, I'll be able to help you.' She gasped in surprise as her mother pushed her violently away.

'No, don't you interfere! Do nothing and say nothing, understand?' Amy's face was pale and almost wild-looking as she repeated, 'Understand?'

Eleanor nodded, but the rejection hurt.

'Don't you worry,' Amy's smile was rueful and her voice more normal as she went on, 'it'll just be a bootlace job, that's all.'

'A bootlace job?' Eleanor had no idea what her mother meant.

'When I'm really down, I tell myself I have to make more effort, heave myself up with my own bootlaces!'

The two came together again, arms around waists, secure at least in the knowledge of mutual support. But when her father arrived home later that night, Eleanor instinctively looked out of the kitchen window. There was just one crow flapping lazily around looking for scraps and, as she watched, it settled on the post and seemed to regard her with a baleful eye.

Reuben Lewis looked almost debonair when he first returned home, and if there had been any contentment in his mind he would have been handsome. The women tried, but their greetings neither fooled nor disturbed him, as he ran his eyes over them and his home before throwing down his kit and going off to The Hunters for his ale.

'You look like two damfool songbirds put back into their cages,' he snarled, mocking their discomfiture, and went laughing to his evening with the men.

'Why is he so?' Eleanor demanded. 'Why should he take pleasure in humiliating everyone?'

'I only know his father beat him almost daily,' Amy said woodenly, 'or so Clarrie Sansome's mother once told me.'

Eleanor worked at the village hosiery factory with Clarrie, and the Sansomes not only lived in the same yard as the Lewis's, sharing path, pump and privy, but were authorities on village gossip throughout the generations, having grandparents and one great-grandparent still alive. She decided to ask Clarrie about the long-dead, Lewis ancestors.

'Oh, yes,' Clarrie confirmed, pushing aside a batch of government-grey army socks they had examined and repaired. 'My mother says you never went by the Lewis's but someone was getting a belting, and the same with his father, always being knocked across the blacksmith's shop he was.'

'Then my father should know enough not to do it to others,' Eleanor said grimly. 'He really should know better.'

'He's started has he?' Clarrie nodded with a wisdom far outstripping her sixteen years. 'My mother wondered how long it would be.'

Eleanor did not answer because she was not sure. 'She's not very well, my mother, coughing and shivering.'

'Hope she's not got this flu,' Clarrie said. 'Then her voice dropped with some embarrassment. 'My mother said I was to tell you . . . that if ever your Dad tried to . . . touch you, you was to run across to our house.'

'He never has,' Eleanor said, and was surprised both by the offer, and the realization that her father never had raised his hand to her.

'Well, if he does ever try anything,' Clarrie closed her lips on the subject with a superior kind of worldliness that would have been a credit to her own grandmother.

There was a shade of meaning to this conversation that Eleanor did not grasp, but she was certainly not going to ask a girl a full twelve months her junior to explain. The Sansomes were superior enough with four in work, and bought fruit and biscuits at weekends.

But Eleanor was to value the extras, the basins of beef tea and the calves-foot jelly that Clarrie and her brothers brought in as Amy had to take to her bed, racked with alternate bouts of icy shivering and increasing feverishness. But always when anyone came she tried to make light of how she felt. It was not until Aggie Sansome heaved her great, dropsical weight away from the support of her kitchen table, from which she ruled her domain, that Eleanor really realized how desperately ill her mother was.

As Amy had to be nursed through the night, Reuben began to sleep downstairs. During the long, dark hours, Eleanor made many trips to the kitchen for drinks of honey-sweetened barley water, for tea for herself and Aggie, and for clean flannels and dry sheets. Each time she carefully shielded the flickering candle flame as she opened the stairs-door into the parlour, where her father stretched out on the couch. She was at pains not to wake him, yet resented his sleep, resented the way he threw his boots, jacket and trousers about the best room. His thick, heavy-buckled belt had been carelessly pulled across the oval elm table, scarring the top her mother took such pride in, beeswaxing and rubbing its dark surface until she could see her own reflection. Most of all, Eleanor resented the beery, sweaty smell of him there and the sound of his snoring, when her mother lay so quiet, and so ill, above his head.

Bathed in perspiration, but as cold and pale as marble, Amy weakly smiled her gratitude of all they tried to do for her. Eleanor and Aggie willed her to live, but neither of them thought of fetching her husband when suddenly and unexpectedly, the crisis came and she began to drift away from them. Amy had one last lucid moment before the end when she lifted a languid arm towards her daughter.

'Kiss me, my girl,' she whispered, and as Eleanor bent to her she added, 'best look after your father.' The last, brief smile was rueful and her hand fell with the weight of a death wish on her daughter's dark hair.

Eleanor felt numb, unreal, as she sat by Aggie that first

evening after her mother had died. Mr Sansome had gone immediately to help keep vigil over Amy, but shortly afterwards they heard the sound of boots on the cobbled yard, as her father went for his usual evening drink. Eleanor saw Clarrie and her mother exchange glances.

'One thing,' Eleanor said, recognizing now at least one emotion, 'she's safe from father. He won't be able to get at her now.' She turned to Aggie feeling that at least this was one slender revenge.

'No, love, that he won't, not at your mother. . . .'

'No. . . .' Eleanor's low reply accepted the apprehension in Aggie's voice. She knew in that moment, even though she sat in the house of her friend, what it was to feel totally and utterly alone.

'Eleanor can always come here,' Clarrie put in hastily, 'can't she, our mam?'

Eleanor looked at Aggie, who held out her arms, and very slowly Eleanor lowered her head on to the ample bosom and there shed the first tears for the loss of her mother. As if to give her privacy, Clarrie rose and unhooked the bellows from their nail by the fireplace and stooped to blow the embers of the neglected fire. Aggie rocked Eleanor gently as tears became sobs. Clarrie pumped the bellows harder and kindled the fire until the kitchen glowed warm in the deep twilight, then she swung the trivet over the fire and put the kettle on.

Eleanor's thoughts kept returning to her mother's last moments. 'I have to look after my father,' she said, and the bleakness in her voice chilled the two who tried to give her comfort.

If Reuben mourned he gave no sign. For Eleanor, the stark and bitter harshness of the interment in the iron-hard January earth, when those at the graveside were lashed by an icy wind, was played out all through the long, terrible winter.

The influenza epidemic spread world-wide to claim over twenty million lives, and funerals became almost a daily event even in the village. Eleanor was soon helping to nurse the Sansomes and four other neighbours as whole families, their resistance lowered by four years of war and bad food, lay sick together. As she wearily changed sheets and coaxed drinks down aching throats, her mother's last words lay like a whole lifetime's burden on her shoulders.

As effectively as she could, she took over her mother's role: cooking, cleaning and mending. Although her father still never raised a hand to her, and he usually spoke only to give her orders, she became increasingly uneasy when he was in the house. She would look up suddenly to find his dark, brooding eyes upon her. It became a kind of cat-and-mouse existence, as she in turn began to keep a wary eye on him.

'Will I do then?' he asked suddenly looking up from lacing his boots one evening. 'You've been sizing me up for long enough. What for, I wonder?'

He came to stand over her as she sat finishing the toes on a batch of his homemade socks, and putting a hand under her chin forced her face upwards to look at him. She tried to turn away, but his hand tightened over her chin, keeping her head rigid. 'Fancy your old Dad then, do you?'

When she closed her eyes, he laughed mirthlessly and jerked her head away, out of his hand, and went, still laughing coarsely, to spend what little profit he did manage to make at The Hunters.

Fearfully she began properly to undertand Aggie Sansome's offer of refuge if her father ever 'touched her', and yet she could hardly believe even him capable of such a thing.

Her working hours at the village factory soon became the only time she felt at ease. As the warmth of spring began to come, she even jollied Carrie along a little, for although Clarrie had not caught the flu she had not seemed her usual perky self all winter. Her mother was concerned about her listlessness, and had arranged for her daughter to go to her sister's home near the factory for something more than just a sandwich at midday.

But one morning in June, when the sun warmed their backs even as they walked to work in the early morning, and each dewdrop sparkled with its own little rainbow, it was as if Clarrie was making a special effort to be really well, joking and laughing about the latest man to be released from the forces. This was a very special young man in their lives, the son of the factory owner, who was beginning to learn the hosiery business from the shop floor up. Gregory Hamson was already the subject of much giggling and day-dreaming among the factory girls.

'I reckon he comes through our mending shop far more times than he needs,' Clarrie exclaimed, giving Eleanor a playful push. 'It's you he comes to see!'

'He's never even spoken to me!' Eleanor protested.

'But you like him though. Go on, don't you?'

'How do you know whether you like someone when you've never even looked at him properly?' Eleanor reached up to the hedge and self-consciously plucked an archly curved spray of sweet woodbine.

'Bet you don't even know what colour his eyes are?'

'No,' Eleanor admitted, 'I daren't look.'

They had giggled helplessly then, until Clarrie said, 'It's time we got a move on. Come on – tram horses!' They each crossed an arm over the other's back and moved in step together, like the horses harnessed side by side to pull the city trams.

'Bet you'd sooner play tram horses with Gregory,' Clarrie said, as they ran on to work in the growing heat of a sun rising in a brilliant blue sky.

'Now's your chance,' Clarrie whispered as the whistle sounded for the midday break. She threw aside (with exaggerated distaste) a bundle of the grey socks with the deliberately misplaced red stripes, still being made for the German prisoners of war, and nodded towards the doorway. Gregory Hamson and Henry Attersley stood talking, both looking towards Eleanor and Clarrie.

Eleanor thought what a contrast the two men were. Greg was young, slim, with remarkably golden hair, and handsome in a pleasing way. Just by looking at him, you knew he was a kind man, generous too, she thought as she lowered her gaze. Henry, on the other hand, must be well over thirty, for he had served in the Rifle Brigade all through the war, and come home limping from a leg wound. This he attempted to disguise, but as he walked home at the end of each day it was noticeable. A heavier built man altogether than Greg, he made jokes with the older factory women that Eleanor did not understand, and then, to her annoyance, always seemed to be looking at her for some response. Besides, he had dark hair slicked down with a centre parting which she did not care for at all. Moreover, she believed dark-haired girls should prefer fair-haired boyfriends. Clarrie thought so too.

'Go on! You know,' Clarrie hissed and jerked a finger in a kind of pecking movement towards her own eyes, then slipped off the mending-hook kept around her neck on a piece of string. 'See you after the break, and I shall want to know!'

In spite of her leg-pulling, Eleanor thought her friend had looked pale ever since their energetic run to work that morning. She watched Clarrie go, then took her sandwiches and went to stand near the back door of the factory which looked out on to a newly mown hay field. Already workers were wandering into the field, but she stayed near the door. Greg might come out, it was such a lovely day, and his father was rumoured to be away on business. But as she lingered, it was Henry Attersley who came out and began to walk towards her.

Casually she began to walk further away.

She noticed one of the wool-winder boys leaning on the field stile, and with a sudden pang of compassion realized that it was Herbert Briggs, a boy from a family she had tried to help, and again he had no midday snack. He stood in his habitual attitude, hands thrust in pockets, shoulders as hunched as an old tortoise, head down.

Only his eyes were raised, watching the grass fights beginning to develop. Even that looked too much effort for him.

'Want a sandwich, Herbert?' she asked.

Herbert neither moved nor replied.

'I only want one today. Go on. It's lettuce.'

He shook his head.

'Go on,' she pushed the packet under his nose. 'I shall throw it away if you don't have it.'

A curiously pinched and old-looking hand came from one pocket and grasped a sandwich. Eleanor took the other piece of bread and was prepared to eat and enjoy the snack with Herbert, but as she saw the boy try to restrain himself from gulping down the food in huge bites, but quite unable to once his famished frame had the taste of it, her own bread suddenly seemed blacker and drier than usual and she had hard work to finish her slice.

She knew it was no use offering that to Herbert. There was a point where a person's pride was more important than hunger. As it was, Herbert's muttered thanks were embarrassed, and his face reddened as he glanced at her before moving away. His hunched back looked even more shell-like as he went to lean on the sun-baked brick of the factory wall.

'That was a kind thing you did,' a voice said behind her.

Gregory Hamson stood the other side of the stile.

'Giving away your lunch . . .' he said smiling, as if she had not understood him. Eleanor's heart was beating almost too loudly for her even to hear him. She felt her colour rise, but as he continued to smile at her she found herself smiling back, and blinking because she suddenly wanted to cry from inexplicable happiness. His eyes were dark, with dreams, warmth and kindliness all mixed there.

'I don't think Herbert ever has anything at midday,' she said, and at the look of genuine concern on Greg's face was bold enough to go on, 'you see he was the only one of their family to survive the flu. As it was, he lay ill with five dead and waiting for burial in the house. Now his aunt has taken him in, but she has ten . . .' she stopped suddenly aghast as her own prattling and finished lamely, 'so I don't suppose there's food for midday as well as an evening meal.'

Greg was frowning now, he turned slightly towards her, and quite naturally they fell into step and walked further into the field.

Eleanor was slightly apprehensive then, feeling she might have done Herbert Briggs some disservice. You never quite knew about people with money and charity could be as hard to accept as need was to bear. 'Mostly he won't take anything from anyone,' she said. 'He has his pride. I know perhaps he looks a bit comical, but I like little Herbert.' She felt and sounded defensive.

Greg stopped and looked at her, for a moment she thought he was going to touch her arm. She swallowed hard, wondering if she had gone too far. What if she lost her job? She might never see Greg again.

'You're Eleanor Lewis, aren't you?' he said. 'Your mother died of influenza too, didn't she?'

'How did . . . ?'

'I asked,' he interrupted, then added quietly, 'I think Herbert Briggs is very lucky to have you as a friend.'

She felt then as if he *had* reached out and touched her, and the moment had an intimacy which seemed to attract the attention of the other girls in the field. They suddenly became aware that they were being closely observed. Girls were poised with armfuls of hay at their shoulders, but were watching instead of continuing their play.

'I'd better go back,' Greg said. 'I think the foreman may want a word with me.'

She glanced to where Henry Attersley still leaned casually in the mending-shop doorway, and realized that Greg had restrictions of propriety that hemmed his life as surely as necessity directed hers.

'Perhaps we shall have the opportunity to talk again

some time.' His smile was gentle, but his eyes seemed to search her face for a more positive response than the answering smile she gave.

As he walked away, she felt madly happy, quite capable of as many crazy antics as a lovesick March hare. She saw Henry Attersley move aside for Greg to go into the factory, then Henry began to walk into the field. Eleanor grasped up her skirts and ran to join in the more abandoned fights developing in the hay.

She laughed as the girls questioned her. 'What did he say? What were you talking about?'

But the bubble of excitement inside her could only be expressed by gathering a great armful of hay and throwing it up above her own head, squinting at the sun through its falling strands, suddenly wild with its smell, and the spring and the thought of Greg Hamson's dark eyes looking so kindly down upon her. The others fell on her laughing reticence, burying her in the hay, shouting and screaming.

Neither their free time nor their energy lasted long, but it was sufficient to upset the whole factory for the afternoon shift. There was much giggling and surreptitious slipping from department to department, as a competition grew to find the longest piece of grass still clinging between skirts and aprons, or even in blouse tops, where the cheekier boys (from homes where nourishment was better managed) had dared to thrust them.

Poor Clarrie was regaled several times with the story of Greg's conversation with her friend, and to Eleanor's mind seemed to tire of it more quickly than she need. The girl hardly spoke as the working day drew to a close. She took her quietness for sulking, but as they left the factory gates together that night, Clarrie's knees seemed to give way under her, and she crumpled quite slowly over them. Eleanor swiftly dropped to her knees, lifting and cradling her friend's head in her lap, calling her name gently, urgently. She put her hand on the pale forehead but drew it away as if she had been bitten, gasping with shock, for she had felt the same marbly coldness there as she had on her mother's forehead.

She called Clarrie's name again and again, but the eyelids never stirred.

'Clarrie! Don't die!' she implored. 'Please don't die!'

A man's hands reached down and lifted Clarrie's slight weight from her knees. She was aware of a lot of people now, of a trap being stopped and of Henry Attersley carrying Clarrie to it.

'She's not dead, is she? Where are they taking her?'

'Home, Eleanor.' It was Greg Hamson's voice that finally made sense to her. 'They're taking her home to be cared for.' He raised her up, put his arm around her waist and supported her back to his father's office, and made her sip a glass of brandy.

'But she was all right this morning, laughing and talking, and she's not even had the flu or anything.' The heat of the unfamiliar alcohol, coupled with her acute anxiety loosened her tongue.

'I've heard of cases where people have fought off the infection for a long time and then suddenly collapsed, like Clarrie,' Greg said quietly, adding even more gently, 'Often they are even iller. They lose their strength by keeping going when others have given in and gone to bed.'

She looked up at him startled. What was he trying to tell her, was Clarrie really so ill? She remembered the icy cold forehead. Greg gestured for her to finish the brandy, which she did in one gulp. Then she found herself saying: 'But Clarrie and I are going to be bridesmaids for each other, when we find boyfriends and . . . and . . . .' She stopped, suddenly realizing what nonsense she was talking.

'I think you need someone to look after *you*,' Greg said. 'Will your father be at home?'

2

Clarrie's death seemed, in one blow, to take the last joy from Eleanor's young life, and make the shadow of her father more overwhelmingly threatening.

Even the simple task of washing herself became a great ordeal. Shortly after her mother had died, she had half stripped for her nightly wash in the kitchen sink, when the slightest of sounds had made her turn. She had thought her father had already gone out for the evening, but the latch of the kitchen door was slowly lifting. By the time the door was pushed wide enough for him to get a good look at her, she had her clothes in place, and the flagstone brush in her hand as if she was preparing to scrub the floor. From that time, she never washed more than her hands in the kitchen, carrying all her personal washing water to her bedroom and placing a chair to scotch the door.

She had confided in Clarrie at the time, and without fuss had been invited to share Clarrie's bath-water in front of the Sansome kitchen range on Friday nights. She missed those Fridays: for the bath, for the talk, for the laughter as Aggie, tears streaming down her cheeks, prepared huge pans of fried onions and cut thick slices of bread for her 'ladies' evening'.

She grieved for Aggie as much as for her own loss, but came to realize her presence in the Sansome house only brought the memory of Clarrie more painfully alive for the family. In her own home, she knew better than to show any emotion. There Clarrie had been mentioned only once.

Her father had been tying his neckerchief before the mirror propped in the kitchen window, when she had returned from Clarrie's funeral.

'Reckon I'll miss all the giggling you two did

together,' he commented. 'She was a right chirpy little thing. Reckon she knew what was what.' He paused, his voice full of salacious meaning as he went on, 'well, she would with those great brothers of hers, wouldn't she? Wouldn't she?' he repeated, as Eleanor lowered her gaze.

'I suppose so,' she whispered, not understanding what she supposed.

'You suppose so!' The lewdness of his own insinuations seemed to excite Reuben to fury.

Eleanor forced herself not to cringe as she felt his spittle on her face, and as he bent over her, it was as if her mother cautioned her not to look up at him in any kind of challenge.

'You suppose so!' The goading scorn was repeated. When he still drew no response he contented himself with hurling a bundle of work at her chest. 'I shall want those toeing for tomorrow.' Then he left the house repeating the three words as if they were some great, stupid joke. 'You suppose so!'

I hate him! I hate him! She thought the words then, as she often thought them, but knew better than to voice them aloud. She had come to know that, not only did he try to spy on her, but he lingered behind doors listening for just such revelations after she imagined he had gone. While she certainly hated her father, she feared him too.

She began to spend as much time as her work allowed taking flowers to the new cemetery, begun when the village deaths in the influenza epidemic finally swamped the three-hundred-year-old churchyard. It became a morbid ritual with her, the flower-laden, half-mile walk, the careful arrangements of flowers on the as yet unsettled and unturfed mounds of Midlands soil, thrown up here as yellow as potter's clay. Even the sexton, a mild round man who whistled cheerfully about his tasks, and usually kept much to himself, made a point of coming to talk to her, lecturing her gently about spending more time with the dead than with the living. 'T'aint natural for a young gel,' he admonished.

Eleanor felt there was very little that was natural about her life. Natural parental love and affection had died with her mother, and she had been unable as yet to open her heart to another in either love or friendship. This situation came abruptly to an end one July evening as she came back from the cemetery.

The sky was heavy and golden with late hazy sunshine, and the trees and the land were luxuriant with full green growth, near their greatest abundance before the maturing, and gradual death, which is the ripening of harvest. Where the dirt road gave way to the tarmacadamed village street, a derelict three-storey farmhouse stood, its extensive brick-built barns telling of Georgian prosperity, and of much land, now long included in neighbouring holdings.

Eleanor scarcely ever gave it so much as a glance, but this evening as she passed, she was startled by the sound of falling masonry, and as she looked clouds of brick dust billowed from the broken windows. She grasped her skirts and ran to the doorway.

'Is there anyone there?' she called, waving her hands in an effort to see through the dust. Even as she spoke, there was another rumbling slither of bricks. She felt her way cautiously in at the door, thinking fearfully of the children who, as she herself had done, played there in spite of adult warnings to keep away.

She repeated her call.

'Yes, but keep back.' There was some hurt in the voice that answered, and the sound of bricks being pushed aside.

'Where are you?' In spite of the warning, she moved further into the house, and as the dust began to settle could see that a dividing wall had fallen in. There was someone, a youth she thought, lying near the fallen bricks. She ran to him and, with his help, began to throw aside bricks and plaster.

'I'm all right, I think.' He struggled from the last of the debris. 'I was lucky, the wall is the old lath and mortar at the top.'

Eleanor bent to pull the last of the old laths from his legs, and supported his arm as he rose, then, as she looked up at his dust-covered face, gasped in astonishment.

'Mr Greg!' she automatically used the factory name. 'What are you doing here?' Then, as he arched his back and grimaced, she said, 'Come to the doorway, we can see what you've done then. You can sit on the old mounting block.'

Hesitantly she took his forearm again, and he leaned towards her as if glad of the support, while at the same time laughingly protesting that he thought he was not badly hurt.

Outside, she carefully pulled splinters of wood from his hair and brushed away dust from his shoulders, then stood back and looked anxiously at him.

'There's a scratch on your face and on one of your hands,' she said, then asked, 'Can you move everything – fingers and toes. . . ?'

'I can, thank you,' he said, after he had experimented, and bent forward to rub and shake the dust from his hair. He looked up at her with a smile. 'Don't look so worried. I'll be a bit stiff probably, and have a good few bruises, but otherwise. . . .' He spread his arms and looked so ridiculously pleased that Eleanor had to smile back.

'In any event, I don't mind being a little black and blue – in the circumstances.' His dark eyes seemed positively to glow with pleasure, and while she puzzled as to his exact meaning, he went on. 'I have great plans for this old place. Have you time for me to show you?'

When she nodded, he took her arm and led her round the house. 'Perhaps it will be safer if we go in from the back.'

'What can anyone do with these old buildings?' she asked, following Greg as he flattened a path through the tangle of grasses, docks and nettles that grew solidly up to the house's foundations.

He stopped, putting a hand on one of the windowsills almost with affection. 'I want my father to buy it! I can see this place as a means of livelihood for this village, and a way too for my family firm to make real progress, not just stagnate in one factory.'

Looking up at him, she felt what a zest he had for life. He seemed to look fearlessly into the future, almost inviting trials and tribulations to triumph over. The thought brought a twinge of anxiety. Was he too hopeful, too venturesome, she wondered, but it uplifted her just to look at him, and suddenly she noticed how warm the last rays of the sun were, how the stored heat radiated from the old walls, how dry the brick dust smelt – centuries dry – and how warm her cheeks felt as she looked up at Greg Hamson and he looked so directly back.

'I want to convert all this,' he made an expansive gesture with his arms, 'into a dyeworks. Instead of having to send our work nearly thirty miles to the nearest dyers, I want to do our own here, and eventually other hosiery and woollens manufacturers will send their goods here too. You see, the secret of success in business is, I believe, based on two things: looking further ahead than your competitors, and finding the right man for the right job, and I know a chemist who has specialized in dyeing techniques, who knows how to make stockings white without bleaching holes in them! We could be years and years ahead of our competitors. If only I can persuade my father to buy!'

'Oh! he must,' she said, carried away as much by Greg's presence and enthusiasm as by his ideas.

'I felt you would understand,' he said. 'We both want to help others. If I could feel that no one in this village would ever be hungry or unemployed again, for unemployment will come, I think I could leave the world a happy man.'

'Don't talk of death,' she said, bleakness coming into her voice. 'There's been so much.'

'Eleanor, I'm sorry! For a moment I had forgotten Clarrie and your mother.' Impulsively he took her hands, held them tight between his own. For a moment her lips parted with the shock of that unexpected, kind, contact. Since her mother and Clarrie had died, there had been few warm, casual, handclasps or brief embraces to help her through the days. Until that moment, she had not realized how much she had missed them.

He seemed to want to prolong the hand-holding, or to emphasize what he said, for he kept hold of her hands as he went on speaking. 'You see, in the war, when we were at the front, we had such high-flown dreams of putting our country to rights. A land fit for heroes to live in, you know what everyone said. I had a particular friend, William, William Day-Orton, we were at school together first, then all through the war. We sort of vowed that, just as we were *fighting* for old England and her ideals, we would put as much time and effort into the peace, and I want to start here, in my own village.'

'And your friend, William?' she asked, wondering if Greg would possibly know how much this extraordinarily prolonged handclasp meant to her. How she wished to have Clarrie to tell about it!

'He's in London, studying to become a doctor. He wants to help open free clinics for the sick there.'

'I hope you both succeed in your ideals,' Eleanor said, and felt an expanding sense of gratitude that he had identified her own small act of kindness to Herbert Briggs with this greater, more positive plan he had for improving the whole village. They shared a caring, but here was a man who looked way beyond himself and his own interests.

She was so proud that he was discussing his ideas with her, and seemingly took such pleasure in her interest, and in holding her hands. She wondered if his friend, William, could possibly have the same shining enthusiasm as Greg.

He led Eleanor into the old house again, explaining how the first two floors could be made into one vast room. He had seen such a factory, with great wooden vats (complete with wooden stirring paddles), standing in graduated line, each vat bearing a painted name after the man who tended it, and called into action not by capacity or vat colour, but by the man's name.

He seemed to find romance in business, even in what he called the primitive beginnings of the stocking trade, when a man made his own wares and peddled them on his own shoulders from village to village. She laughed at his astonishment when she told him that her father did exactly that, only he used the trains. He obviously found that fact romantically quaint, and Eleanor did not disillusion him, though she knew that there were many families who would be glad to be able to make their last payments on socks and woollen underwear to the morose and growingly belligerent tallyman.

As they talked he became aware, and concerned, when he realized that as well as working at the factory she toed and seamed all the work her father made at home.

'It's too much.' He opened her hands as if seeking evidence for his remark. 'We want work for everyone, but not drudgery. Your father won't be able to compete with the new factory prices much longer. Would he consider a job in our factory? Shall I come and see him?'

'No!' She heard the same peremptory command in her own voice, as had been in her mother's when *she* had thought of intervening between husband and wife. 'No,' she repeated more gently. 'It would do more harm than good, he's . . . he's a stubborn man.'

'Like my father then, stiff-necked and old-fashioned. I sometimes think he believes progress stopped when Queen Victoria died.'

They had laughed together then, but prompted by thoughts of her employer, and his old-fashioned attitudes, Eleanor said she must go home.

Greg wondered if she often walked that way in the evenings. They parted almost solemnly, shaking hands. 'We shall meet again, soon,' he said.

They would meet the next day and every day at the

factory, but Eleanor dared to hope this was not what he implied.

That late summer, the time when Eleanor learned to feel again, brought conflict and sharp division into her life. Never had she felt so repressed as when she came under her father's scrutiny, never so released, so happy, as when she saw that Greg waited at the brook bridge beyond the cemetery gates. She always felt taller than her five-foot-three as she walked downhill to him, and far from feeling self-conscious as he watched her approach, felt as if she floated rather than walked, drawn effortlessly on by his joy in her coming.

She discovered other things about herself which astonished and delighted her, as they walked first along the lane, discreetly apart, then along field paths and finally seeking unfrequented ways, pushing aside the ancient overhanging willows to walk and sit by the swift, sweet brook where great beds of watercress grew. There, in summer deep as green water, Eleanor learned true communication of speech, of heart, of mind, each aspect of their growing relationship a source of wonder and amazement, not least the capacity she found she had to weave dreams to match Greg's ambitions.

If he could build factories and dyeworks and delivery networks, she could dream beautiful houses, with farms, orchards, herb and kitchen gardens. They laughed at each other, and wondered if they could ever be happier, than in the stolen hours they spent sitting and lying under the willows, talking, planning and laughing. But once as she lay, eyes closed, engaged in one of those daydreams, she felt a dark shadow over her face and opened her eyes to see Greg bending to kiss her. Surprised, she closed her eyes again quickly, but was not sure how to respond as his lips touched hers. Her own lips remained flat, almost stiff, pressed to her teeth. The thought that he must think her a fool vanished as he whispered, 'I love you, Eleanor.'

He bent to kiss her again, and this time she parted her lips slightly and was startled at the difference her own response made. She sat up hurriedly, feeling shaky.

'Eleanor,' Greg gently questioned, 'you're not upset?'

'Yes,' she answered looking down at her lap. 'I am upset. So upset, I want to run about, I want to shout, to tell everyone Greg Hamson loves me!'

Greg rolled backwards, laughing, and now it was Eleanor's turn to lean over and whisper, 'And I love you, Gregory Hamson. Perhaps I won't ever be able to tell anyone else, but I do love you.'

Greg sat up then, suddenly sober. 'Oh! yes,' he said, 'we shall tell everyone eventually. When it's possible for us to marry.'

'Marry.' There was the utmost bleakness in the word as she repeated it, but before he could speak again, she added, 'Think of your father, then think of my background. Your people are businessmen, property and landowners – gentry. Mine – my father – why, if he sells an extra pair of men's stockings on his rounds, he just drinks the extra pennies away. What chance can there ever be for us? I guess your family already has someone in mind for you to marry.'

He did not deny this, but instead grasped both her hands and pulled her to her feet. 'Don't ever doubt that I shall marry you, Eleanor. There's a saying, what you care, you do, and I care very much. Nothing will stop us being together.'

Again, when he was at his bravest and strongest, looking as if nothing could possibly daunt him, a shiver of apprehension made Eleanor feel great love and great anxiety for him. She was sure he was too good for her – too good for this world – but that was a saying she did not repeat. He was certainly too good to have to tangle with her own father. She vowed she would *never* let the two come together, if she could help it. She knew instinctively that her father would find some way to demean and poison the beauty of their relationship.

'If only. . . .' She smiled at him, tears brimming to her eyes. 'We've started a lot of daydreams together.'

'Open your heart to those dreams, Eleanor,' he pleaded enthusiastically. 'Don't be afraid. We can make anything we truly want, come true.' Then he explained, with step to step practicality, how he would learn the dyeing processes, then when he had the dyeworks under his direct management and had some financial independence, then there would be no obstacles to them finding their house, the one she had dreamed of, and marrying.

She shook her head at him. 'You make it sound so simple.'

'It is, don't you see. I'll *make* it happen.'

She stood solemnly, believing him, yet with a conviction that *she* would be the one who would have to make it happen. Not really understanding why she should feel so, she gently shook her head. Greg looked at her and her doubts with mock exasperation. He glanced round as if searching for something to convince her.

'Ah!' he exclaimed with some satisfaction, and drawing her after him, as if she were some reluctant schoolgirl, he led her to the bole of a sturdy oak in the middle of the brook-side field. She protested, laughingly, as he took out a penknife and began to carve a large heart on the tree, all the time saying he really could not understand girls who had to have everything written down before they believed them. When an arrow piercing the heart, with the initials 'E.L.' and 'G.H.' at head and tail stood out startlingly white in the dusk, he turned back to her.

'Well,' he asked with fake severity, 'will that do until such time as I can give you the marriage lines?'

Eleanor went to the tree and leaned her cheek on the carved heart and put her arms around the trunk.

'Lucky tree,' Greg said huskily.

She was up early the next morning, singing gently to herself as she went to fetch water from the yard pump.

The crispness of night still lingered in the air, and a single lark began the dawn chorus, throwing a solitary note into the amphitheatre like a conductor tapping his baton.

She was so early, she had even beaten Mr Sansome. She heard the pump rattle dry as she raised and lowered the handle, and suddenly remembered it always ran dry in the night. Still humming, she turned back to the kitchen to find water from a kettle or jug to prime it.

The rattle of the privy latch made her start, and the sight of her father's unkempt figure, trousers pulled on over the shirt he had slept in, silenced her. Her father must have collected a little more money than usual from his rounds the day before, she thought. An enforced trip to the privy was the only thing that ever made Reuben rise before she left for her work at the factory. Even as he followed her into the kitchen, she could smell stale beer on his breath.

She turned away, wondering if there was water in the kettle on the hob, but as she moved towards it, her wrist was caught and she was spun round to face her father. Then he gripped the other wrist, and with sounds that were half grunts of amusement, half of anger, he pinioned her wrists to the wall high above her head.

'Singing!' He spat the word like an accusation. 'What have we to sing about then?' When she only turned her head away from him, he banged her hands hard back against the wall again. 'What have you been up to? You've had trouble keeping your heels on the ground this last week or two, wanting to skip here and there, I've seen you, wanting to sing! What have you been doing? Hey!'

'Leave me alone. I've done nothing,' she whispered.

'Perhaps it's time you did do something, then.' He twisted his head until his face was inches from hers. 'Perhaps it's time,' he repeated, and she sensed he was very gradually leaning his body closer and closer to her.

She lost her fear in the intensity of the loathing she felt, and as his breathing became ragged and disturbed, she was reminded of the nights she had listened when her mother had been at this man's mercy, of Clarrie and Aggie Sansome's message: 'If he tries anything, run in to us.' Of their innocent, girlish speculation about Greg, of her love for Greg, and in that instant she knew the difference between love and lust, and her scorn erupted. She turned her face to her father's, eyes wide and challenging.

'Leave me alone!' she ordered, not loud, not urgent, but carrying that positiveness that expects to be obeyed. 'Leave me alone,' she repeated.

Perhaps it was her scorn that shamed him, or her anger that cowered him as his own father's inveterate rages had always cowered him, or perhaps in her voice he heard the echo of some diminutive but respected schoolmarm, for he looked away, the aggression dying from his eyes before the immutable order, the waiting-to-be-obeyed impassivity of her face. He stepped back, looking almost stupidly bemused, and did not speak again until he was out of sight on the stairs, only then finding his courage to shout back that she had better watch her step because he wasn't having any goings-on behind his back.

She did not move until she heard his weight fall upon his bedsprings, then trembling, she sank into a chair. Perhaps he'll leave me alone now, she thought, knowing her victory, but pushing to the back of her mind the fear that it might well have been a very different ending if the encounter had been in the evening, when either he was fresh and eager for his night's drinking or fiery and expansive with ale on his return.

The worry that came most persistently to her mind now, was the fear that her meetings with Greg should be discovered. Then, almost as if the fear gave its odour to the world, Greg told her that *his* father had cross-questioned him about the many evenings he spent away from home and his companions. Greg had told his father everything, his ambitions, his intentions, and had met his father's disapproval and intimidations with unswerving determination. In the end they had compromised. Greg was to leave immediately for Honsfield, where he would join the chemist he knew who was researching into dyes, and if in two years the young couple felt the same way about each other, then Bertram Hamson would relent.

'Relent?' Eleanor queried. She had seen much in Greg's expression as he told the story and could almost hear his father's disbelief – his son and a factory girl!

'We will be married,' Greg stated. 'In two years I shall open a dyeworks for my father's firm, and we *shall* be married. You don't doubt that?'

Looking at Greg, who as always seemed ablaze with love and energy, she doubted nothing.

She still believed in their future, even when Bertram Hamson met her face to face before the factory gates, and told her bluntly that he trusted his son would come to his senses while he was away. She felt she knew better.

On the evening Greg said goodbye, when they lingered late into the evening, each reluctant to make the parting, there were no doubts, just unease as she stood for long moments in his arms. Once she shivered violently, as if someone had touched her back with an icy hand.

'Someone walked over your grave,' Greg said lightly, holding her closer. 'I have a little present for you, another proof in *writing*.' He pulled a small velvet jewellery case from his pocket. Inside was a dainty gold brooch with the word 'kismet' spelt in seed pearls. 'It's a Turkish word. It means destiny, that distance, time and men's feeble wills, are as nothing, it is all ordained in the stars. It means you are my destiny, Eleanor.'

The words stayed with her as finally she watched him go away into the dusk, and she returned home. Only as she neared the cottage, did she have a sudden pang of apprehension lest her father should be home before she could reach her bedroom.

Everything was dark and silent, as clutching the warm velvet box in one hand, she quietly pushed the key into the front door. She used this way because it was a more private entrance in the evenings, when back doors stood ajar, and someone or other would be sitting on their back step, enjoying the peace of evening after the hard working day.

She had been wrong about the cottage being in darkness. A light shone from the kitchen, but there was no sound, only a certain awesomeness in the silence. A little breathless, she pushed open the door to the kitchen. The gaslight was dim, too low, the flames around the mantle guttered and smoked. In the carver chair by the table her father sat as if asleep. He had taken off his jacket and neckerchief and rolled up his shirt sleeves. Eleanor took two steps further into the kitchen and could see then that his eyes were open, but fixed unnaturally, unblinking, staring into space.

She dropped her cardigan on to a chair and walked slowly round the table, heart thumping faster, then she stopped and drew in her breath in surprise.

In front of the fireplace, ready for use, was the big zinc bath. The surface of the water still rippled and lapped gently, as if the filling had only recently been finished. Eleanor kept her eyes on Reuben's face as she tried to understand. Was he drunk, or ill? There was no movement, no change of expression, but she could smell drink as she watched him over the widening and stilling ripples.

'Father . . . are you ill?' she asked, but did not approach within his range. He was breathing, for she could see the rise and rall of his chest.

She was on the point of going to his side, when she sensed rather than saw, a flexing of muscle, a tension, the spider anticipating the fly, and she backed away, apprehension giving way to fear.

'Get Mr Sansome.' Disconcerted, she spoke her intention, and Reuben exploded into life. She turned to see what later was to haunt her: two cruel hands, clawed with rage, raised and seeming too huge, as they stretched forward to reach her. She tried to get to the back door, but splashing heedlessly through the bath in his eagerness, she felt her father's hands fall like talons on her shoulders, tearing at her clothes. She opened her mouth to scream out her terror, but the back of his hand fell across it, knocking her to the wall.

'You little whore!' His voice was low, full of evil, full of intention. 'So now we know where you go. I've seen you! I've watched you letting him paw you about!'

'Watched?' Heart racing, she pushed herself up from the wall, disbelieving.

'Yes!' He snatched at her closed hand, and in proof prised Greg's present from her. 'Kismet!' he ridiculed the word, and threw the little blue velvet box into the water with all his force. 'Foreign mumbo-jumbo.'

The box bobbed to the surface, spotted with beads of water not yet absorbed into the material. With a cry of protest and outrage at the thought of him spying on her and Greg, Eleanor swooped to retrieve it. 'Leave me alone! Leave me alone!'

'No! I made that mistake before. This time I'm going to teach you a lesson you'll not forget.' He grasped her blouse sleeve and swung her towards the bath. 'I'm going to wash your paws for you – you dirty whore! I'm going to scrub you clean!'

Eleanor wasted no more breath on words, she fought to free her sleeve, fought to escape to the back door, but every blow she landed, Reuben redealt twice as heavily. Tears threatened to blur her vision, but she blinked them away as another bruising blow forced her back towards the bath, and she had no time to cry. She needed all her wits and faculties about her.

He was laughing at her now, enjoying tormenting her, and as she began to try to call out for help, he redoubled his enjoyment by clipping up her chin every time she began to shout. Then she saw the false playfulness leave his face, and she knew she would not repel him as she had before. This time there was desire and lust in his eyes, that nothing she could say would quench.

The tactics changed, he held one arm, seized the front of her blouse and tore it from her. Then off came her bodice, and his hands plunged and wrenched at the waistband of her skirt. Tapes, hook-and-eye fasteners and buttons bruised and burned her body as the garments were torn from her in a violent tug-of-war.

He stood for a moment as he held her last garments in his hand, devouring her young body with his eyes, catching his breath. For a moment her reaction was to cringe before him, to try to cover herself with her hands. Instead, pride, or bravado, prevented her and she drew herself up, scorning him for his attack by her lack of embarrassment. She pulled back her shoulders, enhancing the line of her breasts as she raised her chin and looked defiantly at her father.

'Ah!' the noise was low and appreciative. He reached to the mantelpiece and grasped a half bottle of whisky, from which he drank the last mouthful. 'My beauty. You've a bit more spirit than your mother used to have. I like that.' Before she could move to prevent him, he ran a hand up from her hip to her breast, catching and pinching the nipple.

'I am your daughter!' she screamed at him, and slammed her hand as hard as she could across his face. Reuben threw himself forward at her, grasping her round her hips, lifting her bodily and flinging her into the bath. Next moment he was over her, wielding the scrubbing-brush used for the kitchen flagstones.

'Not my daughter, but a little whore who's got to be scrubbed clean!'

She fought then, forgetful and heedless of the outcome or consequence. She bit his shoulder, and dug her nails into the back of his neck as he thrust her repeatedly down into the water, feeling his skin curl into and fill her nails as he tried to draw away. As she was pushed back again and again into the cold water, she was unaware of any sensation of pain or cold, the water a neutral element in the fight. She was conscious only of the arms and hands that with strength-sapping regularity returned her to the bath every time she tried to rise, and of noise like a torrential waterfall, coupled with the animal-like grunts and gasps they made as they struggled.

Above all, she was aware of the abrasive scrubbing-brush which her father vigorously applied to all and any areas of her back and legs she was unable to defend. Then it was her breasts he attacked, and as she must protect herself, he thrust the punishing brush between her thighs with deep, sensual, dragging withdrawals, his own excitement making him half rise from his knees, shouting, 'Whore! Whore! Whore!'

She had no strength to resist him now. She alternately gripped the sides of the bath and tried to cover herself, sucking and sobbing her agony through clenched teeth.

Then suddenly it was over. So quickly that she still fought against arms and hands that no longer plagued her. Then she realized that there were other voices, other men in the room, shouting, angry, pushing her father from her. It took long moments for her finally to emerge from the hell that had encompassed her, to see Mr Sansome and his two sons, made grimly determined by their revulsion as Reuben turned on them, fighting with the strength of a maniac as they tried to pull him away.

Mr Sansome pushed a bundle of her torn clothing at her. 'Get across to our mother!' he said. 'And stay there.'

Clutching the clothes to her, she ran from the kitchen, across the cobbled yard, glimpsing curious neighbours as she went. Aggie stood in the doorway.

'God Almighty!' she cried, as she saw the girl coming towards her.

3

Aggie, having shut her door in the faces of the distressed, curious neighbours, hobbled to where Eleanor crouched on the horsehair sofa.

'Ooh! Look at your back!' she exclaimed, hesitating to put her arm around the scratched and scored back for fear of causing more hurt. Eleanor looked up into her face, mouth open to speak, but no sound came.

Her father, she thought, her father had done this to her. Her father which art in heaven. No. Her mind, more distressed than her body, swirled as irresponsibly as if unleashed by sleep. No, she corrected herself, her mother which art in heaven. Her mother, who had said to look after her father. 'Best look after your father.' She glanced panic-stricken at Aggie. Aggie cried out at the expression on the girl's face, then took her into her arms and cradled and rocked her for a long time, as if she were a tiny baby.

'I'm going to get something to cover you now, and some salve for that back,' Aggie explained, as she slowly withdrew her arms.

The thick, green salve was spread as gently as possible over the deep scores on her back, the raised red weals between her thighs, and on the cuts and bruises where she had been thrown on to the sides of the zinc bath. For a time, Aggie exclaimed involuntarily over the injuries, then, more shocked, she became silent, anger locked in her. Eleanor felt isolated, and despised by everyone who had seen her humiliation.

Surely she had not deserved such punishment? She wanted to ask Aggie why he had done this to her, but she seemed as incapable of speech as she was of understanding Aggie's mumbled words of comfort, or George Sansome's conversation, once she was enveloped in a cotton nightdress, and the Sansome men allowed back into the kitchen. Only odd phrases reached her consciousness. 'Laid him out with a chair leg.' 'He wasn't punishing the girl, he was enjoying himself!'

Then Eleanor found herself being supported by George, who helped her to her feet and up the stairs, taking her into Clarrie's old bedroom, and that seemed wrong. She turned to George to make some protest, but he nodded to her that she was all right.

'Mother'll make us all some tea directly,' he said.

But when the tea came there was whisky in it, and Eleanor saw again the hand reaching for the half bottle, the smell of alcohol on her father's breath, and clenched her teeth tight so that none of the liquid should pass into her mouth. She would never take alcohol.

'Is it the whisky?' George guessed after a moment. 'You don't want the whisky. I'll get a fresh cup, if that's it. In the meantime, there's this. He put down the tea and took something from his pocket, pushing the object into her hand and closing her fingers around it.

For a moment the box lay unrecognized in her palm, then as her fingers closed on the soft wet velvet she remembered it. 'Oh!'. The noise was low, but startlingly poignant, like the first pangs of imminent birth, and she curled herself round the memory of her evening with Greg, and like a child with a comforter she gripped the box to her lips and quietly began to cry.

'Ah! that's better lass,' Mr Sansome said with some satisfaction. 'You cry – cry your bloody heart out.'

It was much later, far into the night, that she recalled that she had never heard Mr Sansome swear before. She had always seen George Sansome as a figure in the background, believing Aggie to be the dominant member of the household, even though she was bound by her sick bulk to the kitchen, but in the next two days she quickly realized that it was George who held the household together. He it was who fetched water and washed Aggie before anyone else was stirring, establishing her with all she needed for the preparation of the day's meals, fuel for the stove, everything to hand before he cycled to his work as boilerman at the town asylum. He it was who dealt with her father, telling Reuben Lewis that he was lucky they had not fetched the police, and that his daughter would be staying with them. Eleanor sensed that he would take quiet pleasure in having her permanently in the house, and Clarrie's bedroom no longer empty, but having once cried herself out of the shock of her father's attack, she knew she could not stay, knew she had decided to go and find Greg as soon as George had pushed the 'kismet' brooch into her fingers.

The composure which Eleanor managed to acquire in her short stay with the Sansomes was quickly tested by her journey north. The threat of a rail strike had hurried her preparations. George read from the newspaper that new proposals for railway workers threatened a reduction of fourteen shillings a week in some men's wages. On 24 September 1919 there were stern warnings from union officials that an ultimatum would be sent to the Government giving notice of the commencement of a 'Great Railway Strike' unless new negotiations were promised.

George put her strapped wicker basket on the handles of his bicycle and walked with her to the local station early the next morning. Train times and connections were unsure, and George was not at all happy with her going, but she was determined.

It would have been easy to slip into the Sansome household. She would have been content to wait for Greg there, if it had not been that every time she heard her father's footsteps passing, or pausing, in the cobbled yard, her heart and breath seemed to stop in fear. She was his daughter, and well under age, and she supposed he could force her to go back home. She dreaded encountering him, and hurried away from the yard that close, misty morning, thankful to be away, every step she took creating a joyful distance between herself and her father.

The only person they saw on their way was Henry Attersley, who, responsible for opening up the Hamson factory, was always there first. Eleanor saw him stop, rivetted by his interest in them, as they passed, to watch them go by. He raised a hand in greeting but, engrossed as they were, neither she nor George returned his wave as they hurried along. Eleanor was later to think of the way he had stood to watch her go and to wonder if she had imagined the air of sadness about him.

The threatened railway strike engendered an exhausting air of anxiety among those travelling. There were rumours of goods trains not leaving destinations, or being abandoned in mid-journey, and certainly there were many unscheduled stops between stations. The gloom of an overcast evening overtook her long before she reached Honsfield. To reassure herself, she took from her purse the slip of paper on which Greg had written the name of the firm where his chemist friend worked. 'Drummald & Sons, Dyers, Honsfield'. It had seemed quite sufficient while she still travelled through the familiar, calm, green hills of her native Midlands, but as the landscape grew harsher and more rugged, she valued Aggie Sansome's advice, and the money she had reached down from beneath the bobbled brown mantlecloth. 'Keep that by you, in case you need your return fare.'

The town itself was alien to all that she knew. In her tiredness she soon became completely lost in what seemed to her a profusion of narrow, steep, cobbled streets, some no more than sinister looking alleyways. Nowhere did she see a sign showing the willingness of anyone to take in lodgers, however temporary, and the little money Aggie Sansome had given her did not allow for a hotel.

Hesitantly she walked to the front door of one of a small but respectable looking row of houses, where a light showed in a fanlight, and knocked. She waited some minutes, then the light went from the hallway. She walked further along to a house where lights burned in several rooms, calculating that whoever was inside would be unlikely to put all those out before answering their front door. A man like an ex-army sergeant major came, and roared with laughter when he heard her enquiry. 'Not with fourteen in the house, love!' but as he went back inside, stooping to deal with two of his brood who were fighting behind his heels, he called, 'Go to Gunson's corner shop.'

Left alone in the dark street, shut out from family warmth and laughter, Eleanor thought she had never felt so alone in all her life, but then grimly judged that she had been far more alone when her father had stood vicious and evil over her. Resolutely she looked to either end of the street, and once more hoisting the weight of her worldly goods on to her hip, she put on as brisk a step as she could muster, towards the end of the street which had the most light. The light turned out to be coming from a public house. She turned and forced her legs back uphill to the other end of the street, her sore feet seeming to burn on the contour of every cobble and ill-set flagstone.

The shop was so dimly lit that it was hardly visible ten yards away, but at least it was open. A bell jangled harshly from its spring above her head, and a small old woman rose from behind the counter, where she was eating her supper of cold tripe doused in vinegar. She was neither welcoming in manner nor appearance, taking in Eleanor's weariness, her luggage, and the fact that she was unlikely to be a customer, in one business-like sniff.

'A gentleman further up the street said you might be able to give me lodgings, at least for tonight?' Eleanor said doubtfully, not at all sure how clean any lodgings offered by this woman (who wore a man's cap on top of her grey, wispy bun of hair) might be.

'That's a bloody tale for a start,' Mrs Gunson said, cutting herself a strip of tripe, which was almost a perfect match for the colour of her skin. She looked as if the full light of the sun had not fallen on her for years. 'There's no bloody gentleman in this street! What's tha' name lass?'

To her surprise, even as Eleanor answered, Mrs Gunson was opening a curtained door through to the back of the shop. 'Well, come on then!' she prompted.

'This *is* good of you.' Eleanor noted with some relief that the back room was spotless, with a degree of shine on the furniture and the metal fender rail that had only been accomplished by years of elbow grease.

Mrs Gunson waved aside her formality, pushing the

kettle over a range that shone more as if it had been lacquered than black-leaded. 'You're in trouble, I've a spare bed, and if your need is for free board and lodging, well mine's for another pair of hands.' She stretched out her hands for Eleanor to see. They were swollen and cruelly deformed with rheumatics.

Eleanor felt she must offer frankness for frankness. She told Mrs Gunson how she could no longer live at home, and why she had come to Honsfield, adding, 'I'm not a bad girl, Mrs Gunson.'

'I know that, luv. I know right here,' she tapped the middle of her thin chest. 'There's some as comes in my shop with hands so black you'd think they'd gloves on that I'd trust with my last brass farthing, and there's others, fat with their own importance, that I'd trust no further than I could throw 'em – and that wouldn't be far!' She cackled with laughter, flexing her bony arms. 'No, luv, stay while you've a'mind, and I'll be glad of your help while you're here.'

The following morning, a note from Eleanor was sent to Drummald's factory with a boy who had a bicycle. He had been promised a halfpenny worth of sweets (and that was four choices, at two a farthing) from Mrs Gunson's assortment if he was back in twenty minutes.

'I said it was from Gunson's,' he reported to Eleanor, who was established in a long, white apron behind the shop counter when he returned.

She spent the rest of Friday in a fever of anticipation so much so that in the end Mrs Gunson propped the door open between shop and parlour and went to sit out of the way of her restless assistant. From here, she could direct Eleanor to goods people wanted, often before they entered the shop. 'And call me Gunnie, everyone else does,' she instructed.

Before the day was over, Eleanor realized that Gunnie was a well-loved personality in the neighbourhood, both men and women came to her with their troubles and gossip, and most with promises to pay. It was hard work, everything had to be weighed, from stones of flour, slices of lard, to small measures of tea in screws of paper. With such shortage of money, the aftermath of food shortages from the war made little difference here.

It was an exhausting day, and Eleanor wondered at Gunnie's stamina for so slight and crippled an old woman. No wonder she looked as if she never went out, there could never be enough spare time! Eleanor's only disappointment was that Greg did not come.

'He'll come, brasses clanking like a May hoss, when he gets the message,' Gunnie reassured. 'Like as not he'll not go to the factory at all until Monday. Possess your soul in patience. Like me!' And Gunnie went off into one of her cackling laughs again.

Eleanor knew the old lady might be right. Greg had said he would take a few days to find his way around first. Even so, she spent every spare moment looking up and down the street and already she was on waving terms with some of the neighbours.

On Saturday afternoon, it was she who saw a familiar motor car coming along the street, very slowly, obviously looking for the shop. Even as she started forward, heart thumping, she was questioning why Greg's father's car should be in Honsfield. Unless Greg had borrowed it! In the instant of that exciting thought, she saw that it was Bertram and not Greg Hamson at the wheel. Drawing in her breath in a great gasp, she stepped back from the window, clattering into the big set of floor scales. Her father, *her father*, sat next to Greg's father, in the passenger seat.

In complete panic she fled in to Gunnie, who for a few seconds could not make sense of the girl.

'Get thy sen upstairs,' she said, grasping at least the essentials of the story. 'I've dealt with murderous husbands in my time, so a father or two shouldn't set me fast. Keep away from that window!' she instructed, as she went into the shop, closing the door firmly behind her.

Eleanor flew upstairs, stealthily closing the bedroom

door. She sat on the bed, frantically gripping at the bedspread, and expecting any second to hear her father's voice and his footsteps on the stairs. She sat tight with apprehension, closing her eyes to listen more intently, but she could hear nothing that passed in the shop.

How had her father learned where she was? She shook her head with impatience. Nothing stayed secret in a village for long! So he, in his spite, had gone to Greg's father, no doubt with some story which would blacken her name. Bertram Hamson had driven up to Drummalds, and – her eyes opened wide at the realization – had read her note to Greg! Thankfully she recalled that she had put only that she could be reached through the shop, not that she was staying there! Everything now seemed to depend on Mrs Gunson.

After what seemed aeons, she heard voices outside on the street. She crept on her hands and knees to listen beneath the window.

'If you see the girl again, you may tell her that she is unlikely to see my son. If she stays in Honsfield, I shall make it my business to see my son comes back home. She would be well advised to do the same, to return home to *her* father.'

If there was any answer, it was inaudible upstairs, and seconds later two car doors were banged. Only when she could no longer hear the engine, did Eleanor get shakily to her feet and go downstairs.

'Eeeh! your mother must have been a nice woman!' Gunnie greeted her. ' 'Cos, by God, your father's a wrong 'un!'

Even in her shaky state, Gunnie's remark surprised her into a brief smile.

'They'll not come back here,' she added. 'Think I'm the village idot, they do, and when I got me cow 'eels out and started to have a bit of a snack, the posh old boy nearly had a fit!'

'Oh! Gunnie,' Eleanor said between laughter and tears. 'What am I going to do?'

'Wait here for your man, of course. We'll send another note to Drummalds, Monday!' She swung a hearty, bony fist into the air in a gesture of certain victory. 'He'll cum, never fear!'

Very late that evening, Eleanor was making herself toast at the bars of the range, sleepy with the aftermath of emotion and heat from the glowing embers, when Mrs Gunson, who was making her last tour of inspection before finally deciding to close, startled her by suddenly opening the shop door an inch and hissing urgently: 'There's another motor coming. I can see t'lights. It's stopping . . . .' The door closed, and the bread dropped from the toasting fork with a great scattering of crumbs on the hearth.

Eleanor heard a man's voice. The next moment Gunnie was pushing open the door again, her old face beaming.

'Here's t'man you're waiting for!' She gave a convinced nod of approval as she stood aside to let Greg pass her. The door, swinging into place as Gunnie went back into the shop, was for a moment all that moved in the room.

'Greg!' Great relief flooded over her, there was such comfort in his presence in that northern back room.

'Eleanor?' He came quickly to her, held her fast, savouring the closeness, the dearness of her, before explaining. 'We were away in Bradford, looking over some faulty dyeing. When we arrived back the man on the gate at Drummalds told me some garbled story about *my* father and *your* father coming.' He hesitated, as if expecting her to deny it. 'Then they read a note that had come to me from Gunsons. The gateman knew Gunsons, and . . . .' He stopped, concerned, questioning. 'Eleanor, why are you here? Has something happened?'

She had given no thought as to how she would explain her journey, and would have turned away.

'No, you must tell me. I know it must be something serious, and yet,' he held her hands and spread her arms so he could look at her, 'and yet, here you are, before me, whole, *nearly* smiling.' Then more urgently he asked: 'No one's harmed you?'

She did not move, not sure how to answer, how to tell her story.

'Eleanor!' his urgency surprised her, and as she looked up at him the truth was in her eyes.

'Tell me!' he said, and something in *his* face reminded her of how recently he had returned from the trenches.

At that moment, Mrs Gunson came through from the shop asking Greg if she could make him a drink or some supper before she went up to bed, but Eleanor went to take her hand.

'No, please stay, I want you to know . . . .' She urged Gunnie towards her favourite chair. 'You may be able to help us decide what we should do.'

She tried to tell her story calmly, but was so conscious of the blaze of Greg's eyes, and those of Gunnie moving first from her face and then to Greg's, her voice was little more than a whisper when she finished, and in the silence that followed even the soft movement of ash from the embers was audible.

'I could kill him,' Greg stated, without emotion. He sprang up then, and after squeezing her shoulders for a reassuring second or two, began to pace the room. 'We'll be married right away,' he decided. 'You are not going back there!'

'Then your father will have nothing more to do with you. I won't be the cause of that.' Eleanor shook her head decisively. 'You with your wonderful plans for the family business – no.'

Gunnie listened quietly, as each of them suggested, and urged the other to unacceptable courses, each wanting to do what was best only for the other. At last Eleanor appealed to her.

'What should we do, Gunnie?'

'You mustn't waste your lives,' she said. Her voice was very low, very calm, quite unlike the brisk business-like banter she affected in her shop. 'I waited fourteen years for Gunson, fourteen years for his domineering mother to die, and,' she laughed briefly, shaking her head at the memory, but Eleanor saw swift tears in her eyes, 'we were married one week – one week – and old Gunson went and fell off the shafts of our delivery cart. Silly old bugger, wasn't he?' She dashed a forearm across her eyes, and waved Eleanor away when she would have come to her.

'No! I'll tell you what I'd do. Buy yourselves a sixpenny brass ring. I'll find somewhere the two of you can tuck away until you can be married proper. How old are you both?' she paused to receive their answers. 'Twenty-four and eighteen, you may have to wait three years until Eleanor's twenty-one, but *don't* waste your lives waiting.'

'I've no intention of being separated from Eleanor now, not after what's happened, what her father has done . . .' Greg said.

Full realization of what Gunnie was suggesting only came slowly to Eleanor. She recalled hearing whispered, awe-filled comments about strangers who had come to the village to live during the war. 'They're not really married!' She had dismissed the gossip as being too incredible. People didn't live together unless they were married, did they?

She looked across at Gunnie to make sure it was not one of the old lady's jokes, but the face was solemn. Then, she thought, the precious sanctity of marriage had hardly been anything to boast about as far as her mother and father were concerned. The dawning light of a possibility made her look shyly across at Greg, who too seemed not a little shocked at the suggestion, but sounded as if he might be trying to come to terms with it. He vowed he would on no account be called home like an erring schoolboy, and that Eleanor was certainly not going back.

'Silly old bugger,' Gunnie repeated from her rocking-chair, with quiet, but deliberate, calculation.

* * *

Greg returned to his lodgings to find his father's car parked outside. He went hurriedly in, and heard voices coming from the front parlour. He was pleased this confrontation was to come while Eleanor's quiet tones, as she retold her awful ordeal, were still fresh in his mind. He was only sorry that it should be here, where he had found both lodgings and new friends, but when he burst into the parlour he found only his father and Reuben Lewis.

'Gregory.'

'Father.'

The words were formal, like the customary and preliminary salute of duellists before a fight.

'I'm afraid we've come with disturbing news for you,' his father began. 'Eleanor Lewis has decided to quit her home and decent society. She has defied her father and acted in a thoroughly immoral way, such as cannot be forgiven, or even countenanced by her *own* father.' Bertram Hamson gave much weight to the last words.

Greg, inwardly raging, drew deeply on his experience of disciplining men in the army, of listening and observing, of not allowing them the advantage of seeing their officer lose his temper. Reuben Lewis took his silence as an invitation to begin his story.

Greg heard the beginning of a malicious, moral condemnation of Eleanor. He gripped the back of a chair to retain his self-control, as Lewis made his own daughter sound like nothing more than a woman of the streets. He took a moment to find a modicum of control then, eyes blazing, he turned on the man. 'You,' he said with ringing emphasis, 'are a sadistic liar! If it was not for involving Eleanor, I would expose you for what you are.' He gave no opportunity for the man to reply as he turned away and addressed his father. 'If *you* have anything further to say to me I shall be in the garden.'

He walked swiftly through the small, semi-detached house, out of the back door and to the end of the long, narrow garden. He was surprised to notice that his hands were steady as he slowly lowered them on to the coping of the back wall; he felt his whole frame was shaking with suppressed rage. He did not turn until he heard his father's voice behind him.

'Where is Eleanor Lewis now? I feel her father should be told.'

'Never!' Greg vowed. 'He's forfeited all rights as a father. She's my concern now.'

'No! I think not! This girl has shown herself to be an opportunist of the first order. She used her position at the factory to enthral you, then as soon as you leave the village, she shows her true appetites, her true colours.'

'You don't know the truth! Can't you see that it's the father who's a brazen liar, a twisted sadist!'

'Gregory, I will not be shouted at. If you pursue this . . . person, you will earn my extreme displeasure. I won't have it.'

Greg suppressed the volume of his voice but not the anger in it. 'You can't stop me, father, I intend to marry her as soon as I am able. I love her.'

'Love!' His father began explosively, but then paused, shook his head, and continued in a quieter tone. 'Greg, since your mother died you have meant more to me than anyone else in the world, you must know that I have only your interests at heart. When I see you about to make a fool of yourself over . . . some social climber, *condemned* as completely immoral by her own father, what do you expect me to do?'

'You believe the father without hearing Eleanor's story. . . .'

'I am of her father's generation,' Bertram Hamson retorted, 'a generation who respects elders and betters – *that* is the generation I want to deal with.'

'That is the difference between us then, father. I belong to a generation who saw many who should have been "elders and betters" push them through a senseless and bloody war, perhaps we've come back without any automatic regard for those who are older and supposedly better. We've certainly come back more determined to make our own decisions about our own futures.'

'Make them, then, but don't expect me to cushion you when you fall. If you persist in this. . . .'

'I'm going to marry her, father, make no mistake about that,' Greg interrupted.

'Then your wage from Hamson's ceases unless and until you return home, and to your normal work at our factory.'

'Very well,' Greg said, 'You have to learn, father, that the time is passing when people who have money are looked up to as gods. I'll find employment here, and be content with an ordinary wage, if it means I'm with Eleanor.'

His sons words were like a slap across the face of all Bertram Hamson's principles, and momentarily his features betrayed his hurt. 'We'll see how long it lasts, particularly as Reuben Lewis will refuse to give parental permission to his under-age daughter.' His feigned aloofness did not quite cover the sneer of contempt in his voice, and left Greg smarting at the unjustified slur cast on Eleanor's character.

This he felt he would never forgive his father for – besides which old Gunnie's words kept repeating in his mind, 'Don't waste your lives waiting.' They seemed strangely relevant and important to him.

4

Eleanor had always supposed she would have a village wedding with posies of flowers, Clarrie as bridesmaid, relations, friends, and the rest of the villagers as witnesses to fill the church. But now there would be no wedding. Instead, quite alone, she paused, mistress of two strange attic rooms.

She could not quite dispel the feeling that she was a child again, playing at 'house'. An innocent game of preparing meals, sweeping out unwanted things like grasses and boys, making the 'house' beautiful with flowers, and being able to order one's companion to go shopping while the householder proper prepared 'the dinner'.

The only thing was that everything was frighteningly real, and certainly larger than life. She stood wide-eyed, looking at the heavy Victorian sideboard and table which had been painstakingly dismantled at the bottom of the two flights of stairs, and reassembled beneath the low ceiling of the attic room, so the furniture now looked more as if the house had been built around it. The only small things seemed to be herself and the tiny iron fireplace with its miniature hobs, which was to serve them for heating and cooking.

Eleanor listened intently, exploring the stillness around her, and the silence which stretched to the limit of her hearing. She leaned on the door frame between the two rooms, feeling curiously remote. She imagined this was how a producer might view the stage for a coming play. The lifeless set was meaningless until the curtain rose and the play was brought to life by the characters.

Yet again she wondered if they were doing the right thing. Everyone in the community would condemn them if the truth became known, but Gunnie had been clever on their behalf. Already in the shop Eleanor was known as Mrs Hamson on the strength of Gunnie's word and a small brass ring, and she found sadness in the ease of the deception. She had been treated with great respect by their landlady, too.

'We'll be moving in later today, Mrs MacGee.'

'I'll be right pleased to have you, and Mr Hamson.' Their landlady had clasped her hands reverently over four shillings, the first week's rent, and gone away down the dark passage to her back room, as smug and compact in her black dress as any well-oiled landlady.

If the exposure of their deception was to come, Eleanor

knew it would be from those who might have heard of the visit of her father and Bertram Hamson to Greg's lodgings. Eleanor felt terribly guilty at being the cause of Greg's separation from his family and rightful inheritance, and had at first tried her hardest to encourage Greg to return home, while she stayed with Gunnie, working in the shop for her board. She had argued that they could meet as often as possible and perhaps in three years his father would relent and be agreeable to their marriage. 'After all,' she reminded him, 'he did say *two* years when you first came to Honsfield.'

Greg had been silent a long time, but finally he had shaken his head. 'I learned to live for just the moment in the war,' he said, 'and there's Gunnie's experience – but it isn't just that, Eleanor. I don't know, but something, a feeling, or an instinct, tells me that we mustn't wait, we must make the most of our time.' He had pulled her to him then and whispered in her ear, 'We'll make a bargain. If you can thatch Groby Pool with pancakes, I'll agree to wait.' She had tutted, but had to laugh, surprised that he should use a local expression of the impossible. She supposed he must have heard it in the factory.

Then came a letter from Aggie in reply to hers reassuring the Sansomes that she was all right, telling her that it was fast becoming a village scandal the way her father was entertaining the 'easy' woman of the village at his cottage until late into the night. Eleanor knew then that there was no danger of *her* father coming back to Honsfield to force her to return home – it suited him too well to have the cottage to himself.

She sighed, and went to assure herself that the coal she had heaved up the two flights of stairs was sufficient for the evening, should they decide to light a fire, and to boil a kettle for tea the next morning. Greg was to pick her up from Mrs Gunson's later, and then they would return to begin their life together as husband and wife. Her heart beat quicker at the thought, and she could not quite dispel the childhood fancy that the action invited damnation.

When she arrived back at Mrs Gunson's she packed the last of her clothes into the strapped wicker basket and went to sit quietly in the back room. Even Mrs Gunson seemed slightly nonplussed now the situation she had sparked off was to come about. She took refuge in grumbling, and pushing bits and pieces of groceries into a bag for Eleanor to take to start her pantry off. 'Rubbishy odds and sods,' she called them, as Eleanor protested that she was giving them too much. They both paused and looked at each other as they heard a car pull up outside. Gunnie nodded. 'You're doing the right thing, lass,' she said.

Eleanor smiled and shook her head doubtfully.

'You can trust old Gunnie,' she folded the girl in her arms. 'Let's say I have a nose for what's best for folk. Learned to pay heed to it when it was too late for me and Gunson, but . . . .' She shook her head to hide the quick flick of pain that came into her eyes, then gave Eleanor a squeeze. They were both smiling as Greg knocked and came through from the shop, bringing a smell of petrol and exhaust smoke with him.

Greg bent to kiss Gunnie as they left. 'I'll never forget what you have done for us,' he said.

Gunnie bustled them out, embarrassed but bursting with pleasure.

'I'll be back to help you in the afternoons,' Eleanor promised, as Greg swung the starting handle of the Model T Ford, borrowed from his American chemist friend. The motor car produced a healthy sounding backfire and they were away, amidst much waving and kissing of hands.

The collapsible roof of the car was folded back over the rear seat, and the October evening air was chill and as exciting as a first snowfall, as it streamed at speed over their uplifted faces.

'I thought we would . . .' Greg paused, and laughed a little self-consciously. 'Well, I thought we would go out of the town and then come back in again,' he said, as they left first the back streets, then the wide main road of the town behind them. 'Is that stupid?'

'No.' She too felt the need for some small ceremony. 'I'd like that.'

They were silent as the house lights were left behind. A drift of wood smoke teased their nostrils as they climbed the wooded hills.

'It smells as if someone is burning pine cones,' she said, drawing the fragrant air deep into her lungs and feeling a sudden, ridiculous urgency to know if this were so, to register every fact, to memorize accurately what she instinctively knew would be a time she would remember all her life. 'Do you think they are?'

'This evening they are sure to be pine cones.' She sighed appreciatively, treasuring the knowledge that he knew so exactly how she felt.

Greg stopped the car in a gateway high in the hills and they sat very still, listening to the wind lifting the branches of the nearby firs, and bringing to them the sweet-scented smell of green foliage mingled with the more pungent pine smoke. It seemed to bring sermon to ceremony. His hand reached and gently held hers and for a long time they let their minds be soothed and tutored by the stillness and the age-old sounds and smells.

But in listening, Eleanor suddenly found fear, and was a child again listening from her bedroom to the pleadings of her mother, and the noises of the animal her father always seemed to become in those dreadful times before sleep claimed her; listening to the sounds from that closed order of adulthood she was about to enter.

'What is it?' Greg asked, feeling her fingers suddenly tense.

'We should not have said our name was Hamson. They'll be able to find us . . . and. . . .'

'No, no. If anyone enquires, Gunnie will say you still lodge at the shop, and Lloyd will say I'm still with his family. Don't let the phantoms of the night spook you. Let's stand by the gate for a little.'

He unbuttoned his jacket so she might put her arms beneath it, close to his warmth, and he held her secure, stilling her panic with his positive calmness, his measure of things greater than their own worries.

'It's a great wonderful world, Eleanor, full of mysteries we barely glimpse. Our minds contain powers we can't begin to imagine.'

She looked up at his face as he stared at the dark outlines of hills and woods and at the lights of a hill farm far across the valley. He had good features, reminding her of a silhouette of Byron in a classroom book of poetry. The lift of his head was always so eager, and he found an excitement in life which thrilled and lifted her soul. She felt her fear of sharing a man's bedroom disappear as she dispelled the memory of her father, and filled her mind only with thoughts of this man she truly loved.

'Go on,' she whispered, wanting his thoughts and the sound of his voice to mark the evening as indelibly as the scents and the touch of his hands.

He turned to face her in the darkness. 'I would rather have been able to marry you in our church, to show to all the world what I feel for you but, believe me, Eleanor, I could not revere you more than I do now. If you stood in some great cathedral, resplendent in the most marvellous wedding gown, I could feel no more pride at having you by my side than I do here, now.' He lifted his face again to where the dark foliage of the firs was interspersed with distant stars. 'Before God, I swear it!'

She stood quite still in his arms, letting his words fall upon her like a blessing, and truly she felt uplifted.

'Shall we go home?' he asked quietly. They turned from their place of vows, not speaking as they drove back to their attic rooms.

They carried everything from the car in one load up the two flights of stairs, but as Greg struggled with the large basket and a bag of groceries, he dropped their key. In falling, it almost disappeared under the door. He bent to retrieve it.

'We were nearly locked out, before . . .' he began, then both of them dissolved into nervous fits of giggles, and in the urgency to get into their rooms before anyone heard them, they dropped the key again. Finally they had to put down the basket and bags, and very deliberately and very elaborately Greg finally opened the door, while Eleanor smothered her laughter, both hands tight over her mouth. Once inside they abandoned their belongings and laughed until tears ran down their cheeks.

'I've got to sit down,' she gasped. 'My sides hurt.'

Greg sprawled in a chair opposite, across their table.

'Look at this,' she indicated the mahogany top she had polished that afternoon. 'There's acres of it!' They spluttered with laughter again.

'Stop it!' Greg ordered, hands spread over his aching ribs, 'and come here.' He indicated his knee. 'You're much too far away, across all those acres.'

She went to him, and he drew her up on to his knee, holding her for a moment as a parent might cradle a child. Then, as she pressed her head close to his, he bent his lips to her neck, and with a swift catch of breath, as if his own emotion took him by surprise, Greg lifted her fully into his arms, and carried her to their bedroom.

He laid her gently on the bed and lay beside her, kissing her eyes, her cheeks, her lips. Then with shaking fingers he began to unbutton her blouse, and she to undo his tie. They helped each other to undress, in moments eagerly, in moments shyly. When she stayed her bodice on her shoulders, he smiled, kissed her hands, lost his face in her unpinned hair, and slowly she revealed her breasts to him.

When they lay naked beside each other there was still a momentary awkwardness, a social reserve not discarded with their clothes, but as their mounting passions rose, unconsciously they moved and responded to the lightest thrill of movement one against the other. From embarrassment they flowered to desire, each wanting to please and to give to the other. Their young bodies were aesthetically perfect, and soon ecstatically one.

'For once in my life I feel as if I'm really doing things and going places!' Greg spun his trilby on to the table.

'Even just as an ordinary wage-earner?' Eleanor queried, bending over the stew she stirred over the fire. The quality of the meals she could offer him troubled her, and in five weeks stews seemed to be the most satisfactory and nourishing meals she could manage.

'As some kind of wealthy visitor, I would never had had the chance of working with anyone like Lloyd, not as closely as I am doing now. I should have just acquired a superficial knowledge of dyes, enough to see me through, but now . . . .' He would have pulled her away from her cooking. 'Come and sit down, let me tell you.'

She kissed him lightly on the lips, then held up her hand to restrain any further advances. 'Eat first,' she said. 'We can't afford to let this burn, and you need your food. I think you're even thinner!'

They sat together across one corner of their table.

'I never realized what a fascinating thing research could be,' he said. 'The effort that's needed! The concentration and precision. The disappointments and failures that in a way just make you more determined to succeed. Lloyd's attention to detail is . . .' Greg searched for a word, 'meticulous!'

'What is Lloyd like?'

'Oh, great, and so is his wife Sophie. We're invited for Sunday lunch, by the way.'

She put down her spoon, and looked nervously at Greg. 'I've never met a chemist, or an American.'

'Oooh!' Greg spooked her. 'He'll have you pickled and in a jar with stars and stripes on in no time.'

'Eat your meal,' she said, treating his remark with mock disdain, and hiding the apprehension she felt at accepting hospitality that somehow they would have to return.

No one could be apprehensive long with the Irvings. Lloyd was a small, slightly built young man, deceptively vague-looking behind large, tortoise-shell-rimmed spectacles, and Sophie was a smiling plump young woman, as friendly and disarming as her three roly-poly, tumbly, baby boys.

'Greg is coming along just famously in the laboratory,' Lloyd told her, giving no opportunity for awkward pauses at the dining table. The eyes twinkled behind the round spectacle lenses. 'He's a great experimenter. A dash of this, a little of that!'

'Now be fair,' Greg interrupted. 'It is a *measured* dash of this, and a little of that!'

'He's improving,' Lloyd admitted. 'But, seriously, what he really brings to the science of dyeing is a sort of controlled imagination.'

'Even my father admits that if someone could invent dyes that came up the same colour twice in a row he would make a fortune,' Greg said.

'Or one that would just stay in!' Lloyd said with a comical grimace, 'but we'll manage it, eventually. We'll make a good team, Greg and I, with time and patience, and quite a lot of the firm's money of course.'

'We just have to convince them that it will pay big dividends in the near future,' Greg said with confidence. 'Industries are crying out for new, reliable, dyes.'

Eleanor thought Lloyd felt doubts, but with the Irving babies competing for attention, serious conversation was never more than momentary.

Eleanor came to think of all the times they spent with the Irvings as occasions, times when the hours were full of living and laughter, times that Greg made special for her. He discovered a passion for fish and chips, and insisted on inviting Lloyd and Sophie for the evening to eat small, whole battered haddock and chips from the paper they were bought in, accompanied by a bottle of wine he had chosen specially as being 'delicate and pleasing, suitable for parties, dances and luncheons, seven shillings a bottle'. She had felt a traitor to Greg's exuberance, when she silently calculated that *that* was nearly two weeks' rent.

It was a great, moving occasion when they all met outside the main church in Honsfield to observe the 'Great Silence', arranged on the eleventh hour, of the eleventh day of the eleventh month of 1919, the first anniversary of the Armistice. Curiosity as to how the idea could possibly work was as much on everyone's minds as any other emotion. In spite of explanations that it was to be in the nature of the silence observed at vigils for the coming of a new year, Eleanor felt they all approached the time as spectators rather than as participants. It was only as the crowds grew in intensity beneath the standards of the local regiments that the sense of awe began to be felt.

She and Lloyd both spoke to Greg, but he was quite lost in the spell of the occasion. Floral tributes now had to be passed overhead from hand to hand, to find a place among the growing piles of flowers of every kind mounting on the steps of the church. Great wreaths of lilies and greenery from expensive florists were placed side by side with sprays of chrysanthemums, Michaelmas daisies, Honesty and Japanese lanterns from many humble gardens.

As the eleventh hour approached, there was a hush of anticipation and, as the maroons exploded signalling the beginning of the silence, men snatched off their hats and straightened to attention, the women following suit. It seemed as if the whole empire held its breath, and the spirit of remembrance was raised by their thoughts, like a huge banner that would endure until the memory of all those present, and the generations who would tell, and retell, of their losses and suffering, all passed away.

The two minutes was unbelievably long and, as they stood, the clouds that had all day rolled over, grey but with threatening ochre hearts, began to release their snow. The flakes fell softly, settling on hair, lashes and overcoats, as if in answer to the thoughts sent heavenwards to those lost to their families, sweethearts and friends. At last, at long last, the maroons sounded again, but while shoulders relaxed a little and one or two replaced their hats, there was no general movement. Eleanor slipped her hand into Greg's. He gripped it tightly, but none of the four moved until a middle-aged woman in front turned to them shaking her head. 'All those boys,' she said, eyes brimming with tears, 'facing their ends, and no one to give them a last cuddle.'

Eleanor gripped the woman's forearm in sympathy, and after some moments Lloyd murmured one soft, awe-filled exclamation, 'Gee!' The four turned away at last, Sophie and Eleanor searching for dry handkerchiefs.

By evening it seemed that nature was planning some special silence of her own, for the snow fell steadily, blanketing the northern country under several feet of snow. Greg stood for a long time at the window, watching the huge spinning flakes, until Eleanor left the warmth of the fireside to join him. He slipped an arm round her waist, and they stood looking at their world of white roofs and grey sky.

'It was strange this morning, when the snow started so gently at first. I was suddenly back in the trenches, when the frost and cold were a blessed relief, after the unending mud up to your knees as you tried to make your rounds. It snowed then, like this, gently at first, then much more heavily. One of the men came to me, asked me to take a diary he had kept, to make sure it reached his family if anything happened to him. He did not come back from a big push we had to make the following morning. When I looked in the diary for details of where he wanted it sent, I found he had foretold his own death, with almost uncanny accuracy. This morning seemed to hold something strangely prophetic too.'

Eleanor thought of Gunnie and what the old lady had said about learning to pay heed to her instincts. The chill she had felt creeping over her, ever since she had left the tiny range of the heat from the fire, turned into a full-blown shudder.

Immediately Greg was all attention. 'Sorry, I was getting quite morbid, all that remembering. Where's that stone bottle Gunnie gave us, let's go to bed.'

She unscrewed the top and handed him the hot-water bottle, which he filled from the kettle always hot on the hob.

'Lloyd says he's going to take us tobogganing tomorrow evening if this lasts,' he said.

'That's for children!'

'Oh, we let grandmothers come, if they're good!' He pushed the bottle gently to her middle, so she must catch hold of it, then swept her off her feet.

'I want to undress by the fire,' she protested.

'No! That way we never get as far as the bed!'

If the freezing wind had not driven some of the snow from the hill slopes, it would have been far too deep for tobogganing. Drifts were high against walls, and frozen in looping waves by houses and gates. Sheep had to be found and dug from this early winter downfall.

By the time the four had reached the tobogganing slopes, lamps flickered from the highest hill, and already a crowd of laughing young people were calling and directing each other as the sledges hurtled downhill. Some kind of contest was developing to see which sledge could make the longest run.

'Hey, I bet we'll win this,' Lloyd declared confidently. 'This toboggan's a real goer.'

'If the weight has anything to do with it, you're right!' Greg panted, surrounded by clouds of his own breath and yards of woollen scarf, as he took his turn to pull the toboggan the last hundred yards to the top. By the light of the paraffin lamp Lloyd had fixed to a crook, Eleanor thought he looked like a Christmas card illustration.

'Sure! That's right!' Lloyd agreed. 'More velocity.'

'There speaks the scientist,' Sophie laughed.

'Prove your theories then,' Greg demanded, pointing to the toboggan. 'You're first!'

Lloyd was somewhat unceremoniously shoved on board, and all three put their hands to his back and headed him off downhill. He gave a shout, which lingered on the wind as he swept downwards, but as the sledge reached the steepest part of the slope, the cry wavered, was muffled, stopped.

'He's off!' Greg roared, 'but he's proved his point. There goes the toboggan! Wow! What a champion!'

Soon they were all glowing with the exhilaration of the speed of the downhill runs, and the exertion of pulling the sledge back to the top. Scarves were hung on the pole under the lamp, and the fun continued until Sophie declared that they must go home, to allow their elderly neighbour who was looking after the babies, to go home to bed.

'One more run then,' Greg said, grabbing Eleanor's hand. 'Come on, we'll make this the longest yet! Lie on top of me.' Greg lay face down, and amidst much laughter and ribald remarks, Eleanor balanced herself on top.

'Come on!' Lloyd urged those around. 'Last try for the longest run!'

Eleanor felt many hands on her backs and legs as they fairly hurtled to the brink of the downhill slope. They were off, with a cheer behind them, the wind singing in their ears, the speed and the cold air taking their breaths. On, and on, they went, down the ice of the well-used run, past the point where the marks of most feet and runners stopped, breaking through new snow, leaving the sound of voices far, far behind. A world of soft, cushioning night and deep, white stillness, through which *still* they moved, until at last they ploughed sideways into a huge drift that completely buried the wall edging the huge, hill field.

They toppled from the toboggan, and lay breathless, laughing up at the stars bright and high in the velvet blackness. Greg reached over and hugged her, then kissed her cold lips and put his glowing cheek next to hers.

'Oh, Greg!' Tears of happiness made her nose prick, nervous laughter pulsed in her throat, and lying under the great, wide heaven she knew her own spiritual growth, felt the last vestiges of social guilt slip from her shoulders. 'I do love you.'

He sat back on his heels and scooped up great handfuls of snow, throwing it high above their heads. 'Ah! to be part of it all, this wonderful, wonderful world! I'm sorry for everyone who is not us!' He rolled over in the snow like an abandoned puppy, revelling in the sensation. She laughed at his ridiculous antics until he caught and silenced her with a kiss. Then he pulled her to her feet, and slowly, arms wrapped about each other, they began to pull the sledge uphill.

Christmas bloomed with festivities centred around the Irving children, and Sophie seemed to bloom too, in a new olive-green dress that emphasized her glowing complexion. Eleanor told her she looked like a decoration herself. 'Like holly,' she said, 'with your red cheeks.'

'Not too sure I should feel so well, or like celebrating,' Sophie answered. 'I'm pregnant again, and goodness knows we can't afford it! But with Lloyd like he is . . . .'

'What do you mean, with Lloyd like he is?'

'Well, gee, if I'm standing around, he's terrible. I hardly dare bend over the sink.'

'Lloyd?' Eleanor had trouble reconciling the mild-looking, owl-spectacled, young man with the super-lover Sophie was describing.

'Sure, Lloyd! Some days twice, or he's as niggly as hell!'

Eleanor laughed nervously, and felt a little awkward as Lloyd came into the kitchen at that moment with new shiny pennies to put in the Christmas stockings, together with an apple, an orange, and a sugar pig, for each of the boys. She was a little shocked, having equated such appetites with less amiable and less lovable men, like her father.

'What's this?' Lloyd asked. 'Have I interrupted women's talk?'

'Not entirely,' Sophie answered, and Eleanor giggled at her dry tone. 'I was just telling Eleanor about you,' Sophie went on, but seeing the embarrassment of her friend's face, altered her sentence, 'and me, and our good news.'

'News?' Greg asked, coming through to join them.

They celebrated the coming baby by opening a bottle of Christmas wine there and then. Eleanor watched their two friends over the top of her glass, saw the special look of love that passed between them, and stored away the revelation Sophie had made as a little broadening of her knowledge of men.

She felt particularly moved when they begged Greg and herself to join them at the Christmas Midnight Communion to give thanks.

It was the first time Eleanor had been to a service since Clarrie had died. She was aware heads turned in the packed church as the four found places in the pew Lloyd and Sophie regularly occupied. Sophie seemed to take on a special radiance, and Lloyd was so proud of her. Soaked in the atmosphere of this family time, beneath the boughs of holly and ivy, the huge tree by the font and the soft light of candles, Eleanor began dreaming of children: golden-haired boys and dark girls.

Until that time, the possibility that she might conceive had been the one remaining fear in her relationship with Greg. A child born out of wedlock was a stigma a girl carried for life, and even though the secret that they were not married seemed secure, there would always be the complications of registering a birth . . . . She had felt she was very fortunate not becoming pregnant. Now she found herself yearning for Greg's child, wondering what he would be like, for she was sure she would have a boy – first, anyway. She found that the mood of the Christmas season had given Greg much the same thoughts.

'If I ever thought of marrying when I was away in the war, I never thought of children,' he said when they reached their flat. 'There seemed no future for *anyone* then, but now . . . seeing Lloyd escorting Sophie like some proud little tug guiding a budding battleship . . . well, when we have our own home, and I have our marriage certificate safely in my breast pocket, then . . . I hope. . . .'

She went to him, holding herself close to his chest. 'Hmmm,' she agreed and later, when they lay warm in bed together, they talked quietly of their plans for the future. Greg was tired and soon asleep, but Eleanor lay awake a long time. She felt so secure, and decided that lying cosily in bed with the one you loved was the very best place in the whole world. As she lay there, she imagined a large family of merry children in one or other of the homes they had planned together, and it seemed like several years since they had met in the deep evening fields of home.

Sophie, Lloyd and the children were being entertained to Christmas dinner by their widowed neighbour, who wanted to repay the Irvings for their many kindnesses during the year. Greg had been amazed to hear that the woman had been paying her butcher an extra few pennies all through the year to buy the joint of beef for Christmas Day.

'Some are never out of debt with their butcher from one year to the next, because of the meat or poultry they have for Christmas,' Eleanor had told him, surprised in turn that he really knew so little of how ordinary people had to scrape in order to buy a few extras.

Eleanor had asked Sophie, Lloyd, the children and Gunnie to the flat for Boxing Day afternoon and evening, and had it not been for Gunnie being determined to supply pork pie and the remains of the Christmas ham-on-the-bone from behind the shop counter, Eleanor's table would certainly not have been so amply supplied.

While Greg went to fetch Gunnie from the shop, Eleanor put the last touches to her room, making an infinitesimal adjustment to the antimacassars she had crocheted for the backs of the chairs, and putting the best ash log on to the fire. 'My first party, my first Yule log,' she said, as the flames began to lick the wood. She stepped back to admire the grate which she had black-leaded until it shone like a blackbird's wing. It was all very Christmassy she decided, surveying the new green plush mantle-cover she had made, with green crochet edge and small red pom-poms suspended on red, silk thread. She had also made and hung up a Christmas hoop, (there being no spare money for a tree) covering the wooden ring with red and green crêpe paper and tinsel, and hung from it small presents for the three little boys: small sugar mice and knitted soldier dolls in black bearskins, red jackets with tiny brass buttons, and black trousers.

She heard voices on the stairs as Lloyd and the boys came up, and she could hear Sophie being introduced to Gunnie. They had all arrived together, but Gunnie seemed almost grumpy. As Eleanor took coats through to the bedroom with Greg she asked in a whisper: 'What's the matter with Gunnie? She looks a bit put out.' Greg grimaced and whispered back: 'We met three people who all made comments about never having seen her out from behind her shop counter before, and one who wanted to know whose Sunday hat and coat she had on! She got less and less amused each time.'

Any apprehension Eleanor might have felt about

Sophie and the children getting the wrong impression of Gunnie was soon dispelled, little William and Alistair saw to that. The two older boys were fascinated by Gunnie, as soon as one climbed down from her knee, the other was up there, and she in turn loved every second. From the bottom of her capacious black handbag, she drew a small, silver propelling pencil, and showed the boys how to peep through a tiny glass in the top to see a view of the Crystal Palace. 'Gunson bought me that when we first met,' she said.

Baby Ronald slept once high tea was over, but Alistair and William continued to be spellbound by Gunnie. Lloyd was then prevailed upon to sing, and they all joined in to sing carols and some of the still popular songs from the war, 'Keep the Home Fires Burning' and 'Pack Up Your Troubles In Your Old Kitbag'. When Gunnie raised her completely tuneless voice, the two boys went to stand open mouthed before her, and William's face creased into a most comical scowl as Gunnie reached for somewhere near the high notes. Eleanor loved every minute, and knew it was a gathering they would long remember.

New Year, the dawn of the twenties, brought out again the red, white and blue bunting that had celebrated the Armistice, the Peace Parade and the first Great Silence. Even the balloons that descended on the revellers at the factory party at midnight were red, white and blue.

Excitement reached heights of social abandonment as Greg, dressed as old Father Time, paraded the dance floor, to be led out carrying his scythe over his bent back, before Lloyd was pushed around, in the Irving's old coachbuilt perambulator, dressed in a nappie and sucking a huge bottle of milk labelled '1920'. Everyone was kissing, shaking hands, and greeting people they barely knew with tears in their eyes.

Eleanor strained to see where Greg was, wanting to

give him a hug and a kiss for the New Year, wanting to tell him how happy he had made her. Not finding him in the ballroom, she wondered if he was having trouble getting out of his costume. She made her way around the noisy merrymakers to the cloakroom used to dress the Old and New Year characters. She stopped short in the doorway.

Greg was there, he had pulled of his wig and beard, but sat slumped on a bench still draped in the druid-like robes of Father Time. Her greeting changed instantly to concern, yet there was a quality in his stillness that kept her silent, that she could not fathom. It was as if he had gone several steps beyond weariness, as if the slightest movement would be too great a tax on his strength. Panic moved her at last to him.

'Greg?' She ran to kneel by his side. He blinked several times before he seemed able to bring himself back to reality, then he straightened with what seemed real physical effort, and smiled.

'Felt suddenly tired,' he said, smiling. 'Stupid.'

Almost fearfully she felt his hands and brow. She could never quite rid herself of the fear of touching the marble-like coldness she had known twice before, but Greg was hot, too hot perhaps.

'I'm all right,' he answered, seeing the concern in her face. 'Don't look so stricken! I'm just a bit overtired, all that extra work when that last commercial quantity of new dye didn't match the laboratory specimen. There's nothing like a disappointment to make you tired.'

Grudgingly she accepted his explanation, particularly as he whirled her into the last waltz and 'Auld Lang Syne' with his usual vigour. But from this time, she began to watch him more carefully, and as the early days of 1920 went by and the brisk days of snow turned to more chilling sleet and rain, she became convinced there was more to Greg's tiredness and lack of appetite than overwork and disappointment.

She mentioned it to Sophie, but she seemed equally

concerned about Lloyd. There were things about the factory Greg had not told her. Money problems were becoming acute, their parent company was feeling the pinch since orders for woollen garments for the forces were fast disappearing. There were rumours that this unprofitable dyeing division was to be severely cut back.

When she asked Greg about it that evening, he shook his head. 'It's worse, I'm afraid. We've had confirmation today that our factory is to close at the end of the week.'

'This week?' she asked incredulously, then was silent as the implications of the news began to build up. 'What will Lloyd and Sophie do, with three babies and another coming? With all this unemployment, will either of you find other work?'

'Lloyd has seen it coming for a long time, and he's been looking around, but there seems to be nothing in his particular line. He has written to a friend back in America who he thinks might be able to help him. There's one big company there experimenting with dyeing as an offshoot of their gunpowder and chemical interests. They have control of a lot of different companies, and more important, plenty of money. But Sophie knows nothing of all this, yet.'

It was a concerned little group that gathered in Gunnie's back room a month later. Lloyd had at last persuaded, and had taken, Greg to see a doctor, and had arranged to pick up Eleanor on the way home.

Lloyd came, not with Greg, but with Sophie, and the news that the doctor wished to do some further tests which would take a little time. Greg had asked Lloyd to go on without him, to put Eleanor's mind at ease, saying he would join them as soon as the doctor was through.

Eleanor was curious as to why Sophie had come, and thought she looked fussed, and in a curious way like someone with a guilty secret. She was more than a little tense herself, beginning to feel there was something they all knew and were keeping from her. Yet she did not see how this could be, with Greg not yet finished at the doctor's.

'We thought we'd all wait here for Greg, if that's okay with you Gunnie,' Lloyd said.

The old lady nodded. 'There's times when it's good to have friends around you.'

'What do you mean?' Eleanor's anxiety made her voice sharp.

'These are not easy times for the four of you, are they?' Gunnie said evenly, looking at Eleanor as if challenging her to deny *that* statement.

Lloyd made noises of agreement, but when Eleanor looked sharply at him, he frowned and brushed imaginary particles of dust from the knees of his trousers. Gunnie made them tea and cut into a seed cake, which Eleanor guessed she had baked specially because she knew it was Lloyd's favourite.

Greg arrived while the tea was still hot. He greeted them all and sat down next to Gunnie, smiling around.

'What the matter?' he asked.

'The tests,' Eleanor began. 'What did the doctor say?'

'Oh! He just said he would let me know the results,' he said casually.

'When?' Eleanor demanded.

'I never thought to ask him.' Greg dismissed the matter. 'Probably shan't hear any more.' He looked around the room as Gunnie sniffed expressively and noisily balanced her refilled kettle over the flames. 'What's the matter?' he asked again. 'Nothing's happened has it?'

'We were worried about you,' Eleanor began.

'Lloyd!' Sophie interrupted, as if urging her husband to some urgent action. All eyes were immediately turned in his direction.

'Yes, well, we do have some news . . .' he began a little diffidently.

'We sail for America in three weeks,' Sohpie interrupted, then burst into tears. 'Oh! I don't want to leave you all. All you darling people.'

Questions and answers came quickly then. Details emerged of the offer to Lloyd of an excellent post with prospects of early promotion, in the dye research department of a huge American concern. The family's passage was paid for, a company home was waiting for them and, finally, confirmation and the steamer tickets had arrived that day.

'The one nice thing is that the plant I shall work at is almost opposite Wilmington on the New Jersey side of the Delaware River, and that's where Sophie's folks all live,' Lloyd said, 'and mine are only a hundred miles from there.'

He handed Greg the tickets for inspection. The strange pieces of paper and card were examined with respect, and their excitement died a little as there, passing from hand to hand, was the proof that the Irving family was really leaving England.

'You see, America even sought to bargain with Germany during the war, for enough colours to print stamps and paper money,' Lloyd explained, as if in further justification of not only his going, but also for the millions of dollars being poured into research. 'And of course, this company's interests all spring from the same basics: gunpowder, coal tar, cellulose . . .' he broke off, spread his hands. 'But gee! I hate the thought of leaving you all, Greg without work and everything.'

'Don't worry, old boy!' Greg went to put a hand on Lloyd's shoulder. 'There'd obviously be no room for an amateur like me in such a set-up, and I've a little money from my grandmother's estate I can get at if need be.' He went then to where Eleanor and Gunnie stood close, and moving between them, put his arms around their waists, and drew them both close. 'We'll see this bad patch through all right.'

'Yes, and people are travelling more,' Eleanor said, wanting to drive the sadness from Sophie's face. 'You never know, perhaps one day we'll come to America to see you!'

'Sure! Sure!' Lloyd grabbed at the suggestion as if it was some kind of moral lifebelt. 'We'll all meet again.'

'We ought to celebrate,' Greg decided. 'Fish and chips and a bottle of wine at our place at seven.'

There were mock groans. 'Not again!' Lloyd pleaded.

'Maybe we should just open a fish and chip shop,' Eleanor declared.

'You too, Gunnie,' Greg said, carried away by one of the bursts of enthusiasm so characteristic of him, but which Eleanor knew would now probably mean he would be utterly exhausted later. 'Lloyd will pick you up,' he volunteered.

'I'm not gallivanting about at all hours of the night!' Gunnie wagged her teaspoon first at Greg, then at all of them, as if censuring the lot for irresponsibility. Then she clattered it back into her saucer. 'Ah! get on home with all of you – and take the rest of that cake with you!'

'Say!' Lloyd turned to Sophie with sudden consternation. 'Can you get caraway seeds back home?'

5

'You say goodbye here! Then you can get straight on wi' what should be being attended to.' Gunnie's tone was tart as she interrupted a discussion between Greg and Eleanor as to whether they should go to the docks to see the Irvings off.

'Less time for tears,' Greg tentatively offered.

'Less tiring! See them to the train if you must. Then come back here and I'll have your tea ready.'

'We're always eating here!' Eleanor protested. 'We mustn't keep coming.'

'Work here don't you.'

'There's just no argument when you sniff like that.'

Greg shook his head at the old lady, adding quietly, 'And I know when you've got me cornered.'

'Aye, I'm glad you do!'

Recently, Eleanor decided, there were times when conversations between Greg and Gunnie reminded her of the jokes Henry Attersley used to tell at the factory – they held meanings she could not appreciate. Although now, of course, she realized, brightening a little, there was a whole lot more she did understand.

The day of departure hurtled towards them. There was so much to say, and yet so much that could not be put into words, and finally they were at the station helping the Irvings to load into the train a seemingly impossible number of bundles and bags. Even the boys looked twice their normal size they were so layered with extra clothes, topped by the little cloth coats Eleanor had spent every spare minute in making.

At the last moment, Sophie pushed a cloth-wrapped box into Eleanor's hand. 'I knew you would argue if I tried to give you this before. Goodbye, my dear – my dear, dear, friend. God bless you.'

Eleanor grasped Sophie around the neck. 'God bless you, and keep you safe.' She embraced Lloyd, kissed each little boy goodbye, and handed them aboard.

'God's speed!' Greg called, before the engine drowned every sound with a great surge of steam, took up its burden of carriages with a great clanking of couplings, and set off on its journey.

Eleanor was left with an impression of two windows crowded with tearful faces, interspersed with bundles and frantically waving hands.

The two of them did not speak as they left the station, Greg taking the parcel to carry, so Eleanor had quite forgotten it until they reached the shop.

'Oh! She's given me her beautiful inlaid work-box, and she loved it so much. She used to say she loved running her hands over the wood because it felt like satin.' Eleanor knelt on the hearthrug at Greg's feet, where she had found room to unwrap her present. 'Oh! And look inside!'

Gunnie came to look at the array of new needles, pins, cottons, tape measure and silver thimble that Sophie had assembled for her friend.

'Something loved, for someone you love,' Greg said quietly.

'We'll miss them all,' Gunnie said on a brief, rising note. 'Meantime, I've made tea, and I'll be in t'shop.'

For a few minutes longer, Eleanor remained absorbed by the box, exclaiming over new finds of bundles of tape and elastic. 'It must have taken hours . . . .' She looked up at Greg and smiled at his indulgent expression. He reminded her of a parent watching a child's last few moments of play before announcing bedtime.

'Where's Gunnie?' she asked.

'Eleanor.' Smiling back, Greg ignored the question. He held out his hands towards her. 'I have something to tell you.'

His expression sent an alert, like a distant fork of summer lightning over harvest fields, flickering fearfully through her. She sat back on her heels, not reaching for his outstretched hands as she regarded him. The firelight gave his skin the look of flawless alabaster, but added blackness to the hollows under his eyes. She realized that in all these last three weeks of hectic preparations for their friends' departure, she had not properly looked at Greg. Now she saw a refinement of his features, a delicate planing away of flesh, a look of self-imposed patience – a look of acceptance. The thought sent her hands swiftly to grasp his.

'What is it?' she whispered urgently.

His hands clasped her tightly. 'The tests the doctor made . . . they show I am ill.' He paused as if to let her accept that much, then went on. 'I have consumption, Eleanor. The doctor recommends I go to a sanatorium.'

Her hands would have fallen inert to her sides, but

Greg held them firm as the first shock overwhelmed her like a wave of physical pain.

'I'm sorry,' he said. 'There was no easy way to tell you.'

She felt for certain her heart must be bleeding itself to death. 'I should have known,' she whispered in an agony of self-torment. 'It's my fault. I should have known.'

'Don't be silly.' He folded her into his lap, and rested his cheek on top of her hair. 'How could you have?'

At that moment, she felt certain she ought to have known. All the signs – the unquestionable symptoms – had been there. Then another thought came.

'How long have you known?' she asked, and knew that it was some time, that he had deliberately not spoken until Sophie and Lloyd had gone. Now she remembered that for some time he had avoided kissing her on the lips, and that he had not hugged the babies goodbye, but she . . . she had been too busy sewing. She drew away to see his face. 'Gunnie knows, doesn't she?'

He nodded ruefully. 'Gunnie guessed, and she intended I should waste no time in telling you today.'

'She was right!' Eleanor's knees still shook as she rose to her feet, but now she was beginning to think clearly. 'The sanatorium, when did the doctor say you should go?' she asked. 'And where is it?'

'You go and see the doctor yourself, my lass,' Gunnie said, coming in from the shop. 'Go and get t'story direct. You know what men are.' She poured a cup of tea and pushed it towards Greg. 'He'd not get half the facts right.'

'I assume he is *now* in bed.' The doctor's manner was brusque and, as he looked up at Eleanor, he shook his head. 'Ah! you people make me cross.'

She tightened her lips and lifted her head a fraction, but did not answer.

'Why didn't your husband come to me months ago? And *why* hasn't he been to make arrangements before now?' He consulted his notes. 'It's nearly another month since I first saw him, when he had begun to cough up blood.' He leaned forward, his foxy face questioning, seeming more like a judge than a doctor.

'Where is the sanatorium?' she asked stiffly, too shocked to betray the revelation he had made.

He sighed. 'Ah! well, at least you're not babbling on making excuses.' Then he paused and looked at her with new discernment. 'When did *you* know?'

'Yesterday.'

'Then he is a doubly foolish young man,' he said, but more gently.

'How bad is it, doctor?'

'He's left it plenty late enough, but . . . he's young,' he shrugged. 'the best place is Switzerland, of course. All that clean, cold air, *that* kills the germs, but that's for people with plenty of money, apart from the expense of just getting there.'

'Since he began to cough up blood.' The dry, persistent cough at night – but blood. She had not known. 'He's left it plenty late enough'. The doctor's words kept pace with her steps as she left the surgery, but behind their persistence formed a resolution just as stubborn. She would do everything in her power to defeat this sickness. Its menace made it seem like a separate entity she must fight, and to fight, she thought, you armed yourself with the best possible weapons.

Her step became more purposeful. She went to the nearest newsagent and bought a packet of stationery, then found the public library and the writing room.

It took some time to draft the letter to Greg's father. There had to be plain facts, stark and startling, to bring Bertram Hamson to his son's side, plus the promise that if he came at a certain time she would be out, that there need be no contact between them. She knew Bertram would seize the opportunity to retrieve his son from her 'sinful' clutches, and baited her letter accordingly.

She went quickly to the main post office, brought a 1½d stamp. The elation of action turned into a terrible finality, an awful sealing of her own fate, as the letter dropped from her fingers into the post-box.

The only thing she concealed from Greg about the letter was the promise of her absence at a certain time.

'For the first time, you've made me really feel like an invalid,' he said when he began to realize the implications of what she had done, and that the letter was already written and posted. 'Someone whose decisions are made for him.'

She did not charge him with his own deception, and his criticism, perhaps because it was so evenly spoken, kept her awake long after he slept that night.

On the afternoon specified for her absence, she lingered at the far end of the street long enough to see the motor car arrive, and Greg's father go to the door, before going to do her shopping at Gunnie's. Since Greg allowed himself to be put to bed in the afternoons, she had stopped going to help in the shop, at least until he went into the sanatorium. If his stay looked like being prolonged, it had also been arranged that the attic rooms would be given up, and Eleanor would go back to live with Gunnie, until such time as they could set up house again together. Greg had speculated that at least one good thing might come out of this 'appeal for charity', there might be some reconciliation so they could marry.

Eleanor refused to be drawn into argument at those moments when Greg's frustrations made his tongue unnaturally sharp. He was right in what he said, and she was right too, and without quarrelling each stubbornly stuck to their ground.

His father's visit both excited and exhausted Greg. He did not get up again that evening. His one regret was that his father had called while Eleanor was out shopping.

'But he would not wait,' Greg said. 'He was going

straight to see the doctor himself. If he confirms that Switzerland is best. . . .'

'We *know* it is, the doctor told me that, and the quicker you can be got there, the quicker you will get well.'

'You wouldn't be able to visit me there!'

'No, but it won't be for ever, will it?' She sensed the beginning of his acceptance of the idea.

He would not commit himself verbally, and tried to make Eleanor admit she would rather have him in some sanatorium where she could visit, than abroad.

'I'd rather think of you breathing that pure mountain air,' she answered.

However, events were swiftly swept out of their control. Within days, a long letter came from Bertram Hamson, who had not only seen the local doctor, but had been to London to contact Greg's school and army friend Willie Orton, who worked in a clinic in the East End, and he, in turn, had taken him to see his father, who had a practice at the other end of the social scale, in Harley Street.

They had agreed on the Swiss clinic, and Willie who was long overdue for a break from his work, had volunteered to come to Honsfield, accompany Greg to Switzerland, staying on in the vicinity of the sanatorium for a holiday. He would arrive on Monday.

In three days' time, Eleanor calculated, as Greg finished reading the letter.

'Willie Orton!' He shook his head in mild amazement. 'If I didn't know better, I would think you and my father had collaborated on this.'

'What do you mean?'

'Well, if I *have* to go, then to have Willie as nurse-companion is the next best thing to you going.'

'You will go then?' she tried to keep any shade of emphasis from her voice.

'Yes, my tight-lipped little nurse, I'll go. You've won.'

She closed her eyes in thankfulness, so Greg startled

her when she found him by her side, his arms slipping round her.

'It's not the illness that I find so hard,' he said. 'It's the thought of our being apart. When I've gone I want you to go to Gunnie's right away, don't stay here by yourself. I don't like the thought of that.'

Hardly had she thought of parting, so anxious had she been for him to agree to go. Now she looked at him with all the anguish of love and imminent separation in her heart. This, she thought, is the real moment of parting, now, because tomorrow will bring all the rush of preparation, so many little things to do before his friend arrives. It will be like plunging downhill on that toboggan, only at the end, I shall be alone. 'It has been such a short time . . .' she whispered.

'There'll never be another separation after this,' his voice was firm, intense. 'Never, I promise.'

'No, we must be sensible.' She dare not give way to emotion, or she felt it was possible he would change his mind, and in her own words she found the acutest agony, already she was loosening the bonds between them, preparing his mind, as she would his clothes, for the journey.

Willie Orton came exactly on time on Monday afternoon. Eleanor was surprised that he was very little taller than herself and stocky in his knee-length, square-shouldered overcoat. He regarded her with a searching eye which she judged as having been previously prejudiced against her by Greg's father.

The greetings between the two men were enthusiastic, the handshakes hearty, until William stood back and viewed his friend critically.

'I suppose you've no idea just how much weight you have lost?'

Greg pulled at the waist of his trousers. 'The old clothes are a bit loose, I suppose.'

'I should say you've lost two stones since the army,' William said, but then dismissed the subject. 'Anyway, enough of you. It's this young lady I'm so curious about.' He reached out both hands to Eleanor, and she took them automatically. They were squeezed with a reassuring and friendly pressure. 'You realize, of course, that you are some kind of goddess,' he raised his voice over Greg's burst of laughter and her astonished denial. 'Oh yes! You have to be. I know Greg's ideal of a woman from back in the trenches. I never thought it possible for him to find her.'

'But as you see, I have.'

William looked solemnly from one to the other. 'Yes, I really do see, and she is beautiful too.' The remark held great sincerity, then he sighed deeply. 'All I have is a clinic full of East Enders!'

They laughed and relaxed in each other's company, drawing chairs around the tiny grate. She would have liked to have gone on watching the two men, listening to their reminiscences of actions and the long discussions the two had about life, death and 'Greg's mythology' as Willie called his friend's fearless searching for the perfect woman, and the perfect way through life, but the next day's journey preyed on their ease. Willie took out a notebook to check his arrangements, then left with an almost apologetic confirmation that he would arrive with a taxi-cab at seven-thirty the next morning. Eleanor went out to the street with him.

'Get him straight to bed, mi'dear. The journey's going to take a lot out of him.'

'But it *is* best?'

'It is.' William patted her hand, looked as if he could have added more, but did not.

She lit the fire in the bedroom, and they both went to bed, lying watching the firelight play on the walls and ceiling, making patterns through the bars of the huge, brass bedstead. He made her promise that she would not come to the station. 'The last time I saw my mother was when she came to the station to say goodbye at the beginning of the war. She died before I could return. I don't want to go away leaving you behind on a station platform. Promise you will go to Gunnie's.'

She nodded against his shoulder, remembering Sophie and Lloyd's departure.

'I feel marvellous when I'm in bed,' he whispered. She giggled obligingly. Then she lay, long after he slept, attendant on his every breath, fretting on the one hand that he was not already in the sanatorium, resting and recovering, and on the other pining for the loss of him, though he had not yet gone.

6

Even though she did as Greg asked, every morning she made a pretext to go back to their rooms. After the first three mornings, there was nothing she could usefully do, but she felt the need for this private daily communion with the place they had shared.

It was here that Willie Orton found her on his return from Switzerland, just three weeks after he had left with Greg. There had been confirmation of their safe arrival, a brief note from Greg to say he was settling in 'among the high, cold mountains, and seeing the first doctor later in the morning'. Then nothing until William again knocked on their door.

'Mi'dear,' he began, then stood quite still as if having found and greeted her, he was now at a loss for words. A thousand questions raced through her mind, but she asked none of them.

'You were to have stayed a month . . .' she stated, stepping aside for him to enter.

He held his hands out to her then. 'We were both supposed to stay,' he said, keeping her hands, as she remembered Greg doing when she had knelt over Sophie's work-box.

'Greg!' She looked around foolishly, as if she might

have admitted him without realizing. 'Greg?' she repeated. 'He's not come back. Oh, no!'

Willie nodded. 'To England, but not here. I persuaded him not to come north again. He's at a seaside cottage my father owns on the east coast. The sea air will be better for him than here. I've come to take you to him, Eleanor.'

'Why? Why has he done this? Did he go to the sanatorium at all?' She manufactured a tinge of anger to spur William on.

William nodded, then indicated the chairs. 'Shall we sit down?'

She hurriedly pulled out the dining-chairs and sat quietly, hands folded, like an expectant, obedient child.

'My father had arranged for an eminent Swiss physician to see Greg the morning after we arrived.' William paused, spread his hands. 'All the usual tests were made and X-rays taken under his personal supervision, and Greg's prospects are not good.'

'His prospects?'

'Of recovery,' William added gently.

His prospects of recovery are not good, she put the words together in her mind, like individual jigsaw pieces that should make a logical whole, then shook her head.

'Not good,' she repeated, 'but not . . . .' She looked at William for some sign of hope, but he got up, paced to the window, and stood looking out. She must know everything, all her life she had been able to put name and outline to what she feared, there must be no indistinct shades of dread. She stared at William's back, forming her question, ready to watch his reactions.

'If you were Greg, would you have stayed in Switzerland?'

Although he did not perceptibly move, his stocky shoulders seemed to become less broad. His voice was low, but very clear, as he finally answered. 'I would have come home to you Eleanor, just as Greg has done.'

She was quite still for a moment, letting his answer, the knowledge she had sought, try to submerge hope, but hope was not so easily defeated. She got quickly to her feet, as if to escape the wave of panic that threatened to engulf her. William would have come to her support, but she lifted a hand. She must contain this shock, this grief, herself – and she wanted no one's touch but Greg's.

'How long, William?' She disciplined her head to lift her eyes to look at him, and she felt a momentary pang of compassion for the friend who had to bring her this news.

'Perhaps six months – here . . . longer if he stayed in Switzerland.'

No, her mind refused *this* judgment. She looked with sudden defiance at him, denying this sentence from some Swiss physician she knew nothing of.

William shook his head at her kindly, but with the certainty of one correcting a pupil about to go astray from the truth. 'The disease has gone too far. Only a miracle would work,' he said. 'Greg's lived on his nervous energy for years. It all began long ago, probably in the war. There were many ways of . . . I'm so sorry, Eleanor, so bloody sorry.' He wiped his fingers over his eyes. 'That's a bit unprofessional – it's you who's supposed to cry.'

His words did not register as she counted on six months through the year. 'A summer,' she said. 'One summer.' Her eyes were looking far beyond William, forward into the coming months with Greg. Not one precious moment must be wasted.

'Will you help me?' she asked. 'I must give up these rooms, pack all our clothes, and see Gunnie before we leave. We must go tomorrow.'

In the next hours, she could feel William and Gunnie waiting for her to subside into grief and tears, could sense their arms waiting, almost anxious to cradle her, but she knew she would not give way. With Greg waiting for her, the things to do were too many, and the seconds too few, for squandering on tears that could change nothing.

Saying goodbye to the old lady, Eleanor twisted the

ring on the wedding finger. 'Thank you for these extra months. It was almost as if you knew, wasn't it.'

Gunnie took the young girl into her scrawny arms, and patting her back in one of the oldest, most instinctive forms of comfort said: 'I'll look for you t'come back, when . . .' she shook her head, 'aye . . . well . . . when you're ready.'

Content with nothing less than arriving, the journey was a wearing time. Although she had hardly been still since the moment William had arrived, it was now a special kind of torment to sit in the confines of a railway compartment. The only time she relaxed a little was listening as William told of the times he and Greg had shared: schooldays, outings to London, holidays and the war.

She was avid for every reminiscence, until she realized that she was like someone drowning, grasping at every memory, sketching herself a larger canvas before it was too late.

'Once we arrive, we can walk from the station,' William said, breaking into her sudden silence. 'The local train pulls around behind the hills that surround the bay, and there's a path. It might be quicker than waiting for the local carrier anyway. He's not always at the station. I can carry your personal bag, and the other things could be sent down tomorrow.' She appreciated his consideration and kindness as he talked, but it could not drive the stricken look from her eyes.

The sun was low behind them over the land as they climbed the last marram-laced dune. The sea was calm and flat, with only the slightest ripple of water at its edge, like the movement of the finest silk thrown from the roll. Reflected brilliance from the water made fir trees on the far arm of the bay stand tall and black against the backcloth of sky and water, delicately washed with suggestions of pink, gold and green.

William would have paused to refresh himself at the sight, but Eleanor did not falter until, at last, he pointed to a small flint and mortar cottage, built, no doubt, by some long-forgotten fisherman in the middle of the tiny bay, and copped sides and back by a miniature forest of firs.

'That's the house,' he said. 'With the fields and sea all around, you and Greg will find peace here, Eleanor, and rest.'

'And healing, please God,' she murmured, walking on, erect, almost crusader-like in the dying light.

'Greg's still sitting out. Do you see him?' He pointed again, to the far side of the cottage where a permanent awning had been erected, and basket chairs and a table stood. 'He's seen us,' William added. 'Would you like to go on alone from here? I'll come tomorrow, bring the luggage. I shall stay at the village pub, they're old friends of mine.'

Taking her bag, she stretched to kiss his cheek. 'I'll be able to thank you properly when I can collect my thoughts. We owe you such a lot.'

'You owe me nothing.' He gently turned her on her way, and when she glanced back, he had gone. An unexpected feeling of freedom came to her as she hurried along the path. Now she had time, all the time in the world to be single-minded in her devotion to Greg.

The sun was quite far down now and the only light seemed to emanate from the sea, throwing everything into relief, so that the figure before her looked like a negative of reality, imprinted on her memory for all time.

She dropped her bag and ran as they drew near, only stopping when she was a few yards from him, blinking to clear her eyes, to search for expression. He stood smiling the same smile, and yet stepping closer she saw in his face, in his eyes, added dimensions and knowledge, but still no defeat or bitterness. She felt very humble as she went gently to his arms, her own slipping into their familiar clasp under his jacket, her head on his chest. They were both very still: words were not important.

The irrelevance of asking whether or not he was all right, left Eleanor tongue-tied for a moment then, feeling the enormity of the task ahead of them, she felt she must reassure him. 'We'll be all right, Greg.'

'Yes. I'm content, as long as you're here.' He caught her hand, and led her back to where she had dropped her bag and then to the cottage, but she sensed a reserve in his voice, as if he was keeping something from her.

Pine needles were thick in the sand before the cottage, and as Greg opened the front door, which led straight into the main room, she could see pine cones and twigs piled up by the hearth, ready to bring the bed of red embers to life again. The atmosphere was laden with the scent of pines inside as well as out.

A tall brass lamp with a glass reservoir stood filled ready for lighting on a small tripod table. On the mantelpiece, two new candles had been put into pewter holders, each boasting its own conical snuffer; a small glass-fronted American clock swung its pendulum busily beneath a flower-painted face, and a china cottage held an ample filling of paper-spills in its chimney. On one side of the hearth a brass kettle stood on its trivet, and on the other side were a pair of bellows and a good long toasting-fork.

To Eleanor the cottage seemed to have a half artistic, half utilitarian air. The table had a heavy orange and brown plush cover, and on the bare boards was a single woven mat in the same colours. Four lacquered bamboo chairs seemed to stand nonchalantly around – while in the far corner was a large wooden wash-tub.

'We have everything we need,' Greg said, picking up a corrugated wash-board from inside the tub, and making a pretence of scrubbing clothes up and down it. Then he indicated two huge old fishing skips full of cones and small pine branches. 'I collected all those behind the house in no time, and some driftwood from the beach, too. Every morning the tide's brought up something new!'

She smiled at his new-found enthusiasm for beachcombing, aware that he watched her as she dropped a few cones into the fireplace. Then she took up and examined a piece of driftwood, silvered and weathered into an intriguing piece of art nouveau, which he had preserved on the mantelpiece.

'Eleanor.' His voice was suddenly full of quiet appeal. Her fingers became still, and under her touch she seemed to feel the smooth quality of bone. In the hearth, the first, fresh blaze died around the cones, so it was almost dark. 'I want you to promise me one thing. If in the coming months I want to talk about my illness, about dying, you must let me. I once had an uncle who knew he was dying, and he wanted to talk about things to his wife, but she wouldn't let him. She *jollied* him along, right until the end, wouldn't even talk about arrangements that had to be made about financial and family things. Later she told me how much she regretted her attitude and he, I think, died a poorer man for not being allowed to explore his feelings or his situation.' He paused, then sighed and, as if with self-exasperation, added: 'I feel intensely curious about it all, detached – perhaps not really and truly believing it – and possessed with this crazy feeling that I have endless things to say and do in a very short time. I'm so ridiculously full of life and laughter at times, I keep thinking it's all a joke. Perhaps it is. . . .' The laugh he ended on was light, disbelieving.

She gripped the driftwood with all her strength, and found reserves of imagination to answer him, to give added purpose to the coming months.

'Yes,' her voice came as a mere husky whisper, but the low-beamed ceiling gave it a resonance and almost an echoing quality. 'You must have your times to talk, and I must have my times to dream. Like we did before, Greg.' There was urgency in her tones now, as if she too had caught his sense of time curtailed. 'You remember how, in the fields when we met we invented our houses, your business, our family. We must do all that, all that!'

They came swiftly back to each other then, hardly knowing how their hands moved over each other, comforting and patting. Their needs had been spoken and realized as equal. Only the time left was important – each only concerned to bear the coming trials together.

'Together.' He sought her affirmation.

'We'll do very nicely.' She lifted her face into the warm angle of his neck and shoulder. '*Now* I feel tired, really tired.'

In the early months, Greg's illness was not apparent, or would not have been to a casual observer.

One fine May morning, Eleanor lay listening, a little incredulously, to him singing outside their bedroom window. He sounded as if he was running through his full voice-range in preparation for a public performance. She had not realized until now what a good baritone voice he had and she almost believed his voice had improved. Then fancifulness left her, and she wondered if it was some instinct, some trick of nature, that encouraged him to sing and to exercise his lungs.

She found herself listening critically for any asperity, aching with a tinge of bitterness at the purity of each note, but as he changed from song to quiet, happy whistling she forced herself to relax. This was not to be the way of it. She had promised him. There was to be no wasted time railing against fate. For comfort, she gathered the other sounds of the morning around his voice, like flowers around a central bloom: the murmur of bees in the pink sandflowers beneath the window; the soughing of the breeze in the pines; the gentle long lap and withdrawal of the waves, with the trip and tap of pebbles in each aftermath, telling it had reached the centre of the otherwise sandy beach.

'Mid-tide.' Already this new life had recognized punctuation, and since William's return to London, new friends. A seagull with a dark grey feather in its tail, that swooped for bread from Greg's fingers, and a squirrel, whose courage still failed at the last when they approached with titbits, streaking up its favourite pine, to sit, haloed by its tail, and looking regretful at its own cowardice.

She felt there had been some cowardice, or at least far less than the truth, in the letters she had written to Lloyd and Sophie. She told them of the confirmation of Greg's consumption, of their seaside cottage, and these new fur and feather friends, but nothing about the abortive trip to Switzerland, and the time they garnered ear by precious ear, each day a full harvest.

They had no other visitor, except the local doctor, briefed by William. A kindly old man, tall, discreetly hooding the knowledge and the sympathy in his eyes, stooped it seemed with his many years of ministration over sick beds, and caring a little too deeply for those who lay in them.

Greg had forestalled any visit from his father, by writing to explain, quite matter-of-factly, that he wished to spend his time alone with Eleanor until the end when Bertram might come. She witheld judgement on Greg's wishes, but his father's reply moved her deeply. Behind the almost businesslike terminology at the beginning of the letter was all a father's grief and longing for his child. The second half of the letter was a complete surprise, addressed as it was to her personally. It told of a visit from George Sansome, who had 'in no uncertain terms corrected my knowledge of your father – and of you, my dear. I can only ask your forgiveness. At my age, I should have learned never to judge anyone except by personal knowledge, not even a daughter from her father's word. I would wish you to know that all my thoughts of you are now as of my dearest daughter-in-law.' The letter ended with offers of any help within his power, and was signed with love from 'their father'.

Her heart warmed to George Sansome. George, the

quiet doer, assembling Aggie's day around her, before going to earn the staple wage of the household, and she knew it would have been the letter she had written to Aggie telling of Greg's illness, that had taken him to the factory office to see justice done. She had not expected any reply or reaction from the Sansomes, for Clarrie had been their letter writer. She found it pleasant to be so unexpectedly vindicated.

The second half of the letter seemed to give Greg more concern than that addressed to him, and towards that evening he seemed fussed and anxious. He had a bad coughing spell which left him bloomed with perspiration and exhausted. The next morning he lay in bed until midday for the first time.

'I think we should write to my father and ask him to go and see your father about our marrying.'

'Greg, it's not important,' she shook her head at him. 'We don't want the upset, and he'll only refuse.'

'Surely not now, and it is important to me. My father did offer any help in his power.' He was solemn, pale, and to have tried to deter him would have meant more fuss. She brought him his writing case, and later that afternoon walked over the dunes to the village post office, feeling that if there was such a thing as sweet, exquisite torture, she was surely living it.

The reply came quickly. Reuben Lewis was now not easily found, as he had taken work on the construction of a new branch railway line some forty miles from the village. Bertram promised to seek him out the following weekend, when they would hear again. So the uneconomical stockinger's shop at the back of the cottage was at last silent. Eleanor thought how delighted her mother would have been to have had her man working away from home.

The second letter came promptly after the weekend, to announce that her father had been contacted, and that he was thinking the matter over. 'Perhaps,' Bertram suggested, 'a visit from Eleanor might help.'

'No!' Eleanor shook her head before any discussion could begin. 'I would not give him the satisfaction of being able to refuse me face to face.'

'But if there were to be a child,' Greg said. 'I suppose it's still not beyond the bounds of possibility. You could at least ask. . . .'

The possibility of becoming pregnant had been a worry at the beginning, now to have his child would be her dearest wish. 'Whether or not we are married is surely only important to other people.' She loathed the thought of having any contact with her father again, and least of all the idea of going as some kind of supplicant, asking permission for something he had done everything in his power to prevent.

'I would like any child to have my name in a proper legal manner,' Greg was quietly stubborn. 'Perhaps it's possible to apply to the courts? I think it is! We could ask my father to find out about that!'

'Greg.' She slipped a hand into his. 'Let's not waste these lovely summer days worrying about it, and then I promise you I will go and see my father later.' Even the words were like swallowing the proverbial bitter pill, but she recalled how fussed he had become thinking out and making plans and, however simple a ceremony might be arranged, she was doubtful of the wisdom of it. More and more he needed the calmness and rest of their uninterrupted days and nights. In the mornings when he was rested, he would walk and enjoy the seashore and the fields. After lunch they lay together, close in bed, resting, and often he would make love to her with great tenderness. Her total devotion to him gave restraint to her response, until his final ecstasy became a mutual triumph and pleasure, not just between themselves, but with some added radiance, some unexpected benison, that felt like a trinity.

She would lie in his arms then until he slept, careful not to let her occasional hot tear betray its presence by falling on to his skin. Slipping away, she would ache over the boyish look he had in sleep, the overheated flushed look of a dreaming child. Then, inwardly sighing, she would go to prepare trays for their evening meal.

After they had eaten, as the evening shadows lengthened, they talked, exploring the mysteries of living things, of beliefs, religions, myths and mysteries; or of their love, which Eleanor found difficult to reconcile with any other couple's experience, either her mother's and father's, or even the pleasant domesticity of Sophie and Lloyd.

'Perhaps it is the finite quality of our time that heightens our experience,' he ventured, then softened the thought, 'given pencil and paper we would all make different drawings, some would be masterpieces.'

'Some would have better quality paper and pencil.'

'True.' Greg laughed softly. 'Then, perhaps, it would be a case of better luck next time around.'

'Ah! but we can't know there is another time,' she said, wondering how one who looked so young could sound so wise, who looked so well, could be so ill.

'I believe there are clues.' He anticipated her questions. 'I remember a strange incident when I was in France,' he reached for her hand in the dying light, 'nothing to do with the fighting at all, in fact it happened way behind the front line. We were resting up in a village and there was a baby, only a few weeks old I would say, being pushed by an older child. I looked down into the perambulator, only to step back instinctively, smartly catching my breath, my heart thumping.' He paused, pursing his lips, as if still incredulous. 'What I stepped out of range of was the knowledge in that baby's eyes, it was too overpowering, too complete. I've thought about it many times since, and I wonder whether new-born children have some memory of their source, which dies before they can communicate it. I'm sure that child had. It really was like being in the presence of someone from another world, someone very superior who found my ignorance amusing.'

They sat in silence, then Eleanor recalled an incident from her very early schooldays. 'I remember running in from school, and smiling and nodding at an old man who was sitting in my mother's kitchen chair. But when I asked who he was, I was told there was no one there, and when I looked again, there wasn't.' She shrugged, then was thoughtful again. 'Do you think *we* could ever find each other again in another life? Would there be some kind of recognition?'

'There are these feelings of having met people before, of having been to places before – but would we be the same people again? We could never be *quite* the same, could we?'

'But part of us might recognize something in the other.' She recognized her own desperation, and Greg drew her to him, bending over her to shroud her with his arms, head bent protectively over hers, as he mimicked the northern tones of Gunnie, whispering, 'Eee! luv, thou'rt bonnie – daft perhaps, but bonnie.' She was still.

His acceptance of death she found hardest to bear, and he read her withdrawal in her silences. He supposed it was because he had seen so very many young men die, in such a terrible, unnatural way, that the thought of his own end was more acceptable, 'at least more civilized'.

'You, and the life and family we can only dream of – and know we only dream of – are my only tragedies.'

They often walked to the sea's edge when they reached such point of impasse, and found the gentle durability of nature's rhythms at length irresistible, lifting their spirits, and Eleanor's unextinguishable flicker of hope. Conversations then sprang again. 'If we had a son would you send him away to school, to your old school?' 'I think you should make a garden specially for wild flowers and herbs, you know so much about them.' 'I shall have all these shells among the rocks in the rock gardens.' 'We must have watercress in a stream. . . .'

'I hope you'll find someone else to pick it for,' Greg said quietly, 'someone to love . . . someone to marry after I've gone. Any money I have coming will be yours of course.'

She turned her back on him, her lips parted with shock and hurt at his words, at his almost prosaic tone of voice. She wanted to cry out her protest, to silence him, but she remembered her promise to let him talk of his illness, or of his death, if he wanted to . . . but she did not answer him. She could not talk of it.

'I remember losing a dog, a dear companion, when I was very young. I remember throwing a real tantrum when my mother suggested a puppy, but when it arrived, it helped,' he went on.

Eleanor stood rigid, her eyes closed, until at last she found the right words: 'I think I'm a bit old to throw a tantrum.' He opened his arms to her, and they stood very still, close, sharing their sadness. Eleanor's tears fell swiftly and silently, but then she found a sudden strength for she sensed that Greg too was very near to tears.

The prickly, purple sea-holly had just begun to flower in mid-July when one morning a youth on a large bicycle was seen coming unsteadily, but with some speed, along the cart-track from the village.

'Telegram, sir. Came straight over with it.'

Greg gave the boy a shilling, for which he beamed with decayed-tooth appreciation, and asked: 'Any reply, sir? I don't mind waiting.' He motioned the boy to a basket chair, nodding agreement, before ushering Eleanor inside and handing her the slip of paper.

RAILWAY ACCIDENT. REUBEN LEWIS BADLY HURT. SUGGEST ELEANOR COME AT ONCE CITY INFIRMARY.

BERTRAM HAMSON.

She shook her head at him. 'I don't want to go, Greg.'

'Is there anyone else?'

'I'm his only relative,' she said flatly.

He took the telegram and read it again. 'But . . . it

seems to me you must. My father would not say "come at once" unless it was serious, and . . . if there's no one else.'

She thought bleakly of her mother's last words. 'Best look after your father.' All her thoughts rebelled at the idea of leaving Greg.

'I'll be all right. You still have a duty to him. . . .' When she did not answer he asked: 'Shall I send a reply to say you will arrive tomorrow, Friday? I dare say my father would meet the train.'

There was no peace in her mind, leaving him, even though he declared he had food enough for a seige, and she had alerted the doctor to her absence. He had promised to make extra calls, in case she should be away over the weekend.

She consoled herself with the thought that the journey to Lycester was three hours shorter than that from Honsfield. She would be back so much quicker.

Bertram Hamson was at the station to meet her. Sitting by him as he drove to the Infirmary, Eleanor thought how old he looked, ten years older than when she had last seen him, old and defeated. He had taken her hand as they met, but all Eleanor could feel was pity, mingled with a sense of withdrawal, having to remind herself not to retreat physically when he bent to kiss her cheek.

'My son?'

'He's . . . not too bad, when we're quiet he's happy, and the local doctor is very good, very kind. I shall go back as soon as I can.'

'Your father is quite badly hurt,' he answered. 'I think you should be prepared – he is in great pain.'

'How did it happen?'

'He was standing on top of a wagon loaded with gravel, moving up the line. It's thought the engine travelled too fast over a set of points, it was derailed and the wagons began to topple over. Your father and two others jumped and tried to scramble up the embankment, but they could not climb fast enough out of the way of the falling wagons. The other two were killed outright.'

'Oh!' Eleanor closed her eyes against the vivid picture his description evoked. Her father climbing, slipping, his magnificent body trapped, crushed. She wondered if even he deserved such punishment.

'They are doing all they can, I believe,' Bertram's voice trailed away as he drew his motor car up close to the front entrance of the City Infirmary. The air of carbolic cleanliness, the feeling of suppressed pain, of untold battles discreetly fought, engulfed them immediately, shutting them off from the everyday even before the entrance doors swung to behind them.

'My dear, I'm afraid this is not going to be pleasant for you. Your father is a fighter. He is fighting for every breath.' The Ward Sister paused, as if to let the tone of regret she managed to instil into this information, register, then added: 'A man of less excellent physique would never have survived the initial accident.'

Eleanor, who until now had felt no glimmer of emotion, except a burning desire to begin her return journey, followed the sister as she led them back to a small side ward. Immediately they were aware of someone harshly sucking in air, as if indeed every breath was the patient's last and had to be snatched while there was still time. It was a terrible, violent inhalation. Eleanor gasped with shock and pity, as she saw her father's face ravaged with each agonizing effort needed to draw breath into his crushed chest. A great cage held the bedclothes from him. His eyes were open, conscious, knowing her.

'Father', and in the spoken name was the memory of his scrubbing of her, but she slipped into the chair a nurse vacated near his head, and put her hand over his. For a second, his dark eyes seemed to hold the wish to convey some message to her, but then awareness was gone and the eyes stared sightlessly as he began the battle for another breath.

'Can anything more be done, Doctor?' she heard Bertram ask, and turned to see a white-coated man beside him.

'I would like to talk to you both in Sister's office, next door. Just stay a few moments, and I'll be waiting for you.'

Eleanor was glad to relinquish the chair to the nurse, to leave behind the noise like a great foundering pump; to go to the office, and have the door closed behind them.

'His heart is so strong,' the doctor said. 'This is, I'm afraid, all that is keeping him alive. A terrible tragedy, he has a physique like a champion athlete, but now it is working to his disadvantage.

'How long . . .' Bertram began.

The doctor shook his head. 'I wouldn't believe it could be long.'

It was arranged that Eleanor should be made as comfortable as possible in the sister's room, to rest, and to sit with her father for short spells. Bertram would go back to his factory, where there were wages to pay out and some orders to see dispatched, and then he would return. Later that evening, she heard the flow of visitors and the rise in the level of talk from the ward, and expected to see Greg's father when the door was cautiously opened into the side-ward.

'I thought you might be here,' George Sansome greeted her. 'How are you mi'girl?'

'Oh! Mr Sansome!' The sight of his familiar, friendly face, his awkward stance in the doorway, brought the tears she might more naturally have shed for her father.

'Aggie said to give you her love, and if there's anything she can do. . . .' He looked down at Reuben then, at first implacably, then shaking his head. 'I'd heard he were bad.' He looked back at her, but knew the tears were not for her father. 'Is there anywhere we can talk?'

'I'll get the nurse. I'd be glad to have a walk outside. . . .'

'Through your visit,' Eleanor said, as they slowly paced a central square of grass between the Infirmary's

Victorian buildings, 'Mr Hamson now treats me as his daughter-in-law.'

'Ah! good.' George's face lit with pleasure. 'It was about time things were put straight, but why. . . .' His face became solemn again as Eleanor answered his unspoken question.

'The slightest fuss, the least thing outside our daily quiet routine, makes him so ill.'

'So you'll be wanting to get straight back. This was one of the things Aggie wanted me to come for. She says there's bits of food and a right scruffy mess, dirty clothes and things, in the house – your father's let things go, pretty much ever since you left home. Aggie wants to get in there and clean the place up. Then it can be locked up and nothing'll spoil until you decide what's to be done. At least that'll be yours, you'll have somewhere to come back to.'

'I suppose so,' she answered bleakly.

'We'd be right pleased to see you there,' George answered quietly.

She turned and squeezed his arm. 'You're a real friend, Mr Sansome,' she said and knew they were both thinking of Clarrie. 'Shall we go back now?'

Greg's father was resting in the office, and she was alone with her father when the end came, at a quarter to midnight. There was at first a break in the stentorian breathing. She bent nearer to the bed and was startled as her father's eyes grew wide, at first with panic, then with realization and, to her, most amazing of all, finally with acceptance. At the end, his mouth fell open, his eyes softened almost to benevolence, and with his last sigh Eleanor saw him attain peace.

For a few seconds before calling the Sister, she sat and marvelled that even this violent man's death should feel at the last like a gentle passing to a new beginning. She was full of awe, and wondered if God had decreed this death for her guidance, to provide chapter and verse for the future, the near future.

She travelled back to Greg the following Tuesday, having seen her mother's grave opened to receive her father the day before, and not resenting the intrusion because of the manner of his passing. She felt he had stood trial, paid recompense and been forgiven.

7

The five days of her absence were followed by almost a week of storms. The warm days succumbed to violent thunder and lightning. There was no rain to appease the closeness, only gales which swept the clouds inland, leaving their Midland hearts the wild awesome lashing of the sea for company, and reminding them of the fearsome floods that had devastated the neighbouring county of Lincolnshire earlier that year.

They were glad to shut themselves tight away at the back of the cottage, the wind making the lamp splutter in the gloom. It lifted the sea spray in drenching sheets and drove drifts of sand beneath the front door and into tiny piles through unsuspected crevices in the window frames. For Eleanor it was a spiritual shutting away too, an effort to disregard reality, to ignore what she had seen in Greg when she returned. For looking at him with eyes distracted for a time by different sights, she had seen a mortally sick man.

Bertram Hamson had driven her in his small Model A to the station in the early hours of the morning of her return. She had caught an earlier train than Greg could have expected, and she came upon him without warning. He had a thin, spiralled seashell before him on the kitchen table, and he was studying an encyclopaedia of the seashore. He stretched long, thin fingers to turn a page, then sensing he was observed, looked up. Immediately pale introspection disappeared and his face came back to life as he smiled.

'You're early! Wonderful! It's been terrible without you. Like five long years!'

He was so pleased to see her that she could see he had to remind himself of the sad occasion that had taken her away. He insisted on making tea, while she sat and told all that had happened. She watched as he moved slowly about the kitchen, so painfully thin now, so wan that his sun-bleached golden hair seemed extraordinarily incongruous. Yet his pale face warmed to human contact, was drawn back to animation by conversation and by contact with a sympathetic fellow being.

She exaggerated how well she had got on with his father, how helpful he had been, told of the unexpected visit by George Sansome. As she talked, she wondered how she could do this, how she could move from moment to moment watching someone she loved ageing, it seemed, years in days.

'Look! I have a surprise for you,' he said when she had drunk her tea. 'I've made a catalogue of all your shells and labelled them.' She leaned her head gently against his arm as he put the neatly written and indexed notebook before her, and knew that he was using every minute he had, still learning, still thinking of ways to give her pleasure. This was how *she* must manage, plucking, spinning and weaving each thread of time, like a poverty-stricken spinner at her wheel, anxiously heedful for the use of every fibre.

'Oh, it's beautiful!' she said, as he closed the booklet to reveal the delicate watercolours of shells with which he had decorated the cover. 'And they're not just any shells are they?' She studied the miniature paintings. 'You've made them actual copies of my shells, I recognize them.'

He laughed with pleasure. 'I wondered if you'd notice.'

Oh yes, her heart said, I notice everything.

After a blustery, showery August, September came balmy and warm, the sun with that special autumn gold. It was a mellowness that would ripen apples in Midland orchards, she thought, aching momentarily for the rolling green hills, with the lower browns and gold patchworks of stubble fields and early plough, of cornstooks and late evening gleaners in the fields. She and Greg sat together in a warm, sandy hollow, secluded by low dunes fringe-topped with the round-leaved, seashore grasses, talking of the village and the factory, and feeling like exiles in a far off country. Lulled by the gentle talk and the warm, whispering wind, Greg slept. She too closed her eyes, and gave thanks for the moment, precious with his presence and gifted with the warmth and brightness of the sun on her closed eyelids.

How long she too slept, she did not know, but woke to find him looking down at her.

'I've been watching you for a long time, I wonder I didn't wake you with my longings. You're beautiful, Eleanor. I do love you.'

'Greg!' She stared up at him, half laughing, blinking away the pricking tears. He could have been the Greg she had first known in their secret meetings as he bent to kiss her, but he avoided her lips, and as his love-making began she sensed his immediate near exhaustion. She moved demandingly under him, as she never normally did, surprising and hastening his desire, then again as if to encompass him more. She astonished him to swift satisfaction, and gave false witness of her own. Even so there was a difference in this time for her, a kind of inner listening, and she was still for a long time, aware of something like accomplishment. Rising at last to look at Greg, she was shocked to see him so pale, so hollow-cheeked, as if to raise one finger was beyond his strength.

'I think that was the last time,' he said, and for one moment his fearlessness was swamped with tears, with hurt.

She wished then with all her heart that they both could die at that moment, together there in the warm hollow of sand.

* * *

He seemed to waste quickly after this. The coughing bouts now became nightmarish ordeals, and for the first time Eleanor was there as he coughed up any quantity of blood.

Shock at first made her unable to show any reaction, but as she ran to help him, to bring the bowl and cloths to wipe his mouth and support him as he coughed, the control she needed came and without panic she did what needed to be done.

'Now we come to the messy part,' he said as he lay back exhausted but quiet. 'The doctor knows what to do for me, you've no need to worry. If you need a nurse. . . .'

'No!' she denied quickly.

'I asked the doctor to see the local rector about arranging our marriage. . . .'

'*Please* don't talk, Greg.'

'We still have to apply to the county court.'

'All right, we will, we will, but *please* rest now.'

'Hold my hand.'

They sought each other's hands more and more. Whenever they were within reaching distance as he lay in his bed, their hands came automatically together, perhaps each feeling that no store of memory could give a hand the sensation of the other's lying there.

The doctor now became her mainstay. After each visit he made her go out into the air with him, sometimes to walk a hundred yards or so along the track. This was as far as she would go from the cottage.

'Why does he have to die?' she asked one evening late in September, when the doctor came for the third time that day, and a sea mist coldly shrouded the land.

'There comes a time, my dear, when we can just no longer keep anyone alive, when it would be cruel to do so. A time when those of us who are to be left, have to learn to let go.'

'I want so much to cry – but I must not! I must not! Not

yet, he has enough to bear.' She turned to the doctor who, kind man that he was, had to glance away from the young woman's torment. 'Help me to let him go, doctor. Help me.'

The next morning the doctor made her a gift of a small old print. It showed a unicorn behind a small round fence, secured to a tree by a golden chain. The mythical beast seemed to be listening to a far-off call, an order perhaps for it to return to the magical land from whence it came.

When October came she was alone, their summer had gone, her magic had gone. Bravely he had gone on alone – she felt it would have been easier to die.

8

She had wanted to return alone to the seaside cottage after the funeral, but William would not allow it. She only vaguely registered his deep concern, and no longer cared what happened to herself. She believed she was only an embarrassment. No one knew what to do with her. The one sharp recollection of anyone among the crowd of strangers at Greg's funeral, was of Bertram Hamson, and his discomfort in her presence. She saw even in his grief, the awareness that this village girl who had lived, unwed, with his son, could after all be a great social embarrassment.

William was her mainstay, supporting her physically at the graveside, journeying back with her to the cottage, and with the help of the kindly local doctor, engaging a woman to stay with her until she decided what she would do. There was Gunnie, and there were the Sansomes, and the empty cottage next to them.

'You have only to send me a telegram if you need me quickly,' William told her when he had to go back to his patients in the slums of London. He wrote his address on a page in one of the meticulously kept notebooks and tore it out for her.

When he had gone, she wrote a long letter to Sophie and Lloyd, telling, now it was over, all that she had previously withheld. She wrote to Gunnie, half longing to go back to the shop, where at least she could be useful, half hating the thought of Honsfield without Greg, or Sophie, Lloyd and the boys, and knowing that really it was the last place in the world she wanted to be.

She spent many hours walking the beach alone after William had gone, until one day she found she had said her final goodbye to this place of precious memories.

Late in the November dusk she went to the sea's edge, and looking to where the light faded grey into a darker grey sea, made a last spiritual obeisance. She turned and walked slowly back over the firm, wet sand; across the pebbles that had sounded mid-tide for them; then over the dry sand that flowed with icy coldness into her shoes, and up towards the cottage.

'This is going to be a bootlace job, mother,' she whispered. 'A real bootlace job.'

It was gone midday when she reached the village the following Friday. Walking past the Hamson factory, she felt almost like a stranger. The sight of Henry Attersley standing at the factory gates, in exactly the same manner as on the day she had left the village to follow Greg to Honsfield, gave Eleanor an irrational feeling of irritation.

Then as she passed she had the grace to answer his hesitant greeting, for she realized it was the first time she had felt *any* emotion since Greg had died. But as Henry looked as if he might cross the road to speak to her further, she lowered her head as if battling against the keen November wind, and walked on a little faster.

She had to acknowledge too that this tiny contact with someone from the village did help a little. It made a fine hair crack in the awkwardness she felt at coming back, something she had never envisaged having to do. To the bleakness of her empty life was added the uncertainty as to how she would be received back into the village life; if indeed she would be accepted. Going off with a man was one thing, coming back alone, was quite another. There was also an aggression in her, an anger at her loss, a danger perhaps of antagonizing even those who might be charitable.

She could at least shut herself away, the cottage was hers. She certainly had no wish to see anyone, although she knew she must let the Sansomes know she was back.

When she reached the main village street, she walked straight into the cobbled back yard and, hardly glancing at her own cottage, went straight to the Sansomes' back door. It seemed right that she should knock and wait, although it was the first time in her life she had ever done so.

Aggie blinked in surprise as Eleanor answered her bidding to come in.

'Y'knocked!' the old lady said, as if half reprimanding, then from where she lay on her horsehair sofa, held out her arms for the girl to go to her.

'Oh! Aggie!' Eleanor went to kneel by the old lady, to stretch her arms around her great, warm bulk.

'Y'back?' she asked, 'to stay I mean?'

'I think so, Aggie. I've nowhere else I want to be.'

'You'll be a joy to us, y'know that.' She held her at arms length, and shook her head. 'I don't have to tell how we all felt for you . . . but now,' she gave her a decisive, comforting little shake, 'now, you're due for better times. You've had your sadnesses, your three losses.'

'Four,' Eleanor interrupted. 'Mother, Clarrie, Father and Greg.'

'I wasn't counting your father,' Aggie said bluntly. 'He was no loss to anyone. No, come this time next year, I reckon things'll be a lot different for you.'

She did not answer, only wondered how that could possibly be. Between the present and 'this time next year' seemed a great empty chasm, from which her mind hastily stepped back. If she could keep herself going for just one night, just one day at a time, she felt it would be an achievement.

'Well, I'll have another helpmate now,' Aggie said. 'Push the kettle over the fire. Let's have a quiet cup before the men come in.'

But mine won't come in, Eleanor thought. Even the friends she had left could wound without the slightest intention.

In the next two weeks, she did not so much seem to try to settle into her old home, as to punish it, scouring and scrubbing at every room. There was a savage anger in every attack she made on the floors, with the same scrubbing-brush her father had used on her, and she felt a perverse kind of revenge in crushing the bristle on each floor. Then she asked Mr Sansome to buy her whitening, and found malicious pleasure in hammering the football-sized ball to a powder, mixing it with water to a thick wash and re-whitening the back scullery and the outside privy.

She had become so geared to activity, to hastening to Greg's every need, that now she could not rest – or convince herself that all this activity could not, in some way, be for Greg's sake. In those two weeks, she had turned out the entire cottage, cleaned and polished every piece of furniture, every pan and crock.

Then one morning her energy was gone. The half-conscious pretence that Greg might come and see how spotless the cottage was, at last deserted her, and there was nothing more she wanted to do. She was mentally and physically exhausted, her will to find occupation for herself at an end.

Languid and spiritless, she sat at the kitchen table. When George Sansome came from next door to bring the previous weekend's newspapers for her to read, he urged her to look in on his wife later in the day, stressing again the effort it was for Aggie to leave the sofa. She knew he was very concerned because Eleanor would not go out and meet people.

'Be patient with me, Mr Sansome,' she said quietly, and saw he was reluctant to badger her further. She sat on, after he had left, turning the pages without interest for a start, but then reading the reports of the second anniversary of Armistice day, of the body of the unknown warrior brought from one of the battlefields to lie among the kings in Westminster Abbey, a symbol for all times of the million men who had laid down their lives for their country.

She studied the photographs of King George V pressing the button to release the gigantic Union Jacks draping the permanent Cenotaph in Whitehall, before his ministers, his chiefs of the armed services, ranked choirs and dignitaries, but remembered only the first Armistice Day, the first Great Silence, when she and Greg had stood hands entwined, and the first flakes of snow had fallen lightly on their shoulders.

In a curious way, she thought, she had made her home into a cenotaph, an empty tomb, scouring it of every vestige of the past, both of hatred and of love.

For the first time she contemplated suicide. She reviewed her own end dispassionately, and found the idea as enticing as a warm bed to a weary traveller. If she could have willed her own end, she would have found sanctuary there at that moment, but it was something one had to *do*. It required effort, energy. . . . There were knives, she thought, and her father's razor she had preserved in case she ever had need of anything really sharp. With morbid inertia she contemplated what she would need to do, slowly turning her wrists to examine the veins. Those she could see seemed very thin, and she supposed she would have to cut deep into the throbbing pulse. There would be a lot of blood, but surely, she frowned, irrational and light-headed as she was from lack of proper meals, surely they would not expect the Sansomes to clean up, that would not be fair. Then she tutted annoyance with herself. What was she thinking of! She rose and straightened the piece of bone-white driftwood in the middle of the mantelpiece. There was the gas stove!

Triumphantly she went to the scullery, ran her hands along the front of the black iron stove, raised the iron knob that lifted the oven latch, and held at bay thoughts of Greg and what he might want her to do, or not to do, or of Aggie and her feelings. This was a selfish thing, something for herself, something *she* wanted to do.

She ran to the kitchen, snatched up all the cushions from the chairs and threw them before the stove. She needed to raise her head above the black iron legs to the level of the oven. Then she hurried to the meter. She had a pile of pennies on the top of it, which she lifted and let fall one by one.

'Not enough.' She found her purse on the mantelpiece and sitting down shook the coins into her lap: sixpences, farthings, halfpennies and pennies. Still not enough. She could ask Aggie for pennies, and there was still time to get change from the baker, and the post office if she hurried, and the greengrocer's cart would be in the village. Her heart began to thud with excitement. At last she had something positive to do.

The knock at the front door made her gasp out loud it startled her so. Who could it be? She scooped the money back into her purse guiltily, as if it was positive proof of her intention. Before she could reach the door, the knock came again.

'Good evening.' Henry Attersley stood in the doorway, bowler hat in hand. 'I hope you'll not mind my calling.'

'No, I don't mind,' she said, but her voice was hard. She did not want Henry Attersley on her doorstep, with his hair parted down the middle, his spit and polished soldier-like boots, his limp. She even resented the smell of oil from his clothes, permanently permeated in the cloth from the wool at the factory.

'I hope I am not interrupting anything?' he said.

'No! Nothing! Nothing!' The words were too quick, too defensive. She saw his suspicion sharpen. 'What do you mean?' She questioned the look, rather than his words.

'Perhaps I could come in a moment, I'd like to talk to you.' He hardly waited for her reply, stepping into the parlour as if he had the authority of the law behind him. He closed the front door as she turned, automatically now, and led the way through to the kitchen. She attempted to close the door to the scullery, but he stayed the door with a hand reaching over her head – and stood looking down at the cushions piled before the gas stove.

'It's nothing,' she said. 'Nothing.' She tried again to close the door, but he held it firmly open, waiting silently for her to admit the truth. 'I can't go on, that's all it is. There's no point to anything, any more.'

'It's not what Mr Greg would have wanted you to do.' Henry bent and picked up the cushions, closing the oven door. He stood with the patchwork cushions in his arms, and when she did not reply, added: 'Is it?'

'Mr Greg . . .' she repeated the name the factory workers had called him, and her hands and arms dropped as if leaden and useless, hung by her side as if she would never lift them again. 'Mr Greg. Mr Greg,' she repeated.

Henry immediately put the cushions down, gently turned her, and walked her to the chair nearest the fire. He talked quietly all the time, running words over her in a stream, as if they were some kind of balm, and seeming to believe that if he supplied enough he would effect a cure.

'You see,' he argued with the silent girl, 'if you could prove to me this is what Mr Greg would have wanted you to do, or even,' he paused to give emphasis to his next point, 'if things had been the other way about, and you had died, that this is what *you* would have wanted Greg to do. Well, then perhaps we could talk about it. You should never rush into situations you can't get out of. You know,' he gave a brief humph of laughter, 'I remember when you were just a little footling thing, and the vicar asked for volunteers to go up on the stage to help the choir sing a carol at their Christmas concert. You slipped off your mother's knee, and before anyone could stop you, were up the stage steps. Then, there you stood in the middle of the stage, chewing your pinafore, hemmed in on all sides by huge choristers, unable to get off!'

She looked at Henry, and saw the kindness of the man, the caring, but then as quickly as the spark of interest was gone, she shook her head. 'It's no use, I've nothing to go on living for.'

'You can hardly be twenty, Eleanor! Come on! Think what Mr Greg would have wanted for you – not what *you're* thinking of doing! He would not have wanted that, would he? You think this is the end, but it's not! I . . . I came . . . well, comes the time when you've got to be practical, and I wondered how you were managing for money?'

She looked up at him sharply then, suspecting him of charity, but he spread an appeasing hand.

'No. I came because, as you know, my aunt has a little millinery shop, and she needs a bit of help in the shop, stitching on trimmings and things. Well, you think about it, wouldn't be much of course.'

'I couldn't be in a shop and meet people,' Eleanor said. 'I don't want to see anyone.' She saw he was keenly disappointed, and before he could attempt to persuade her, she went on: 'I'm sorry, I should have asked if you would like a cup of tea.'

'I'll make it.' He rose with eagerness, and went to fill the kettle at the pump. He also filled the kitchen water buckets.

He stayed for what seemed to Eleanor an unconscionably long time, and she began to reassure him. 'I'm all right now. I won't . . . do anything.' Henry was not easily dismissed. He stayed late, and his parting words were: 'I'll call tomorrow, see if you've changed your mind about that little job. It'd be just the thing for you.'

The only emotion Eleanor felt when Henry had left, was surprise. Surprised he should take the trouble, that he should care what became of her. Surprised he should have a memory of her as a child – something even she could not recall, but had heard her mother relate. She realized too that he had been worried enough about her to go to the Sansomes' door. Mr Sansome came a little later to say that if she did not go across for a bit of late supper, Aggie was determined to struggle across to Eleanor. 'And it really is beyond her, now,' George said, adding, 'and she's talking about frying onions – that'll be the first time since Clarrie went.'

Henry did call the next day, and equally embarrassed with the memory of the day before, and afraid of morbid sympathy, *and* feeling queasy after the few onions she had managed to eat for Aggie's sake, she summarily dismissed him, saying he need not come again as she was quite all right. Then, since she could not be quite so hard, she added, 'not unless you really want to, of course.'

He came again four days later at a time when she was experiencing another kind of trauma. She had begun to realize that the queasiness that had hardly left her, except briefly in the evenings, could be because she was pregnant and that against all the odds she could be carrying Greg's child.

The idea had just begun to confuse her with the problems and complexities a child, a love child, could bring to her when Henry arrived. He came burdened with a woman's shopping basket, a large one. He scowled with mock annoyance as if it were only under protest he carried the feminine thing. 'I've brought a sample of the kind of things my aunt needs sewing for her shop,' he said.

She sat down at the kitchen table, but did not speak.

'I feel you must need some money,' he went on gruffly. 'Certainly you need something to fill your hands.'

No, she thought, it's my arms that need to be filled, and now, she gave a sob of wondering disbelief, now it seems they might be. She crossed her arms over her breast, she could imagine the warmth and weight of a child in her arms, and she looked at Henry, needing to tell someone. He stood motionless before her, watching, his sturdy robustness dwarfing the basket of flowers and hats, and the ribbons he displayed in one ungainly handful.

'What's happened?' he asked quietly, putting down basket and ribbons, and sitting in the chair opposite, almost knee to knee with her.

'Keep your gloves on,' Henry advised as he walked her to the doctor's surgery. Eleanor had intended to put the little brass ring back on her finger before she went into Lycester. She nodded agreement. He had arranged this visit for her, from the very first reasoning that there was no point in sitting worrying about something she was not even sure of. He had studiously ignored the outright curiosity of fellow travellers, as he helped her aboard the village carrier's cart (transformed by two rows of wooden benches into the twice weekly bus service to town). He had insisted on carrying her market basket too, which fidgeted her, for he seemed to assume an air of belligerence with a basket, as if daring anyone to comment.

'I'll take the basket now,' she said as they reached the massive portals of Victorian brickwork displaying the doctor's brass plate. Her heart began to thud apprehensively.

'Aye, well, I'll wait outside. The account's paid by the way. I paid when I made the appointment.'

'Henry . . . I . . .' she stammered, then ended in a rush, 'You're very kind.'

'Go on,' he said, 'you'll be late.'

He was on exactly the same spot when she came out,

and they walked together in silence for some way.

'Well?' Henry asked at last.

'Yes,' she said quietly, at last realizing that the reality had many, many more complexities than the total joy she had previously anticipated Greg's child might bring. She had to be careful, or this miracle baby, this love child, could become a thing of controversy and disgrace. She remembered the brilliant girl who had gone from the village to university, to return just so disgraced, and finally she had become so despairing, that she had taken her own, and her unborn child's life.

Walking on, with Henry keeping silent pace beside her, she turned away from the main shopping streets, taking those between the Victorian hosiery, boot and shoe factories, the wool factories, and the dyeworks built in the days of booming markets before the war, then sustained by war orders, now by the post-war boom. She thought of Bertram Hamson, of the home he had offered her after Greg had died, then thought of her child growing up as his grandson, or granddaughter.

Reason as she would that Bertram's generosity and latterday affection for her, had seemed genuine, instinct, and the memory of his detached formality at the funeral, told her that she would be making a mistake to lay herself at his mercy, to ask for a home for her child. On the other hand, though, she would, in the end, always be an outcast and the child would surely have a better future, a brighter prospect brought up as a Hamson? She sighed, then started as Henry gently took her arm.

'Come on,' he said. 'We're going to find a café for a sit down, and something to eat and drink.'

She half turned to protest that she wanted nothing, but his face was determined and looking around she found she hardly knew where she was, so far had they walked from the town centre. 'It's gone time,' Henry added. It sounded as if he had made a much bigger decision than that it was past the time they should eat, and she was glad to let him make at least this decision, otherwise she might well have gone on wandering, body and mind, for hours.

The café they found on a nearby corner was full of men sitting smoking, taking tiny sips from their cups, and relaxing for a few minutes away from the factory. Eleanor recognized them as mostly hosiery workers, since they had the smell and the look of wool about them, oil veneering their clothes, and comfortable old boots and shoes for the constant tramping along the lines of knitting machines, and their scarves knotted loosely around their necks, to be discarded easily in the heat of the factory.

Henry took her to a corner table and ordered a pot of tea and fish and chips for them both, without consulting her. Greg should have been here, she thought.

'What will you do?' Henry asked, and when she shook her head he went on, 'I have a suggestion to make, but when I've made it, had my say, as it were, I don't want you to decide anything – not at once. I want you to think, think until next Sunday, then I'll come for your answer.'

She stared at him, wonderingly, puzzled, and he scowled to hide his embarrassment, then picked up his knife and fork and began to eat. Surprised, Eleanor did the same.

'You see,' he began, looking steadfastly at his meal, 'I've always wanted to look after you, knowing about your father and everything, but I'm nine years older than you, twenty-seven next time. I'm not such a fool as to think I'd have any chance in the normal way of things, but I think I've loved you ever since the moment you ran up on to that platform as a tiny girl.'

Eleanor looked up in astonishment, first at such a revelation, then at the fact that he should be continuing his meal. She then realized that this pretended concentration on his plate was merely the means to allow these disclosures, a ploy so he could reveal his deepest thoughts, a most unnatural thing for such a man to do.

She watched him quite openly, knowing he would not look up until he had finished speaking.

She was surprised too that he was only twenty-six, she had always thought of him as much older, well into his thirties in fact. His hair, of course, parted as it was in the middle (a fashion really of an older generation and already with traces of grey in the short side-whiskers) was ageing. But, if asked to describe an honest man, she thought she might easily choose Henry, and, with his general robustness, she felt he would probably look very little different when he was forty, or even fifty.

She appreciated now that while she had had eyes only for Greg at the factory, Henry had made many of his visits to the mending-shop just to be near her. She saw again how he had always stood where he could watch her, hands thrust into the pockets of his brown factory coat, trying to spark some response from her, even if only from shock at his jokes. Even Clarrie had giggled, but Eleanor had kept her gaze on her hands as they sped in and out of the socks, fingers spreading to examine for flaws.

'More than anything in the world I would like to marry you, Eleanor, to be a father to your child, to work for you both.'

His words brought her sharply back to the present. Now she, in turn, put food into her mouth, pretending normality to hide her feelings. Henry Attersley was indeed opening his heart to her, and she was finding this a book very different to the promise of its covers.

He talked not only of his feelings, but also of his plans – not dreams, he emphasized but plans. He did not intend to remain a factory foreman all his life, when he *knew* he could run a business so much better than a man like Bertram Hamson. He was saving, and trying to talk his aunt into investing a little money in him, so he could start a small hosiery business. 'The only trouble is,' he paused to glance somewhat whimsically at her, 'Aunt Gladys is a great one for taking out insurance, of all kinds, not a body to take risks.' He looked down, and his tone became serious again. 'I'm going to do it, and *now* is the time while we still have the post-war boom. I have a feel for the business. It's in my blood, I suppose. I know I shall succeed,' he paused, and as their eyes met, he gently raised a meaningful eyebrow, 'you see, I'm not afraid to gamble.'

Eleanor knew there had been many occasions when Henry had saved Hamsons money by good organization, making sure the skips of work went smoothly from department to department without delay; being continually on the alert for bad or sloppy work being turned out by the knitters and watching out for too much wastage, or bad purchases of wool. She had seen him do most things from repairing machines to hanging out the name cards asking for the various carriers to call. There was no doubt he knew the hosiery trade as well as any man.

'I'm sure it would not be a gamble if you had the money, the capital,' she said quietly, but aware that Henry's reference to a gamble had included taking on an unmarried mother-to-be.

To both it seemed that for the moment there was nothing more to be said. Eleanor put down her knife and fork, and was astonished to see that she had eaten all her meal.

They drank a final cup of tea, listening as the men called their goodbyes to the proprietor, one or two touching their caps to Henry and Eleanor as they left.

Henry was preoccupied as they made their way back to the market-place for their return journey. Eleanor had given him neither reply, nor sign that she had even heard his proposal.

'I'll come Sunday then.' He slowed down as he caught sight of the queue of villagers waiting for the carrier. 'I just wanted to say that . . . our marriage could be in name only . . . until you felt it could be any more to you.'

'And if I *never* could,' she said quietly.

'I'll take that risk,' he answered, equally quietly.

He again insisted on taking the basket, and was still carrying it when they met Bertram Hamson coming from her cottage door. Henry nodded and stood, gripping the basket handle in both hands in front of him.

'I have something I wish to talk to you about, Eleanor,' Greg's father said. 'If you could spare me a few moments.'

'Yes, of course, you must come in.' She held out her hand for the basket, which Henry reluctantly relinquished.

'Sunday, then,' he said. He nodded briefly again to his employer and walked away, and for a moment both stood watching him go.

'You know Henry Attersley well?' Bertram asked as they went inside.

'I'm beginning to know him,' she answered.

'Really!'

The one word made assumptions and asked questions Eleanor was surprised to find she resented. She did not elaborate until she had shown him to a chair, taken off her coat and hat.

'Henry's a well-meaning man.'

'I'm sure! I'm sure!' Frowning, he resettled himself in the chair, and Eleanor sensed again the change in their relationship. This girl had worked in his factory, and now appeared to be associating with his factory foreman distressingly soon after his son's death. After a few moments further silence, she saw him straighten up, assume a business-like air.

'It was my son's wish – ' he began formally.

'Greg.'

'Yes. You may know that shortly before his death certain monies due to him under his grandmother's will became payable, and, of course, he wished you to have this. There will be several hundred pounds.'

I am grateful to you for the 'of course', she silently commented.

'Are you going to be all right, my dear?' His tone was a

little kinder as she remained silent. 'This money will help, but. . . .'

'I shall be fine,' she said. 'I have the offer of . . . work.' Remembering their shared grief, the news of his coming grandchild nearly tripped from her tongue. She opened her mouth to tell it, but found instead she was breathing heavily like someone sick, panting almost, every instinct telling her that however much she wanted to cheer this sad man, to give Greg's father some joy, it was something she should not, could not, do.

'It was something very special with your son,' she said at last. 'Something I shall never have again.'

After Bertram Hamson had talked further about shares being sold and money sent to her, after he had risen, and she had stood, inflexible, at her door as he formally raised his hat in farewell, she sat for a long time.

The fire was so low now as to be almost past reviving, and as the chill of the November evening crept through the cottage, her mind seemed to encompass the whole vast, mist-laden countryside, seeking solace, finding none, and no one, but herself. Then incredibly she experienced again the inner listening, the same feeling of accomplishment she had so little understood when she and Greg had made love for the last time.

The last time that had brought a new responsibility, a life entrusted, that she must cherish as a witness to their love. She felt the glow of it within her, like a tiny candle flame at the far end of an interminable passage, almost invisible, almost, but she kept spying a glint of it. No, she thought, it was after all more like a star glimpsed through the waving branches of a pine, and she remembered their pre-nuptial vows, and the coldness of another evening full of snow and laughter and speeding silence, and pure extravagant laughter and love of the whole earth. She cupped her hands before her, fingers spread, cradling this sacred thing. She had to live after all.

She rose quickly then, thrusting small pieces of kindling into the embers, wondering if it was too late, and as the first frill of flame caught the dry wood, went quickly to fetch a small log and a few cobbles of coal. Things had to be built up gradually, sensibly and for the best.

9

Later that same evening George Sansome came to sit with her a while, a little self-consciously feeling this was really a woman's job. Something else he did for Aggie, Eleanor thought. He sat quietly by her fire, smoking his pipe, not questioning, not speaking much after his first greeting, just there if she needed him, and quite unexpectedly she found herself confiding in him.

He was silent for some time after she had stopped speaking.

'There'd be a lot to put up with, here in the village, unwed with a child, and as the child grew to understanding. . . .' He shook his head. 'Then if you put yourself in the hands of Greg's father it's a bit like asking for charity, and, besides, I've not a lot of faith in anyone who couldn't see what your father was.' He paused, stretched his feet nearer the hearth. 'You've got a good fire on,' he approved, before speaking again.

'I knew Henry's father and mother, and his grandfather come to that, a kinder man never lived than that old man, spent every spring living out with his sheep, that old shepherd. Gave me my first threepenny bit on my tenth birthday! If Henry's anything like his grandfather . . .' George paused again. 'Whatever you decide, you know me and Aggie will stand by you.' She knew that even this was not an attempt to persuade her. She recognized his words for what they were: the facts as George Sansome saw them. The only positive advice he pressed upon her was not to confide in anyone else, 'not even our Aggie, just yet. There's a lot of people popping in and out of that kitchen during a week, and if she knows nothing. . . .'

The next few days were the loneliest Eleanor could ever remember. In the solitary state of decision-making, she could imagine herself in a deep pit. A pit she knew she had to climb out of – she had decided at least that much – and far, far above distant figures held out encouraging hands, gesticulating as if to indicate the best way, but she could see no foothold, no way.

She met George at the yard pump early on Saturday morning. He asked if she had made up her mind what to do. She shook her head. 'Time's against you, you know.' He spoke without losing the rhythm of the pump handle, filling first his own buckets then swinging hers beneath the gushing spout. 'Go for a good walk, get right way from the house, among the fields. "Lift up your eyes unto the hills".' He grinned almost boyishly as he quoted the old psalm and she looked at him in surprise. 'I was in the choir, when I was a boy!' He pronounced choir self-consciously, in the old local way, 'kire'. 'Now, go!' he repeated.

'I will lift up my eyes unto the hills, from whence cometh my help,' she repeated, as she walked along an old bridle path between great neglected hedges of hawthorn and sloe. Then as the path divided into separate ways, to two neighbouring hamlets, she took the path that led to a narrow stile, looking on to open fields. Behind her, the bare smooth branches of black-budded ash saplings, and the many-stemmed hazel bushes, complained gently in the breeze. Before her was an expanse of green fields.

She stood for a long moment, head bowed, and when at last she raised her eyes, even the dull November day seemed blinding. She felt it had been a long time since she had looked up. She recorded the distant hills, the long lines of layered thorn hedge, the volume of elms, ash and oak, the remnants of the autumn clinging still in every shade of yellow and brown. Her sadness, her loss was undamned a little, spread a fraction thinner over the greenness. She heard a robin sing, sweet high notes in the dull November light, and she knew why her decision was so especially difficult. She knew there could be no compromise. She remembered what Sophie had said about Lloyd, how he became irritable if she denied his love-making. She remembered her father, understanding so much more now the meanings of her mother's pleadings and her bruised cheeks. Had she tried to resist her husband? Would Henry, kind man that he appeared, become just as irascible?

She climbed the stile, and her instinct told her that Henry was not that type of man. Just as his family had been well thought of, and of kindly disposition, so was he. The grass was a bright winter-green beneath her feet. She wondered if she could bear another lover after Greg? Could she bear to lie beside Henry Attersley as his wife?

She walked on and started as some water creature plopped heavily into a still dark pond, the ripples of its hasty dive deep and wide spreading. Perhaps this was how she must decide, suddenly plunging into the rest of her life. She wondered if she had the courage.

She saw grass growing in water-filled ditches, drowned now, and yet as was the nature of grass, always surviving – flood or drought springing anew from every devastation. She stood for a long time looking down into the still, crystal-clear water.

She arrived back just in time to buy a loaf from the last batch coming hot from the bakehouse ovens. She had to light the gas mantle when she went in, to stir the fire. Then she ate the crusty bread, with slices of cheese melting in its middle, and drank milk cold from the pantry.

That night she slept well, waking to wonder at the powers of her own brain, as she recalled her dream. The pit she had previously imagined had become in her dream frighteningly real, and she had scuttered uselessly about in the bottom like a beetle on a saucer. Then Greg's voice had mildly censured her: 'Everyone knows that the easiest way up is by a watercourse.'

She had found the watercourse, grass reaching for the surface beneath its flow, and had walked easily up, up, to where another man waited to take her hand.

So, though it tore her heart yet to do it, she crossed the yard early on Sunday morning, to take up George's offer of a leg of hare. It would make enough dinner for two, with carrots, onions and parsnips.

Henry had tentatively suggested that Eleanor might wish to remain in her own cottage, where there were at least two bedrooms with separate doors to the stairs, unlike his own, where one tiny bedroom led off from the other.

'No, no, marriage is marriage,' she had answered quietly. Henry had not replied, and had made an effort to frown away the slightly abashed look that came to his face, the look of a man who could not quite believe his good fortune.

She knew it would not be easy, was unsure how she would feel when Henry touched her, but she had resolved neither to tantalize nor to frustrate him, she remembered too well the furtive observations of her father before the final outrage of the scrubbing. No, she would not repeat a cat-and-mouse existence, and she always the mouse.

She had come to realize that Henry had a great many qualities she had never noticed, and if Greg's gift had been to open her eyes to the beauty and goodness of the world, then Henry's was to make her see the possibilities of the everyday. It was as if once she had consented to marry him, he had taken her hand and was rushing her apace at ever new ideas. He had a larger than life aura, as he made plans for what amounted to a little honeymoon for them in a small hotel in Lycester until Christmas Eve. She also inadvertently learned from Aggie that he had booked a *box* for the two of them to see the Christmas show at the Palace.

Eleanor and Henry were married just one week before Christmas Day, on Saturday 18 December 1920 at Lycester Registry Office, with George Sansome and Henry's Aunt Gladys from the millinery shop, as witnesses.

Eleanor wore a dark grey costume with a pink blouse high ruffled at the neck. The men both sported pink carnations with an ample arrangement of fern in their buttonholes. Eleanor carried one pink carnation over a new hymn book with shiny white covers that Henry had bought her. Her wedding-ring was a simple but broad band of 22 carat gold. Henry, she thought looked bigger, somehow his nature even more expansive, in a formal dark suit, his grandfather's gold guard across his waistcoat. He carried an air of authority about him, but with a swift wistful memory of Clarrie, she wished again that he did not part his hair in the middle. Perhaps, of course, it might be something she could get him to change.

The authority he exuded at his wedding service, startling her with the loudness and certainty of his replies to the Registrar, he carried with him to the small, but discreet and scrupulously clean, commercial hotel. He dealt with the condescending reception the proprietress at first gave them, and within minutes had turned her disdainful attitude to their wedding attire and the apparent disparity in their ages, to one of respect and obsequiousness.

'Supercilious old dolly,' he remarked after she had shown them to their room. After their evening meal, Henry suggested they should take a final walk in the town before bedtime. As they left the hotel they found the winter evening bitter, a wind had sprung up and met them viciously at every corner, so they did not wander far. He asked her to cross just one more road before they turned back, as they were near a small empty factory he had had his eye on for over twelve months.

'There's machines there standing idle, I could make pay,' he said, peering over the half-frosted windows illuminated by a corner street lamp. 'All I need is more capital, enough to pay a deposit, buy some yarn, and then to tide me over the first few months' wages. I could raise a bank loan nearly up to the value of the property itself.'

' "Keys available for viewing at 136 Market Street",' Eleanor read from a smaller notice beneath the 'For Sale' sign. 'We could have a look round on Monday.'

'Why not!' Henry laughed aloud at the idea. 'Why not though!' He tucked his arm under hers and turned back towards their hotel. 'Come on, Mrs Attersley, we can't have you catching cold.' At the entrance he paused. 'You'd perhaps like a little time on your own. I'll just stroll a bit further. I'll not be long.'

She watched him, for a second feeling strangely bereft, seeing his policeman-like bulk and even stride going away from her. He looked so . . . dependable . . . so much older. . . . She went inside and slowly upstairs, unsure whether she felt saved, or about to be martyred, or just terribly unsure.

In their room, she undressed, hung up her clothes, tidied her own and Henry's clothes into separate drawers of the huge old chest, put a little more coal on to the fire, looked round for more to do, and at last, unable to find anything more, got into bed.

She sat upright between the shiny, cold, flat-ironed sheets, and listened. She hoped Henry had not gone to find a public house, and for a few seconds before she heard the unmistakable sound of a man coming up the stairs, the spectre of her father's drunkenness rose before her.

'It's likely to snow before morning,' Henry said as he closed the door behind him, and not pausing for any reply, he glanced quickly at her. 'Comfortable, are you?'

When she nodded, he hung his coat and hat on the peg behind the door, then to her surprise walked over to the gas light and turned it out.

'I'm not modest,' he said, as he sat on the edge of the bedside chair to remove his boots, 'but I like to do things with a bit of style, and nobody can undress graceful in this rabbit hutch. Single room with a double bed in, that's what this is. . . .'

He went on talking as he undressed. She was pleased he had put out the light when he pulled off both his shirt and vest and got into bed naked. She slid down to lie beside him, feeling like a very small girl. He reached over and took her hand. 'You're not very warm,' he said.

'No.'

'Let me warm you.' He pushed an arm towards her and she lifted her head so he could put it around her. She was glad his breath was sweet; he had certainly not had a drink and she suddenly felt guilty that she had thought of him in the same terms as her father. His face still smelt cold and frosty, like the night air. His body was almost hot against her, through her cambric night-gown. They lay silent and still for a few moments.

'You're sure, this is. . . .'

'Yes,' she broke in quietly. 'I. . . .' She was glad he drew her nearer then, for she was close to tears, suddenly sure that this act would take her one step further away from Greg. Perhaps if she thought of Greg while this other man's arms held her, his hands caressed her? But as Henry reached his free arm over and cupped her waist with his hand, gently pulling her over to lie on her side against him, she had to fight a desire to rebel. Thinking he was about to kiss her mouth, she turned her face on to his naked shoulder, for a moment retreating even from that refuge as the hairiness of his skin surprised her. Then she realized he was whispering to her. Talking, talking, talking, as he had the first time he had come to the cottage, but now the words were a curious mixture of admiration, understanding, promises and plans, which became incoherent as his passion rose, and he lifted her across himself, as if carrying her in his arms.

His tender control surprised her to a response she had not anticipated, and so astonished was she that she found she was still grasping his shoulders fiercely, when he lay relaxed beneath her and was once more murmuring to her.

Like a benevolent father or uncle, or older brother, she thought, and though afterwards she wondered at herself, she breathed the words 'Be quiet' close to his ear in a pre-emptory manner.

'Be quiet,' she repeated to herself, suddenly feeling quite as mature as he, but needing to reflect on this whirl of unexpected emotion. Her physical response to him had *not* been what she had expected, and she had need to come to terms with it. There was no denying that he had some skill, she thought suspiciously, and wondered if he had learned the art of love-making during the war. Without speaking again, he once more held her close, while she silently recalled the many tales of the French madames and the professional houses they had kept for the British Tommies.

She lay awake for a long time after he had fallen into his first sleep, realizing that what she had had with Greg was like a long, pleasant, drifting dream, whereas this man sleeping by her side, the heat of his body seeming almost to radiate across the bed in that cold December night, so that like some unwilling traitress she crept closer to him, was her reality. There would be no drifting or dreaming with this man. It had . . . it had been like being lifted up . . . up, until she was buoyant and breathless in the very breakers of life itself. It was only now that she found herself beached on the remnants of her own emotion.

She could not come to terms with her own body's treachery. She had had to steel herself to come to this man's bed, now she lay replete in every sense, and comfortable in his warmth. She wondered how they would explain if the baby was born with golden hair, and the reminder of why she was Mrs Henry Attersley made her lie staring wide-eyed at the last embers of the fire, which was dying like a cloudy sunset on the far side of the ceiling.

If Eleanor wondered at her own reactions, Henry obviously had no doubts. Glancing up from a meal, she often found him looking at her, his eyes seeming fairly to dance with joy. His look had a particular quality that reminded her of something, yet she could not for the life of her think what. Then at Monday breakfast-time it came. He had said he was a gambler, now he had the look of a winner. She regarded him curiously, to confirm the impression. He looked up from where the maid was putting his bacon and egg before him and, without any change of expression, he winked slowly at Eleanor over the girl's back.

Eleanor blushed and looked swiftly around at the other diners to make sure no one had seen. Henry's wink had a wealth of meaning that she found distinctly embarrassing in company. It really is like starting again, she thought, then ridiculed her own idea. She *was* starting again – although she hadn't known quite what she was starting!

'Shall we go and view my factory, then,' Henry said, for the benefit of the hovering proprietress, as they left the dining-room.

'Of course, and isn't it tonight we have the box at the theatre?' Eleanor said.

The street door was opened for them with almost a curtsey. They both maintained a well-disciplined composure until they were a few paces along the street, then Eleanor clasped a hand over her mouth, suddenly realizing what she had said. She looked at Henry, her hand still concealing the repentant smile.

'Who told you?' he asked.

'Aggie, but she didn't mean to.'

'You'll have to leave life's little deceptions to me,' he said, smiling indulgently. 'You're too honest!'

At the office of the factory owner's agents, they found

they were to be provided with a guided tour of the premises, not just the keys.

'Lot of machinery in there,' a small man explained as he escorted them from the office, pulling on his cap. As they began to walk with him, they saw he had a permanently crooked leg, which gave him a disturbing and violent up-and-down gait, but he had a remarkably cheerful disposition, and a strange habit of always speaking as if in answer to a question.

'No, not had many round really,' he confided. 'Weren't the labour during the war and now I don't reckon it's big enough for anyone to bother with.'

Eleanor noticed how thin he was. He was probably very little older than herself, but he had that special pinched look over the jaw bone that told he had certainly known hunger.

'Yes, its three storeys,' he announced, as he pushed the key into the padlock securing the gates to a small cobbled yard. He undid the back door to the premises and added: 'Yes. I think you should find your way around. I'm not at all easy on stairs, so . . .' he held up a bunch of keys towards Henry.

Eleanor watched Henry as he made his way around the dusty knitting frames. He seemed to step into a different world, she thought, as she saw him run his hands gently along the sinkers as delicately as a pianist might feel the keys before bringing them to life. He strode up the line of machines, looking around, as if in his mind he already saw the room alive again, alive with the chatter and banter of men's voices, machines spelling out their nicknames as they worked, 'Chick-a-chick-Charlie, Chick-a-chick-Charlie. Click-a-clack-Clara.' He turned at the far end of the room and looked back at her, spreading his hands as if saying: 'Look! I only need the baton putting into my hands, and I could bring this all to life.' He drew in a great breath of air through his mouth, as if ready to begin, then expelled it quickly, laughing at himself. 'Well,' he said, 'we'll see it all, anyway.'

He led the way upstairs, where there were several old rewinding wheels, counters for packing and a door out over the street. Eleanor was disconcerted by the sight of a door leading straight out into space. Henry found the key and putting an arm out in front of her, slid the door open. The wind took their breath away, seeming almost gale force at that height. Above the door, he pointed out the pulley wheel on an extended arm, needing only a new rope or chain to allow packed goods to be loaded directly on to a dray waiting in the street below.

Her heart missed a beat in alarm as the door stuck on its runners and he had to lean far out to lever it back into place and lock it again. She knew now was the time to tell Henry a little good news, something she had not revealed before because she had not wished there to be any incentive other than his own wish, to marry her. Now she was glad she could bring him something in return, for every hour she was coming to realize that he was both a kind and an astute man.

'Greg left me nearly three hundred pounds you can use,' she said.

'Three . . .' he began, then laughed as at a child indulging in make-believe. 'Three hundred pounds is a fortune!'

'Will it be enough?'

'Enough? You really have that much! Enough . . . for . . .' he made a half gesture to his surroundings. She nodded, catching his half-disbelieving excitement. 'Well . . . yes, but . . . I mean I can't risk your money, that's your security, or perhaps it should be kept for the child.'

'You're my security now,' she said.

'I couldn't gamble with your money.'

'You gambled on me.'

'Is that why you didn't tell me about the money before?' Henry asked.

'Perhaps in a way.'

'Money isn't that important to me you know. That's perhaps why I can take chances, because I'm always prepared to lose – but with someone else's?'

'I'm not someone else though am I,' she said. 'I'm your wife now.'

He reached out and took her hand, squeezing it warmly. 'You put me at a loss for words.'

'That, I would think, is quite an achievement!' She pulled a face at him, adding, 'Come on, let's go and see what's on the third storey.'

To their surprise they found that the top floor was even larger than the one below, and divided into two by the stairway.

'Looks to me as if the neighbouring premises would have more room on the second floor over the archway into their yard, and here the extra is in the attics,' Henry decided from one side of the stairs.

Eleanor was on the other side, where there were three rooms, two with fireplaces. 'We could live here,' she said as he came to her, 'make a flat.' He blinked in surprise, then looked around quickly. 'Then I could sell my cottage! Now *that* begins to make it all possible. Your money, what I've saved, what we'd get from my cottage . . . we could do it!' He stood nodding his head. 'We really could do it!' Suddenly he picked her up, clasping his hands around her waist, lifting her right above his head. 'Knew you were a winner!' he said. He lowered her gently and she stood acquiescent, guarded by his arms. 'I'll build up a business for this child of ours that he'll be proud to inherit.'

Slowly she lowered her head on to his chest. 'I thank God for you, Henry,' she said quietly, reverently.

They had almost forgotten the young man who had accompanied them. He startled them both as, when they arrived back downstairs, he spoke from where he sat on one of the work benches, his crippled leg under him.

'Yes,' he said, 'you have to go out into the yard to see the boiler-room,' and clambering down, he led the way to another padlocked door. Inside was an enormous old boiler, dirty and looking completely derelict.

'Ah! here's the snag,' Henry said. 'This'll never work again.'

'Don't you believe it, gaffer, bet my brother'd soon have that hissing away.'

'Your brother. . . .'

'Yes, gaffer, he's the best engineer and mechanic in Lycester, anyone who know's him'd tell you that!'

'Where does he work now?' Henry asked.

'He's looking for a job, sir, that's why I mentioned him. He's just four years older than me, a good worker, sir.'

'In the army, was he?'

'Yes, sir, served in Gallipoli.'

'Got an early demob, did he?'

'Yes, sir.' There was a slight hesitation in this reply.

'Why is he out of work then?'

Eleanor looked sharply up at Henry, but the other man answered quickly. 'No, ma'am, he's right. He lost his job, because . . . well, let's say his mouth is his worst enemy, but he's still the best man you could have for this lot,' he indicated the boiler, 'and for those machines in there.'

'I'll make a note of his name, and that of his last employer.' Henry hooked a stub of pencil from his waistcoat pocket, and giving a touch of spit to the lead wrote on the back of an envelope 'Bert Glover, last employer, J. C. Kemp, Wharf Way.'

Although she knew the empty factory was much on Henry's mind, he did not seem to want to talk about it. Just occasionally she noticed he lost himself in a kind of day-dream, still pondering what to do. These moments were only brief, for he was a most informative and interesting man to be with. He knew much of the history of their county town, and had the kind of mind which kept interesting pieces of information bobbing on the surface, and it was never too much trouble for him to relate them.

* * *

At the Palace Theatre, Eleanor found their box rather overwhelming, particularly as several of the artistes playing in Fred Karno's version of 'The Mumming Birds' (the fantasy that had made Charlie Chaplin famous), addressed themselves to the 'gentry' in the boxes, to the raucous amusement of the gallery, and to the added enjoyment of Henry. She enjoyed much more the private engrossment possible when they went to see the picture version of Rider Haggard's adventure 'Allan Quartermain', featuring Mabel May.

Their last two days in town they spent Christmas and window shopping. Henry badly wanted to buy her a gramophone, drawing her attention to the shop windows where a large range of these machines were offered. 'From four pounds to thirty-six pounds,' he read. 'Round and mellow tone sound boxes. Twenty thousand zonophone and winner records actually in stock.' She would not be persuaded that it was something she would enjoy, and in the end he bought her a fur muff and a large fur collar, both of which she proudly put into immediate use.

They spent some time finding just the right presents for George and Aggie, at last settling on a plaid travelling rug in heather colours for Aggie to use on her kitchen sofa. After Eleanor had studied a large advertisement which proclaimed: 'A most useful and acceptable gift, a source of constant pleasure to the wearer, and bringing to mind the thoughtfulness and sincerity of the giver', and remembered how increasingly George had to angle his newspaper to read, they bought him a pair of spectacles, Henry trying them on until they found a pair with what they thought was suitable magnification. The two Sansome boys, who were both courting strongly, were to receive handsome knitted ties.

Eleanor found herself looking at a display of glossy New Year postcards, with pictures of Lycester cathedral, or Lycester clock tower, surrounded by snowstorms. 'Is there someone you want to send one to?' Henry asked.

'I was thinking I should send the news of my marriage to some people Greg and I met in Honsfield.' She had been thinking of Lloyd and Sophie, and Gunnie, but then wondered if she ought to write letters giving more of an explanation – though that could be difficult.

Henry sensed her dilemma. 'Good idea,' he said. 'There's not enough room on a postcard for long explanations, but they can't say you didn't let them know.'

They chose three and went to the post office to write and post them without delay. The extra one she sent to William. She felt that being a doctor, and having known so much about Greg's illness, he might be the one who would guess the true reason for this sudden marriage.

Eleanor feeling at once extravagant and in a holiday mood, bought two extra presents, and very shyly presented Henry with a matching pen and propelling pencil, and a businessman's notebook, and was moved when she saw him blush with pleasure.

They went back to the village on Christmas Eve, and spent Christmas Day with George and Aggie. The two boys were both away, spending their holidays with the families of their girls.

They had a splendid dinner of home-reared cockerel, surrounded by onions, stuffing and potatoes, brought hot from the bakehouse oven where the majority of village Christmas dinners were cooked, and seemed to draw extra succulence from the mass of festive meat and poultry cramming the huge bread ovens. The smell of Christmas exploded on to the village nostrils as the first batch of dinners was drawn at twelve-thirty, and placed into the teatowelled and clean sack-clothed hands of the waiting crowd, jovial but bustling and anxious to reclaim the correct meal.

A plum pudding rescued with the clothes tongs from the back copper, divested of its clothes, and set alight with brandy, made the end to a splendid meal, and when Henry and Eleanor washed up, and when they had all dozed away a little of the after-effects of the meal, Henry told George about the factory.

I don't want to put a damper on everybody,' George said after some consideration, 'but you can't ignore the signs, most industries are having longer Christmas holidays this year. I read that some of the county hosiery people have closed until the 10th owing to bad trade. I'm afraid the post-war boom's almost over, Henry, people are not earning the money they did in war jobs, particularly not the women.'

'I know, I know,' Henry sighed, shaking his head, 'but then again you can read that Lord Derby says foreign merchant princes want to buy goods from this country, and are stopped because we can't promise to deliver. The trouble is you see, I feel that if I don't do this *now*, perhaps I never will. Now is *my* time, do you know what I mean?'

'Now, or never. Yes, I do understand,' George answered, and a glance passed between him and Aggie. 'So, if Eleanor here is willing, you go ahead.'

'I want him to,' Eleanor said, but looked curiously from Aggie to George.

'Tell them about us,' Aggie said.

'Well, it was a long time ago, when we were expecting our Clarrie, and the boys were both small. I had the chance to go out to New Zealand as a sort of gamekeeper. I was real keen on that kind of thing when I was a young man, the open air life, dogs, animals. It was a long, long voyage to New Zealand in those days. Usually it meant you never saw the homeland again, as more often than not it still does, and Aggie belonged to a big, close-knit family. There seemed a lot of good reasons at the time why we shouldn't go.'

'And regrets?' Henry asked.

'There's always the might-have-beens at the back of your mind.' George got up and stood over the fire before lowering another log on to the glowing embers, the firelight emphasizing the long lines in his cheeks. 'It would certainly have been very different to . . . what I do now.'

Eleanor thought of the long hours he spent shut inside stoking the boilers at the local asylum. She looked across at Henry. He had pulled himself upright in his chair, and was sitting very straight, very still, looking at her. She nodded decisively at him, and felt a thrill of almost sensual anticipation as he quickly returned her nod.

10

By mid-May, Eleanor was amazed at just how much Henry had accomplished, not only were they comfortably established in their flat above the factory (complete with gramophone), but he had surveyed his newly leased property, analysed at least some of the reasons it might never have been a successful business in the past, and rectified them.

'People have to be able to see to work properly! Mistakes take time to put right, and time's money!' The knitting machines had been duly dismantled for servicing, and reassembled on the first floor as near the windows as possible. The old work benches from the ground floor had been hauled up to the top floor to make a new examining and mending department on the opposite side of the staircase to their flat. Packaging, dispatch and, Henry's office were now on the ground floor.

She enjoyed hearing the girls clattering up the stairs to work at their benches, particularly as her increasing pregnancy made her less nimble. She always looked in to say good morning, and when one day she found a girl working on her own, two being away sick, she was just about to take up a bundle of socks for examining, when Henry came upstairs. He seemed disconcerted to see her there, neither returning her smile, nor her greeting, merely nodding to the other girl and asking if he could speak to Eleanor in their private quarters. She was surprised to notice his hands shaking as he closed the flat door behind them.

'I don't want you to work,' he said quietly, 'not in the factory.'

'But, I thought you would be pleased.' She could hardly believe that he could really mind. 'Two of the girls. . . .'

'I don't want you to do it! It made me feel sick inside to see you at that workbench. I want something better than that for you.'

She was astonished to see how upset he was. 'I wanted to help. You've done so much.' She spread her hands in a gesture of helplessness, but found it impossible to put into words the need she felt to compensate for her pregnancy. He had given no sign that he found her in any way unsightly, but to Eleanor the bulk of her pregnancy seemed grotesque, particularly so, she supposed, because it was not her husband's child she carried.

'Not doing the old things.' He was so upset as to be curiously inarticulate. 'Not mending.' He took her hands. 'You're not discontented?'

'I feel so useless. All around me, below me, across the stairs, there's a hive of activity, you running about, up and down, racing across town – now even thinking of going to London for orders – and here I am, crocheting, and dusting and polishing things that don't need it.' She glanced around. The flat was as immaculate as she could make it, comfortable with the two easy chairs Henry had bought, the gramophone, and the nicest things from the cottage Henry had sold. Her print of the tethered unicorn hung near the window, and her mother's dark green, ewer-shaped vases stood on the small, cast-iron mantelpiece. Henry had refused to let her sell her cottage, in case the business failed, and they needed somewhere to go back to. She had let this to the eldest of Aggie's sons, who had had to be married earlier than he had planned.

'You should be resting,' he stressed each word, 'with the baby due any time, *and* I'm still not happy with that midwife. She's too old.'

'Henry, she's delivered every baby born within two miles of here, and I've got to know her. She's a homely soul. I feel comfortable with her.'

'I feel comfortable with a lot of people, but that doesn't mean to say I would trust them with bandaging a finger, let alone having a baby! She's old-fashioned, Eleanor, and a bungler. You only have to watch her coming up the stairs to know that. She's a clumsy, lazy, old howdie. I always feel all she has in her bag is a bottle of gin and her knitting. I've got about as much faith in her, as I have confidence Bert Glover could keep a still tongue, and both together wouldn't brighten a single soldier's button!'

'Ah! now, Henry, that's not fair.' She seized the chance to divert the conversation. 'I know he goes on a bit, but I don't think he'd ever betray a confidence, *and* you certainly wouldn't have all those machines moved and working by now, but for him. Certainly you wouldn't have managed to renovate that old boiler.'

'Ah! well, no, I grant you that.' He drew her to a chair, placed her crochet-work on her lap. 'If you really do want to help I could certainly use some with the book work. I could start showing you how they have to be set out tonight.' She agreed enthusiastically. He left the flat with a backward look of mock severity, marred only by the wink he popped back to give her, before rattling down both flights of stairs whistling loudly.

She went to her writing-box, uncorked her ink bottle and taking up a pen wrote: 'If I can't work at a bench, then the boss shouldn't whistle like a common foreman on the stairs.' She sealed the note in an envelope and went to ask the girl on the mending bench to pop down to his office with it.

* * *

On 26 May she woke with a niggling pain in the lower part of her back, but did not mention this to Henry. By midday, the pain had increased, and was beginning to form a slow, but regular, time pattern. She served up and placed their meal on the table, but Henry was immediately aware of her slightly cautious movements. He insisted on running down to find one of the workmen to go and tell the midwife. He came back saying Bert Glover had gone.

'You told him to say there was no urgency?' she said.

'I told him to tell her to come,' Henry answered. 'Do you think you should go to bed?'

'No, no. I feel better on my feet, walking about, for now anyway. But I don't think I want anything to eat.'

Mrs Bates came at three o'clock. Henry, who had been on his way to find out where she was, ran upstairs first.

'Sairey Gamp's here,' he announced. Eleanor laughed between holding her breath as pains took hold of her again. Henry came to her, supporting her around her waist. He would have led her to a chair again, but she waved it aside.

'No, I really do feel better on my feet. I feel everything stops when I sit down.'

He walked with her to the window, and for a moment both stood looking out, watching the drays calling for the factory's hosiery to catch the evening trains. She looked up at Henry and knew he was impatient for the day when his goods would travel further afield than to neighbouring counties, and to his, as yet, solitary customer in Manchester. The door was at last tapped, but as the knob was unsuccessfully fumbled, Henry gave a snort of disgust and, leaving her to lean on the back of a chair, he went to open the door. Eleanor's eyes sought the little print of the unicorn. This is for you, Greg, she thought.

'What's this?' Mrs Bates was aghast to find her patient still on her feet. 'Now away with you,' she bustled Henry towards the door. 'We want no men about, do we Mrs Attersley?'

Henry opened his mouth to reply, but seeing Eleanor's minute shake of the head as she was ushered to the bedroom, he was silent. Eleanor heard him going slowly downstairs as Mrs Bates helped her to undress.

Once in bed, Mrs Bates wrapped the bedclothes around her as if settling her down for the night, and to Eleanor it seemed to have the psychological effect of slowing down her labour. She heard the workers going home, and the street traffic sink to its evening hush as the last of the horse-drawn drays belonging to the London, Midland and Scottish railways rumbled past on their way to their stables.

In the stillness, the labour seemed to take a sharper focus, her body moving to the need for more critical effort, although she was still not sure what was expected of her. She gripped the rails of the brass bedstead above her head, and called for Mrs Bates' attention from where the sat by a small fire, lit to keep the room warm as the evening progressed. As evening became night proper, Eleanor realized that Henry had been right about this elderly midwife. Her appeals for attention were constantly met with a cursory examination, a little sympathetic brow wiping and advice that nature had to take its course, or that when the fruit was ready it would fall, but as Eleanor lay, wet through with perspiration and heard the town clocks tolling midnight, she could at last no longer contain the agony of so much unproductive pain.

'For God's sake, tell me what to do!' she cried out.

She heard the door of the bedroom burst open before Mrs Bates could rise from her fireside chair once more. Henry almost elbowed the old woman out of the way in his anxiety to reach her side. He took one look at Eleanor's tossing head and gripping hands and turned on the midwife, gripping her shoulders and instructing her to do all she could while he ran to fetch the doctor.

'She'd better come to no harm while I'm away,' he added, overruling the woman's now half-hearted platitudes.

'Henry. Henry, help me.' Eleanor begged in a whisper as she heard his footsteps running outside. 'Please help me!'

'Old Mirrie's here, don't you fret. So much fuss! First 'uns always take their time, breaking new ground.' She cackled at her own humour, and Eleanor, now Henry was out of earshot, screamed with anger, frustration and pain. She was so tired. Didn't this woman understand? She didn't feel she was capable of one more effort, and yet still her body demanded more and more. She knew instinctively that something was wrong, terribly wrong. Make Henry quick, she prayed.

She was wild-eyed and desperate by the time she heard men's voices on the stairs. Henry and a younger man came into the room. The doctor ignored Mirrie Bates as she stood defensively over her patient.

'How long has this been going on?' he asked after instructing Eleanor to pant and not to move if she could possibly help it. He grunted a reply to the midwife's answers and lengthy explanations, then turned to Henry. 'How's your stomach?' he asked. Henry swallowed, but nodded.

'Take your wife in your arms and hold her fast. If we're to save this child it has to be done quickly. The cord is tight round the neck, it'll never be born like this. I'll have to try something a little unorthodox so I can get between the cord and the child's neck quickly. You!' he turned to the old woman, 'make up your fire and keep out of my way, or you and I will disagree again!'

Henry's arms were around her shoulders, tears came to her eyes as she whispered, 'Make them save the baby.' Henry nodded, as instructed by the doctor he tightened his hold on her, half lying across her as reality distorted in a swift ecstasy of pain and she heard herself making a noise like the terrified whinnying of a horse as she thought she felt herself being cut. Seconds later it seemed the whinnying had become a different noise, and there were voices again, happier, reassuring voices, and the sound was that of a baby crying.

She could hardly believe the ordeal was over, but dared to open her eyes. Henry was smiling down at her, then as he read the sudden question on her exhausted face, in her anxious eyes, he said: 'A *perfect* little boy.'

'A boy,' she breathed, and aware that Henry saw on her face memories and impossible yearnings, she closed her eyes, keeping close to herself this joy and this grief. Greg's son.

'Come on, Mrs Attersley,' the young doctor said. 'It's all over, you have a beautiful baby.' The child was laid in the crook of her arm, and she cried for pity of the helpless thing, the tiny trembling hands, the red face whose tiny bottom lip trembled with the shock of this traumatic experience, this life, this new beginning.

'There,' the old woman drooled indulgently, seeming quite unaware of her inadequacies, or of the antagonism felt towards her by the two men, 'just like his father with his dark hair.'

Eleanor became increasingly enthralled with the child, rapt in his every movement, hanging over his cot to listen for his gentle breathing when he was quiet, and rushing to him when he cried. One day Henry attempted to detain her as she rushed to the baby.

'Let him cry, a moment or two at least. You're not giving him time to exercise his lungs.' He had held her gently from the crib, his arm around her waist, gently restraining. 'Look! Little as he is, he's pausing to listen for you, waiting for you to pick him up. You mustn't spoil him. Give him room to breathe. You'll smother him with love!

But as little John's cries had increased she had pulled away and picked up the child cradling him close to her face, traitor enough to think that after all he was not Henry's child. Lost in gazing at the pacified child, she barely registered Henry's sigh of resignation as he went downstairs to his office.

Aggie told her much the same thing on the day the Sansomes arranged a Sunday tea to follow John's christening at the village church. The old lady shook her head at Eleanor as she lifted John from his basket crib for the umpteenth time. 'You're making a rod for your own back, my girl,' she said softly so the company who were taking a first cup of tea in the parlour should not hear, 'and making a big mistake letting that mite push Henry's nose out so much. He is your husband, even if. . . .' Aggie left the rest unsaid.

Eleanor wanted to protest, but as always when the soft bloom of John's warm cheek touched hers the world seemed to contract into that small sensation. It contained all she wanted at that moment.

'Madonna and child.' Eleanor looked up to see William who had come from the parlour carrying his tea and stood looking at her. He nodded, smiling approval at the picture he saw. Although no word had been said about Greg, the fact that William had immediately offered to be godfather when he knew of John's birth was proof to Eleanor that he knew whose child he was.

Gunnie too came through to see the baby. Eleanor had been surprised and touched at the speed she had accepted the invitation to be the child's godmother. She refused, however, to stay with Eleanor and Henry, insisting that she must travel back to Honsfield by the evening train. 'They'd all think I'd died in my bed, if I wasn't open by six-thirty Monday morning.'

George, the other godfather, came through to join them, Henry following. 'Might know we'd all finish up in the kitchen,' George said a little awkwardly.

William, who was next to Gunnie, quickly dispelled any strangeness they still felt in each other's company by stretching his free arm across Gunnie's thin shoulders and saying: 'We're just the right size for each other.'

Gunnie snorted with laughter, 'We're a bloody funny assortment, the lot of us!'

'You can say that again,' Aggie agreed from where she had collapsed back on to her usual domain, the sofa, one bloated hand gesturing between herself and Gunnie: 'Look at us two! Like characters out of "Comic Cuts".'

In the laughter and flow of conversation that followed, Eleanor thought how strange it was that the people in that small kitchen were the only ones in the world to know who John's real father was. She glanced at Henry. He was quieter than usual, but he was consciously striving to make everything as normal and easy as possible. This effort, as well as his obvious affection for Eleanor and John, soon made him the centre of the gathering, rather than the interloper he could easily have felt in the midst of her friends. He even made a little speech thanking William for the silver christening mug engraved with the date and the names 'John Henry'; George and Aggie for the tea, and the carrying basket that had been waiting for John when he arrived (complete with new blue silk, quilted lining and hand-knitted blankets), and Gunnie for the dresses which were to be shortened into more practical lengths for when the little boy was crawling.

'You can bring him to see me in one of them,' Gunnie told them.

'We will, we will,' Henry promised.

Before William left, he took the opportunity to find Eleanor alone. 'I shall take my role as godfather very seriously,' he said. 'This boy has a lot of living to do for . . .' he patted her hand, 'well, never mind, but if ever you need help, you or Henry, you know where I am.'

She nodded her thanks and hugged him, as Gunnie too came to say her goodbyes. William was to give her a lift to the station.

'Look after yourself, Gunnie,' Eleanor said and in answer was instructed to do the same for herself 'and that bairn and the man'. They embraced, and in the moments' extra pause as they held each other was the acknowledgment of all the memories, good and sad, of Honsfield, Greg and the Irvings.

The next moment Gunnie was neatly tucked into William's open-topped two-seater and, as they roared away, all Eleanor could see was William's motoring-cap and the merest tip of Gunnie's best navy straw, and two hands waving a last goodbye.

Eleanor and Henry were to stay the night at the Sansomes, sleeping in Clarrie's old room, then rising early to walk the three-and-a-half miles to the electric-tram terminus, where the line, speared out to the very edge of the city's outer reaches, was being used more and more by country people having to find work in the city.

John developed into a more contented baby as the months passed, squirming his delight rather than, as other babies might, chuckling or shouting aloud with pleasure, spending hours watching with dark, quiet eyes all that went on around him, and loving the walks in the park to watch the leaves blowing above his perambulator. She wished Henry would occasionally walk with her, on a Sunday, at least, but 1921 was becoming the year when older, established businesses were finding trouble in keeping up profit levels, and Henry was combining the work of traveller, office manager as well as owner, because he dare not take on the burden of another wage.

Realization of the exclusive role she had made for herself came to Eleanor when an elderly lady who often spoke to her as they walked in the park, tentatively asked if she had lost her husband.

'My dear, I'm sorry, you must forgive me, but you are always alone – and the way you dote on the child. I thought perhaps you were a widow like me.'

Eleanor went into an over-lengthy, over-detailed, explanation. When she had said goodbye and was walking home, she realized that what she had been doing was trying to justify herself to the old lady. To give reasons why her husband was working, even on a Sunday, while she was out taking the air so regularly with her baby. She looked down at John beneath his meticulously correct crochet blankets, perhaps, she thought, even over-warm in the new bonnet and coat she had just finished making.

Reaching the road that would take her directly home, she turned aside and walked slowly the other way. She needed more time to take a new look at herself.

Henry had made no attempt to make love to her since John had been born, although she knew the time said to be normal for abstaining had passed. She knew his feeling for her had not changed, for he found many ways of showing she was always in his thoughts. Even the little outfit John had on, had been worked from the soft balls of angora wool that he had bought for her, two balls at a time, from a shop near one of his regular calls. She had protested that it was too extravagant, but had delighted in the fairy-like down of the wool, working up each ball slowly, with loving care, then waiting impatiently for Henry's next trip to that part of town. Just yesterday the outfit had been finished.

'I wonder whatever you'll find to be working on next for him?' Henry had asked when she had taken John to the office to show the outfit, to him before setting off for their walk.

Now she forced herself to remember the other things in that office, to look outside the cosy world of John and herself. Henry had looked tired, had worked on a desk littered with invoices, order forms, calculations and costings. All the book work she had been anxious to help him with, the work she had had lessons from him to do, she had abandoned without a second thought once John had been born.

She remembered how when John had just begun to smile, Henry had held him aloft, gently waggling him to and fro between his hands until John had squirmed with pleasure, stuffing his tiny fists into his mouth. Henry had instructed him to hurry up with this growing, because the whole weight of the Attersley business empire would be on his shoulders before he knew it, and they had laughed when the child had suddenly looked very serious and had widened his eyes at Henry. There had been a moment then when she could have put her arm around Henry, and almost it seemed he had waited for some tenderness from her, instead she had taken John back into her own arms.

The old lady in the park had perhaps seen the picture she had unconsciously portrayed, for she had lost the father of her child, and the husband she had taken as a matter of expediency, she had been largely ignoring. It was with some sense of shame that she turned the perambulator round and walked back to their home.

Henry was still in the office, and as she wheeled the pram to its store place, in a corridor behind the office, a shyness came over her, and she lingered over John, watching him stir in his sleep, wondering if he would wake, but then was annoyed with herself. This was exactly what she had been doing ever since the day Henry had taken an active part in helping with John's birth. She placed a hand on the child's shoulder, as if to reassure him, then walked quickly to the door of the office.

Henry looked up as she stood in the doorway, automatically smiling a greeting, but his face was composed in tired, placid acceptance of his role as giver. He anticipated her usual immediate withdrawal, and let his attention slide back to his papers. This moment she knew she must not let pass, and knowing this decision to be as great as the one she had made in marrying him, she walked into the office and going behind him, laid her hands on his shoulders. 'I love you,' she whispered. The words and the gesture were more than apology. For the first time she knew she really meant what she said, she did love Henry. It was not the same as her love for Greg had been, she would never expect it to be, they were different men.

Neither of them moved for some long seconds, then Henry put his elbows on his desk and buried his face in his hands. 'I thought I had lost you,' he said into his hands, then he turned, and stood up, solemnly and soberly searching her face, gauging her sincerity.

'I'm sorry,' she began. 'I . . . want to help, I mean with the factory, the book work, everything.'

He laughed briefly. 'I'm not even sure at this moment whether we are wise to carry on. We may lose everything. I think you may have made a big mistake marrying me.'

She stepped closer to him, slowly, experimentally, slipping her arms about him. She savoured his warmness, his strength, but knew that at this moment it was she who must do the reassuring. 'No, I don't think so. I just haven't been doing my fair share, in any way. If I come down to the office I can answer that,' she grimaced towards the telephone he had recently had installed, 'and do the written work while you go and do your travelling with a quiet mind. John can be in his pram in here.'

'Yes,' he looked at her speculatively, considering, 'and I should make Glover foreman, to look after the factory side.'

'And I can sell my cottage if needs be,' she interrupted.

'No, no . . . but . . . it is more than that, isn't it?' He looked down to where her hands lay on his waist.

'It is,' she answered. 'It is.' She noticed for the first time how very dark his brown eyes were, how thoughtful beneath their ample dark eyebrows. She lifted a hand and ran it through his hair, making it lie in a deep wave straight across his forehead, where she had destroyed the centre parting.

11

'It either has to be a cut in wages, or I have to close.'

Eleanor was close by as Henry stood on an upturned packing-case to address his workmen and -women in the factory yard.

'I don't like it any more than you do, but I am not, as you all know, one of your monied bosses living in his country mansion. . . .'

'Not yet you're not!' There was some laughter at the interruption.

'Oh! I hope to be!' Henry retaliated. 'If I work hard enough, I hope to be! But if I fail now, I won't be and you won't have jobs either. I'll bear no grudge against any man who wants to take his cards if he thinks he can do better elsewhere, but I'll guarantee to restore the rate for the job as soon as I'm able.'

'We haven't heard how much this cut's going to be?' Bert Glover shouted from the ranks of men. Eleanor wished, not for the first time, that he would learn to sound more like the foreman she had persuaded Henry to make him, and less like a rank-and-file trouble-maker.

'A halfpenny a dozen,' Henry replied.

For a moment there was stunned silence, then several blasphemed, and there were cries of: 'Slave labour!' 'How am I supposed to feed seven kids?' 'It's hand to mouth now!' and '*You* won't starve, *your* kid won't go hungry!' It sounded as if someone at the back began to remonstrate with those shouting, there was some pushing, tempers began to be lost, and the jostling ran like a wave through the crowd, jolting Henry's temporary platform and knocking him down.

He brushed the wall behind him as he fell. Eleanor was immediately on her knees beside him. 'I'm all right,' he said, but the side of his face and his forehead were badly grazed, blood quickly oozing and running down his cheek. Before he could get to his feet, Eleanor was up and on to the packing-case.

'All right!' she shouted above the din. 'All right! Now listen to me!' She was so furious with them, so incensed by the sight of Henry's hurt face, that she could have taken on an entire army.

There was a startled pause, then the same questioner shouted: 'What do you want? The vote?'

'I may have to wait until I'm thirty for that Mr Glover,' she shouted back, 'but I'm going to tell you a few home truths here and now!' She saw a few turning away at the back of the crowd, and she knew she had to be quick if she was to achieve anything. 'How many of you were in bed with your wives last night?' The unexpected question had the desired effect. Some laughed, some shouted back, some shuffled their feet self-consciously, but they all stayed where they were, and they were all listening. 'I'd liked to have been in bed with my husband last night too, but I was up all night trying to find ways to save this factory. A lot of work has gone into this,' she waved an arm indicating the yard and buildings. 'Eighteen hours a day, for most of the last few months, that's what my husband has worked, *and* we've taken less money a week out to live on than we've paid any of you in wages, so don't any of you whine to me! We've put our time *and* all our money into this, sold everything we had, and if in years to come there are any dividends, we shall have earned them! If you go, we're finished. If you stay we *may* make a go of it, but we have to cut rates to be able to pay our way. . . .'

'It's easy to talk. . . .'

'We know you find it easy, Bert!' The men laughed as she bested the interrupter, and while they were on her side she made one final plea. 'Stay with us until after Christmas. We'll have another meeting then, like this, and tell you how things stand.'

There were murmurs of assent through the crowd, and

one or two clapped. She looked down at Henry. 'Do you want to say anything else?'

'No, I think you've said it all,' he said, holding her arm as she climbed down.

'They made me so mad!' she exclaimed when they were back in the flat. 'Look at your face. I'll get some water to bathe it.' He caught her hand as she was about to move away. 'You're shaking,' he said.

'I wouldn't have believed I could stand up there and shout at those men.'

'*I* was suprised,' he admitted.

'It was the sight of you on the ground, bleeding.'

'Didn't like a woman fighting my battle at the beginning. Then I thought, I should be proud that I've got a business partner, as well as a wife.'

'We'll make it work, Henry', she pledged, and knew it was not just for the security of their livelihood that she would make any effort necessary, but because *he* wanted so much to succeed, to make the dream of his own thriving business a reality.

'We will, won't we,' he brought her hands to his lips, and yet again she realized what a true romantic the rather impassive exterior of her husband hid.

Two weeks later Henry arrived back from Manchester full of dire forebodings. His one customer there, had cut his order by half.

'I've tramped around every wholesaler, every shop I could think of, but . . . nothing! No one's buying. I think we're finished.'

'We said we'd give it until Christmas,' she replied stubbornly.

'I think we shall be throwing good money after bad.'

'Christmas, Henry. We said Christmas to the men.'

'I'm a bit afraid,' he answered. 'You know sometimes it's easier to just go on, even though you know you are only digging your own grave deeper, than it is to stop, take stock and climb out!'

'Yes,' she replied thoughtfully. 'I can understand that with older established businesses. They're in a rut, Henry. We're new, not afraid to try new things.'

'But what? I'll try anything!'

'What are people looking for when they are short of money – *everyone*, rich or poor?' she asked.

He laughed briefly, then answered, 'All I can think of is that they want something for nothing.'

'Yes!' She pounced on his statement, and saw she had his full attention now, as she had caught the attention of the men in the yard. 'When I'm shopping I want the best value for my money. Say I had to go out to buy stockings, I know I would *first* be attracted to those that were beautiful, and *far* too expensive, *then* I'd look along the boxes for the best buy. If the shop assistant told me that with the Attersley brand I would be given a small card of mending thread with every pair, it would certainly encourage me to buy that brand. Women have to make their stockings last, have to mend the mends sometimes – and Henry – we have waste lengths of thread on a good many spools that are just thrown away. Look! I've made a start.' She opened a drawer in the sofa-table and lifted out a double handful of neatly cut cards, each carefully wound with lengths of lisle thread. 'And,' she added with enthusiasm, 'we'll put an extra two cards in each box of a dozen pairs of stockings, and tell the wholesaler, or shopkeeper. Then you've given him the idea to pass on to his customer, or to his salesman or -woman. So the seed is planted in their minds that if they or their wives need a card of mending thread there would be always a spare in the Attersley boxes. It would encourage the assistants to push our stockings, as well as the housewives to buy them!' she finished triumphantly.

'Just a minute,' Henry said, floundering in the excited stream of words and ideas. 'Let me grasp this. Let me . . .' he held up his hands and she tipped the cards into them. On each one she had neatly printed the name 'Attersley's' in a bold arch at the top.

'Every time they mend a stocking, our name would remind them to ask for the same next time.'

He looked at her with open admiration. 'You've done all these yourself?'

'Yes,' she spoke rapidly, not wanting praise, just anxious for him not to give up, to make this one last try. 'Later, if the orders come in too quickly for me to manage, one of the girls in the mending-shop can help.'

'Too quickly!' He shook his head at her, and laughed then sighed, and looked again at the cards of yarn. 'But it's certainly something for nothing, except a deal of trouble.'

She did not answer, for she could see her idea had taken root. She sat down, quietly, giving him time to see the possibilities. She had learned enough about Henry to know that while she could certainly lead him the way she wanted him to go, she would never be able to push him. She also knew that once he made up his mind, nothing, and no one, would deter him.

'I'll go to Manchester again tomorrow,' he said at last, 'then I'll try south, where there may be less short time, and folks may have a little more money to spend.'

They hardly saw each other in the weeks that followed. She wound cards until her hands, wrists and shoulders were cramped, and ached for rest, and supervised the office while Henry retraced every previous call, and made countless new ones. As she worked she could picture Henry waiting to see a prospective customer, not standing passively by, but making himself known, trying to size up the possibility of a sale from the appearance of office, shop or warehouse; not easily put off; certainly impossible to ignore. She was reminded of a gipsy couple she had once seen in a frosty hollow. The man had twirled a rod between his hands, the woman had sprinkled and piled flakes of chaff around the tiny pit the rod had made, and held her breath as the heat blackened the chaff, and smoke became a steady spiral. A few seconds more, and the woman bent to blow, with gentle controlled breath – another sprinkle of dry chaff and they had flames. She piled tiny twigs, then waited, larger sticks – another pause – and finally thick pieces of wood and logs, and quickly then, they had a sizeable fire. With the time stretched out a thousand-fold, she felt this was how she and Henry had to work.

As she worked, she cast around for yet some other way in which she could help. What if she telephoned local shops? Then, if they would like to see their stockings, she could make a list, or maybe take samples out, with John in his pram.

Henry came into the office as she was compiling a list from the advertisements in the evening paper. 'What are you doing?' he asked, and was horrified when she told him. 'No! No! It won't do.' He paced around almost like someone in torment. 'You must have personal contact. It's too easy for them to hang up. And as for putting things in the pram! For goodness sake, what are you thinking of?'

'Survival of this business,' she replied shortly, 'by any means I can put my hand to.'

'It won't survive if we look cheap-skate, like a lot of gipsies traipsing goods from door to door in prams!'

'We could perhaps learn even from gipsies,' she ventured.

'I don't know what! We've got to have *style* to survive, appear confident, not . . . not . . .' he failed to find the right expression. Then he added, 'Just leave this side to me.'

'It'll be a pleasure.' She screwed up the list she had been making and turned to pick up a bundle of time-sheets, thinking he would go. Instead he sat down opposite her. 'God, I'm tired,' he said, 'and cold.'

'I'll make a cup of tea,' she said stiffly, but immediately responding to his need. When she returned with the kettle they boiled on a gas ring in the office, he had John on his knee. He was letting the sturdy seven-month-old tug at his watch-chain, and unable to pull it up, the baby was doubling over to put his mouth to it.

'He'll mark your only decent suit,' she said.

'It'll wipe.'

'We're both tired,' she conceded at last.

He caught her hand and grinned up at her. 'We nearly had a row.'

She began to protest that he had been the one . . . but watching John frantically foraging, head going urgently from side to side in his attempts to push the chain into his mouth, tenderness for both of them took over. 'We nearly forgot what we are doing it all for,' she said, and gently tousled both her men's hair.

'Eee!' he exclaimed with mock annoyance, 'you know I don't like my hair all mussy.' He ducked away.

'Yes, I know,' she answered, reaching to do it again, 'you like everything just so.'

Whether it was the extra effort they both put in, the free cards of yarn, or a little upsurge of business before Christmas, or a combination of all three, they were not sure, but at the meeting of the work people just before Christmas, Henry was able to give better news. Customers hard fought for over the last few months were repeating orders, and most of them slightly larger orders.

'And we at Attersley's are not all having long, extended holidays this year like most in hosiery because here there is work. . . .' Henry was interrupted by loud cheers, and a heartfelt 'Thank God!' from somewhere in the crowd. 'And. . . .' Eleanor could see Henry was enjoying this moment, as he had every right to do. He'd worked for it! 'And,' he repeated triumphantly, 'not only that, but as from the first week in January 1922, I shall be able to restore the rate for the job!' There was gasps of delight, more cheering and much elated talk. 'I thank you all for your hard work and loyalty, and I thank my wife too. Without her we should all have sunk!'

Eleanor was once more hauled up on to the temporary

platform, but this time caught close to Henry, his arm about her.

'Three cheers for Mrs Attersley,' someone called, and the crowd heartily obliged, and then took up a spirited singing of 'For They Are Jolly Good Fellows!'

'There's only been one sad thing about this Christmas,' Henry said two weeks later, as he looked down from their window on to a group of men lingering in the street below, 'and that is that I can't take on the men from Wright's next door. I've had a lot come to me for jobs.'

'I've had men call while you've been travelling,' she agreed. 'Wright's going under, isn't he?'

Henry nodded. 'I tried to advise old Roland Wright to stop trading, pull out with what he had left. He is only making matters worse, but he became abusive, called me an upstart. The man is beside himself with worry, stands to lose his home to his debtors.'

'It is sad, but let's be honest, Henry, it was only the war orders that have kept him going this long. He's mismanaged for years, or so Bert Glover says.'

'Bert!' Henry raised his eyes upwards. 'But he's probably right this time.'

As January passed, each day saw more of Wright's workers laid off, and coming daily to haunt the gates and street, huddling together in drab, great-coated groups against the bitter winds. Eleanor saw the sympathy of their own workers going to and from the factory, and the embarrassed pushing of coppers into hands or pockets for drinks to sustain their vigil. She sensed too that the sight of enforced idleness instilled a determination to keep Attersley's going into them all.

Her own presence, running the factory office while Henry was away, ever seeking new outlets, was no longer a novelty. She was accepted, albeit reluctantly at first by the older businessmen she had to deal with. She also quickly learnt that her appearance could be used as a business asset. She *never* went down from her flat to the office unless she was as smartly turned out as she could manage. However nervous she felt, she never allowed it to show. Her youth and naturally upright carriage gave her poise and attraction. She realized, too, that there was no substitute for knowing every detail of the business, and she set herself to learn every aspect of their trade. The work in the factory was no mystery to her, but the buying of wool and yarn, sending their work for dyeing, costs and outgoings, were all aspects of business she had never concerned herself with before. She found it all a challenge, and a satisfaction. The selling part of the business she did not like. She knew it was irrational, but felt that all the effort that went into producing good quality socks and stockings, at a reasonable price, plus the free cards of mending yarn, ought to be enough, without all the extra hard work that had to be done actually to *sell* the goods. It was precisely this side of the business that Henry loved. 'Case of Jack Spratt and his wife,' he said. He loved the contact with so many people, and was quickly turning acquaintances into friends. He would have dearly liked to have entertained in more style than their factory flat afforded. Eleanor remembered with amusement how he had turned off the gas light on their wedding night. Henry, she realized, was more than a bit of a perfectionist.

She realized, too, that the men Henry attracted around him were like himself – energetic, unafraid and determined not to be victims. The slump was resulting in many small businesses going under, but at the same time the bigger firms like Courtaulds were reported in the newspapers as expanding their premises. Henry was determined to be still on the highway when trade turned the 'corner' everyone talked of.

It was after an evening with a man named Edgar Asher, a wool and yarn factor, that Eleanor woke suddenly from a deep sleep. Her first thought was that John must have cried out. She raised herself to peer at his cot, but the little mound just visible in a shaft of moonlight through the curtains, was still and silent. She snuggled back into her hollow in the feather bed, but was far too alert to relax. The animated talk of the two men went through her mind again. As the evening had worn on, business realities had spun off into dreams of progress. By the time Edgar was ready to walk home, she felt both men saw themselves as merchant princes.

She turned restlessly, but every time she closed her eyes she became immediately anxious. Something *had* disturbed her, she was sure, and now her instincts seemed to be insisting there was something wrong. Something she was not conscious of, was the only way she could find to describe how she felt, and that hardly made sense. She lay for a few more moments, then knew she had to get up and investigate. 'I must be getting like Gunnie, with my instincts.' The thought made her rise quicker. She went through to the parlour. There was nothing amiss there. She slipped on her outdoor coat, and a pair of soft-soled shoes. No sense in waking Henry unnecessarily. She was this far, and knew she would not rest until she had looked over the whole factory. First she went across the landing on their living floor, into the mending and examining shop, all seemed cosy there, then down to the machine floor. The shadows of the knitting machines, the overhead shaft and belts were weird, almost menacing, in the light of the moon, which shone brilliantly through the long ranks of windows.

As she went down to the ground floor, to the office and dispatch, she realized that if there was a burglar on the premises she was being very foolish to go down alone. She listened intently as she reached the bottom of the stairs. There was a noise. A faint, rustle, or creak, just etched on the very edge of her hearing. A mouse, or a rat! She held her coat close around her legs as she went on, wondering quite what she would do if she did find someone, or something. In and out of every room she went, not content until she had peered into every corner and cupboard, and found nothing. Nothing more than the suspicion of sound that vaguely plagued her still.

She wandered back into the examining and mending department opposite their flat door, and moving further into the room she was aware that the sound she had heard was louder here. It was a crackling or a snapping kind of noise. She moved nearer to the wall which joined their property to that of Roland Wright and put her hands on the wall, intending to put her ear to it. The wall was hot. She did put her ear to it, and the crackling was loud, vigorous, erratic. Now she recognized the noise for what it was. Fire! Flames consuming dry wood! She paused long enough to run her hands down towards the floor-boards, and then on to the floor itself. The floor near the skirting-board was if anything hotter than the walls.

'Henry! Henry!' she shouted as she ran back to their bedroom, snatching open the curtains for more light, before half falling across the bed. Henry struggled out of a deep sleep at her cries, while John stirred and murmured protest from his cot. She was thankful Henry just listened without questioning, her urgency making him immediately awake. He was out of bed at once and hurrying across the landing to feel the wall himself. There was no need now to put an ear to the wall to confirm the noise, crackling like a well established bonfire, was clearly audible. He ran to the front and back windows.

'I can see nothing from here, but it must be serious.' He ran back towards their bedroom to pull on shoes and grab up trousers and coat, calling instructions over his shoulder as he went. 'I'll telephone for the fire brigade, then open the front doors to go and look. You collect John, wrap up warm, take blankets and your bag and go down to the front door. Wait for me there! Don't go back for anything else! Understand!'

She nodded reassurance, and thanked God they had a telephone. He turned and caught her briefly to him. 'You'll manage. Do exactly what I said?'

'Of course, you go!'

She heard him clattering down the stairs, doors bang-ing, then she was alone, terribly alone. She stood for just one second, then the sound of glass breaking somewhere in the distance galvanized her to action. She tore the blankets from the bed and bundled them around John, who began to cry loudly as he was unceremoniously picked up and swathed. With her free hand, she threw her small store of jewellery into her handbag, grabbed the coat with the fur collar, and burdened with blankets and baby, stooped to feel in the bottom of the wardrobe for the fur muff that matched the collar. Then, coming to her senses, she reprimanded herself for being so stupid. 'People get burned to death doing things like this!' she muttered to herself.

Holding the blankets high, and the other things piled on top of John, so only his screaming face was visible, she hurried downstairs. She ran to retrieve his pram from behind the office, and hastily settled him into it. She was nearly to the front doors, when Henry came running back in.

'It's bad,' he said. 'The inside's all well alight, and our telephone's not working. It'll be quickest if I run straight to the fire station. Come on, I'll get you out first.'

'You go!' she urged. 'I can get this down the steps.' He held the door until she had the pram through it, then turned and ran. Eleanor was thinking of the business now John was safe. Leaving the pram scotching the open door, she ran back to the office gathered up their order book, men's records, everything she could carry from the top of the desk. She picked up the telephone mouthpiece from its hook, confirmed the line was useless, and threw it down in disgust. She glanced round. There were many other things but no, she must make sure John was well out of the way of the fire engines when they came.

She pushed the papers and books down the sides of the pram, settled John more comfortably, and pulled up the hood, hooking on the waterproof covers. The blanket that would not go into the pram, she threw around her own shoulders. Then there was no more she could do but be a spectator, and crossing the road, she walked cautiously along until she was opposite the Wright factory. The inside was a mass of light. For a few seconds there would just be a steady glowing radiance, then there was a blinding flash of instant combustion as the heat ignited the years of woollen fluff which had piled on every niche, every unevenness in the old walls, along the overhead shafts. Flames ate their way down the leather belts; a field of tiny blue flames grew over the machines as they fed on the oil and fluff that lay there. A pile of skips and packing cases was splitting and spitting flames towards the rear of the building, where the fire was worst, and must have started. Back windows were bursting. She could feel the heat on her face even at a distance. But it was the noise that was the most awe-inspiring: the roar of the flames, the splintering and crackling of wood and the shattering of glass.

She knew she should get out of range in case the front windows began to go, and yet for a few seconds more the awesome sight drew her on. The ferocity of the destruction, the range of the heat and the sudden violence of hungry flames held a fearful fascination for her. Then she felt angry and frustrated at the thought of all this work lost: Roland Wright's certainly, and Henry's possibly. 'What are we doing about it?' The words spoken aloud, made her aware of how isolated they were in this factory area. She was at that moment the only spectator. In the village, there would have been crowds of people by now. She could have shouted for help, done things. . . . She turned and went hurriedly back the way Henry had gone. 'Come on! Come on!' she urged the fire service from between clenched teeth.

She looked at her burdened pram and wondered whether there was anything else she could have brought out? There were the three skips of stockings ready for the railway dray to pick up, perhaps she could drag those down the front steps, and what about personal things? 'Oh!' she exclaimed with the awful realization that she might lose her unicorn picture, and then there was the book of seashells Greg had painted, the piece of driftwood. . . . Almost unconsciously, she found she was retracing her steps to their door.

A tremendous explosion from the rear of Wright's shook the whole street, and stopped her momentarily. She went on again, then heard shouting, a commotion of men's voices and fast revving engines. She finally looked round as she heard Henry urgently calling her name.

'What are you doing?' he demanded, staying the pram.

'I was just going back for some other things. You hold the pram.' She released the handle, but he grasped her arm.

'Don't be a fool. It's worse than you can see from here.'

'It would only take a minute.'

'What do you want to risk your life for?' He turned the pram and still holding her arm began to take them further away, up the slight slope to the end of the street.

The fire tenders roared past them as she was still hanging back. An officer seemed to take in her reluctance and slowed to shout, 'Is everybody out?'

'Yes!' Henry shouted back. Eleanor turned to watch them go, then gasped as from this higher ground she could see the full extent of the blaze. The rear of their factory was already alight, flames flickering in the mending shop next to their flat. She turned to Henry, mouth open with horror, and fear.

'You only just woke in time,' he confirmed her thoughts. 'Another few minutes. . . .' The fire officer who had paused to call to them came running up the road. 'Know anything about these properties?' His dark eyes searched their faces. 'That's mine.' Henry indicated. 'What's the chances?'

'Don't like this wind – gusty,' the officer answered briefly. 'You're *sure* everyone is out?' His glance went to Eleanor again. 'I thought the lady was wanting to go back in?'

'Just for personal things,' she explained. 'I didn't

appreciate how bad it was.' He seemed satisfied, and ran back to where hoses were already connected and beginning to throw water on the further factory, and other men were connecting longer lengths of hose to the street hydrant near where they were standing. 'I'm sorry,' she added to Henry, and was glad he had not known what she thought of going back for.

'We should get John inside somewhere,' he said, but his eyes were constantly drawn back to his property, to his dream. She leaned over and felt John's hands deep in the cocoon of blankets. They were cosy, and with the sides of the pram insulated with ledgers and papers he would come to no harm.

'He's fine, and whatever happens here tonight concerns him as much as us.'

'More,' Henry answered and groaned aloud, then went on as if to himself. 'Must try and save something. There were orders in the front there. . . .' It was her turn to catch his arm now, knowing the same fear he had felt when she had wanted to go back inside.

'No! No! Henry. We're all safe, that's all that matters!'

'I can't just stand here. I have to help.' He turned to a man in railway uniform who was obviously on his way home from a late shift and had seen the flames, which now leapt bright orange against the black winter sky, and lighted the street. 'Would you stay with my wife?'

'Yes, go on mate!' He put a confirming hand on the pram handle. 'You'd be Mr and Mrs Attersley,' the man added as Henry ran to follow three firemen who were going through their front factory door. Eleanor held the question unanswered until she saw Henry emerge dragging one of the full wicker skips, then having to manhandle it over the hoses to the further side of the street. 'He'll be in the way,' she said, and then answered the man. 'Yes, how did you know?'

'I often see you in the afternoons. Pity your place is next to Wright's.'

'Why? What do you mean?'

There was no answer as there was a sudden great fall inside the Wright factory, enormous columns of flames and showers of sparks like giant fireworks burst from every window. Both moved hastily and instinctively back, although they were well out of range.

'That's the floors gone,' the railwayman succinctly commented. 'Your husband ought to get out of that quick!'

The fire was now biting deeper into the structure of both buildings. That Wright's would soon be gutted was obvious as flames began to show almost teasingly, now here, now there, through the roof.

Eleanor's only concern now was for Henry. Her breath was tight in her throat, and her mind cried out: 'Not again! Not again!' and she knew in that moment how much he had come to mean to her. The sight of him safe was the only thing she wanted in the world. She started as her companion laid a hand on her arm and pointed to where smoke billowed from a smaller door next to Wright's. 'Thank God,' she breathed as Henry, escorted by two firemen, came out of the building. He could obviously do no more, and would certainly not be allowed back inside again.

He took a step or two towards where she stood, then stopped to stare again at their business, at their home, as fingers of flame struck ever deeper, engulfing their flat, then the second floor, and finally illuminating the whole building.

'The whole block's going to go,' her companion predicted dourly. Looking from Henry, ever looking miserably back at the destruction, to the flames leaping from their parlour window, she felt grief and yet something else: a steel-like determination that Henry should, somehow or other, make a new start. She pledged there and then that as he had rescued her from the depths of her despair, she in turn would lift him up, give him in turn a new hope and a new life.

'What did you mean about Wright's?' she asked the

railwayman. 'About it being a pity ours was next door?'

'Well, rumour 'as it that the old boy has had one go at setting fire to his place. Tried to make out it was an accident when someone found him, but I reckon there's a good many who knew better.'

'You don't think, this. . . .' She could not believe anyone could create this devastation on purpose.

'I wouldn't tell him that now,' he indicated Henry, still unable to leave the periphery of the action. 'But I reckon you've a right to know, it might be useful should there be an enquiry or anything.'

'Enquiry?' She looked at him properly for the first time. 'Yes, I suppose there might be. . . .' But once more the drama of the fire distracted her, as the wind in a capricious and momentary change of direction sent sheets of flames streaming across the road, seeming to engulf the fire-fighters. Then, just as quickly the fire roared straight upwards again, as if blown by gigantic bellows from underneath, and no one appeared more than momentarily dazed by the freak incident.

'I'm going, mi dear, now your man's here. My missus'll be getting worried if I'm not back – she waits up for me,' he added, as if with apology for such foolishness.

'Thank you for staying,' Eleanor said, 'and I'll remember what you told me.'

She wondered what kind of premonition it was, that made her look with such special care at the man's features, as if it might be so important she should recognize him again.

12

Henry had eventually found them shelter for what was left of the night at the nearby hotel, where they had spent their brief honeymoon. Even then he could not rest, and had gone back to the fire.

In the cold light of early morning he had returned grey-faced, streaked with grime and looking ten years older than the man she had startled from sleep with her first shouts of alarm. 'Henry?' she queried gently, as he sat hunched up on the edge of the bed.

'They saved the roof,' he said bleakly, then putting his hand into his pocket added, 'I just managed to reach this before the fire people made me leave again.' He pulled something small and square from his pocket and held it out to her. If he had struck her she could not have been more surprised. It was the small unicorn print. 'The glass is broken, I'm sorry.'

She was appalled to think that he had gone back for it. She felt she must have failed him in some way, and knew that in the future she would keep memories of Greg for very private moments. She would never have the glass mended, or hang the print up again.

'Thank you,' she said quietly, 'but how stupid.'

'Yes,' he agreed, 'stupid.' And he implied that he did not just mean the venture back into the burning factory.

She ignored his self-denigration, turned back the covers of the bed and knelt to help him off with his boots. 'You must rest. Then. . . .'

'Then?' he queried.

'Then, later, we'll go back and view the damage in daylight.'

'I want to be there when the men start arriving,' he said but lay back on the pillows and closed his eyes. 'It's all my fault.'

'Your fault? How can it possibly be?' she asked.

'It is. I should never have started the factory. I'm not the kind of man who is meant to make good.'

'Oh! Henry, don't! Don't say things like that, don't give up!'

'There's not a lot left to give up.' He turned his head away from her, and she yearned for him to be able to cry. She could easily have wept for him, but it would do no good. Now was the time for her to be the strong one. She lay down beside him and took his hand in hers. It lay unresponsive in her grasp, illusive, like that of someone mortally sick. She remained by him until it was time for them to go back to the factory to talk to the workers as they arrived. She was surprised and gratified when the rather starchy proprietress offered to look after John for her.

As they walked towards their factory, she could understand Henry's personal devastation. Even the destructive flames had held primitive colours, living fear, but now, where there had been employment, hope and a home, was a cold, blackened shell, and before it a growing group of their men and women, familiar faces appalled and made strange by the tragedy, mourners in stark relief against the background of their loss.

'Even Glover's speechless.' Henry's words and his tone of ironic bitterness, only added to the sense of disaster that hung over the factory street.

'Henry! Eleanor!' Their names were called and the tall athletically built figure of Edgar Asher, their guest of only the night before, ran towards them. 'I've just heard . . . I can't believe it! What happened?'

'Mr Attersley?' They turned as a police officer addressed them. '*We'll* be wanting to talk to you about that too, if you please.' He introduced himself as Chief Inspector Langley. 'An insurance man has been here too, looking for you, *and* Mr Roland Wright. I understand both your premises are insured with his firm.'

'I didn't know, no.' Henry was only half listening, his glance going first to the building, then to the group of workers.

'You'll be around here for a time?' Inspector Langley asked. 'I'd like to talk to you again as soon as I've had another word with the fire chief.'

Henry nodded, then went towards his people. There were murmurs of concern, enquiries for the safety of themselves and the baby, much head shaking, and remarks about it 'being a bad business'. 'Can we help with the clearing up, or anything?' 'What'll you do, gaffer?'

This last remark seemed to sum up all the questions in their minds, and there was silence as they waited for Henry to answer. Instead he turned away and walked towards the gap where their front doors had been, and stood with the appearance of a man overlooking a fearsom chasm.

'There is so much to sort out,' Eleanor said, turning so that she filled the space Henry had made. The men closed around her to listen. 'The insurance for a start – we just can't tell yet what will happen.'

'Could we start clearing up inside, missus?'

'Nothing must be touched yet.' The Inspector had returned to the edge of the little crowd. 'Nothing must be touched until certain matters have been dealt with.'

'What matters?' Eleanor asked.

'We'll be in touch with you very soon, ma'am,' he answered, heavily non-committal. 'In the meantime, I am posting constables to make sure no one enters either of the premises.

She suddenly recalled what the railway man had told her the night before, that Roland Wright was rumoured to have tried to set fire to his premises before. She saw a belted and great-coated constable step in front of Henry, who turned away, bemused, like a man denied his rightful grief. Along the street, five other men took up positions before the gaping entrances to Wright's and Attersley's. There was a murmur of concern and protest among the men. Before further questions could be asked, Eleanor saw a tired-looking, fire officer coming towards them, as he did so he nodded meaningfully at the Police Inspector, who went to Henry and took his arm just above the elbow. 'There are some questions we have to put to you Mr Attersley, would you come to the police station with me please.'

'Now?' Henry asked, 'but, my wife. . . .'

'I'll look after Eleanor,' Edgar put in, 'and you must

stay with us until you have found somewhere else to live. We'll fetch the baby. . . .'

'I'll see my wife and baby settled, then I'll come later,' Henry said.

'I'd rather you came now, sir. The sooner we settle a few matters, the sooner clearing up can begin.'

'What matters?' He repeated the question Eleanor had asked earlier. 'Surely the fire service will be able to tell you more than I can.'

'I hope so,' the police officer replied enigmatically.

'What do you mean? What's going on?' Henry swung round almost violently. 'I want to talk to my workers.'

'Later, sir, if you don't mind. It will help everyone if you just come quietly. . . .'

'Come quietly! Am I being arrested? What for? What am I supposed to have done, set fire to my own place. . . .' Henry's voice slowed and died as realization came, and he added quietly, 'that's what you think, isn't it?'

'There are some suspicious circumstances which we must clear up,' the officer said, equally quietly.

'What circumstances?' Edgar asked.

'But the fire started next door. If my wife hadn't woken we should perhaps still be in there!' Henry gestured towards the burned-out flat.

'At the station, sir, would be best.' The officer said firmly.

'What evidence have you?' someone shouted, and there was an angry and growing murmur from the crowd. 'It's Roland Wright you want!' Wright's were finished months ago!' 'It started there!' The shouts became ugly and bitter, as perhaps the realization of lost jobs, lost livelihoods, hit home to the men. 'Attersley's were trying to build a business, not burn one,' one cried, and there was a concerted roar of agreement.

'Do you want to involve your men in trouble?' the Inspector shouted to make himself heard. 'This kind of thing does no good at all.'

Henry faced him defiantly, and for a breath-held moment Eleanor thought he was going either to strike the man, or prod him in the chest to make his point, but he confined himself to words. 'You come with me to see my wife and son settled with Mr Asher here, *then* I'll come with you.' Eleanor's estimation of the Inspector went up a little as the man nodded agreement. Henry turned immediately to go with him, but she saw the anxiety on the faces of their workers, and the rapport she had established with them again made her speak out. 'I'll keep you informed. I'll see notices are put up outside the factory here, and in the newspaper when we know. . . .'

As she walked away with the Inspector, Edgar Asher and Henry, she could feel the wave of concern and sympathy expressed in their calls of 'Keep your chins up!' and 'We're behind you!' For the first time Eleanor saw their business as something more than bricks and mortar or a livelihood. She realized that a business could be a sharing and caring relationship, like a family, spanning and interweaving the fates and fortunes of generations of workers and employers.

Doris Asher belied her appearance, for though she appeared stolid and mediocre, with her medium height, medium plumpness and mid-brown hair, she was quick to respond to both the news of the fire and the needs of the Attersley family. She insisted Henry be allowed to have a hot drink, and while she was preparing that, made him and the Police Inspector bacon sandwiches.

Henry and Edgar left them with confident assurances of their early return, but at eleven o'clock it was a police sergeant who arrived, carrying, rather self-consciously, a long parcel. He asked to speak to Eleanor, then proceeded importantly to unwrap what was no more than an empty bottle.

'I have to ask you, ma'am, if you have any knowledge of this?'

'Well, yes, I. . . .' she began, feeling puzzled and annoyed at what seemed a trivial irrelevance, 'I bought a bottle of this kind of wine at Christmas.'

'One bottle,' ma'am?'

'Yes.'

'Have you ever had this same wine before?'

'Yes,' she answered truthfully, for it was the brand of wine Greg had always brought, 'but not for a long time.'

'Thank you, ma'am, that is all I have to ask.' The sergeant rewrapped the bottle and shook out the chin strap of his helmet before putting it on as he left.

'But, what's happening?' Eleanor wanted to know. 'Why hasn't my husband come with you, and Mr Asher?'

'I can't tell you that, ma'am, but no doubt you'll hear fairly soon.'

'Hear?'

'Yes, ma'am, and I wish you good morning, and thank you for your time.'

She and Doris exchanged deeply concerned looks, but Doris would not let her brood. 'We must be practical. I think for the baby's sake it will be best if we turn the parlour into your bed-cum-sitting-room.'

'I have friends, old village neighbours, I could go to, the Sansomes, but. . . .'

'But you'd feel cut off out there. You'll want to know what's happening, to be on the spot if Henry needs you.'

'Doris, I don't know what to say, you never met me until this morning . . . and your lovely parlour. . . .'

'Do it good to have a change round for once. Come on. It's lucky I have two sofas in there. I kept my mother's. . . .'

They kept themselves busy, and had the room comfortable with a good fire, and the coal box at the side well stocked, when they heard the front door. Before either of them could move, Edgar stood in the parlour doorway.

'Henry?' Eleanor asked, but he shook his head.

'They're keeping him in custody. They found pieces of broken wine bottles that had been filled with petrol, in your factory yard, immediately below your mending-shop window. The police believe the fire was started there.'

Doris told of the sergeant's visit.

Eleanor sat slowly down to absorb the knowledge that she had helped to incriminate Henry. 'But the fire didn't start there,' she could at least refute this. 'It began the other side. Our wall was hot when I found it!'

'Henry told them, but unfortunately. . . .'

'A wife's evidence won't count,' Doris finished the sentence.

'But there are other people. There was the railwayman who stood with me, and the firemen themselves, they must know the Wright factory was more ablaze than ours when they arrived.'

'That could be explained as trying to cover up evidence, and there are apparently other damning facts as far as Henry is concerned,' Edgar told them. 'Henry is, apparently, *well*, or even *over*-insured for a man just starting out in business.'

'Oh! but that's because of his aunt, she believes in insurance. She loaned Henry the money, and he insured the factory well to please her,' Eleanor explained.

'The trouble is that Roland Wright has not increased his insurance for years. The police are weighing up these two facts. I saw Roland Wright at the police station and I felt,' Edgar paused, as if to consider fully what he felt, 'I felt the impression he created, the stunned, but outraged, gentleman, went down well with the police and almost seemed to confirm what they suspected. I think we should be prepared for Henry to be charged with unlawfully and maliciously setting fire to his own property, with arson in fact.'

'Arson,' Eleanor repeated quietly. 'But it's not true. I must go to him.'

Edgar shook his head. 'What we must do first, is to get him the best counsel we can afford.'

Eleanor thought of the meagre amount she had in her

handbag, and the overdraft limit at the bank. 'Yes, of course,' she agreed.

'We'll go to the best firm of litigation solicitors in the city as soon as they open after lunch,' Edgar said.

'How serious is a charge of arson?' she asked as an afterthought.

Edgar edged for a moment, then said, 'I think you have to know the truth – it can carry a sentence of life imprisonment.'

'Life imprisonment?' She laughed incredulously – it seemed so impossible. Life seemed to have a remarkable liking for plunging her into cold water and scrubbing her raw.

13

Two weeks later the King's Counsel was in agreement with Henry's solicitor: the material evidence was against him. What they needed was some witness other than their own work people, their own friends or each other. They had failed to find the railwayman who had been one of the first independent witnesses to the fire; they had failed to find any employee of Wright's who would or could collaborate the story the railwayman had told.

'This man could help considerably I feel,' the King's Counsel had told them at the final interview before the court hearing. 'I could use him to help show the jury your husband's state of mind at the time of the fire.'

Eleanor studied the short but broad physique of their counsel, the shock of grey-black hair, great bushy eyebrows, square jaw, and saw what a formidable man to oppose he would be in court. Edgar would, she felt, have found them a good man. The next moment she was not so sure, as he folded his hands high on his chest and leant back in his chair with satisfaction. 'The police,' he said, 'have, so I understand, briefed Mr Marble. It will give me great pleasure to cross swords with him again.'

It was on the tip of Eleanor's tongue to say that it was no game or sport for her and her husband, but instead she confined herself to saying: 'This business was my husband's dream, and our livelihood.'

The counsel appraised her in silence for a moment, then said, 'And this mine, ma'am.' But he nodded acceptance of her unspoken criticism. Then, stopping his pen *en route* to the brass inkwell before him, he looked hard at her and said, 'And you must remember that this prosecution is being brought by the police, and is not a trial between your husband and Mr Roland Wright.'

She took a moment to consider this, and had to accept his accurate appraisal, rebellious though it made her feel. 'That is just how it appears to me,' she admitted.

'In your mind you are trying to deflect the finger of suspicion from your husband towards Roland Wright, and this is *not* our brief. Our brief is to prove your husband innocent.'

Two things haunted Eleanor in the weeks of involvement with the inexorable process of the law. Whatever the outcome, she would never forget her first sight of Henry in custody, suit unkempt with long hours of sitting and lying, his shirt collarless and tieless. Normally this would all be so abhorrent to him, but he hardly seemed to notice. He looked like a man trying to come to terms with a nightmare. He shook his head often as if to clear it, and sighed unconsciously. The other constant anxiety was that she must somehow make reparation for her statement about the wine bottle, and this in turn was linked with a great feeling of animosity towards Roland Wright, for *she* was sure that he had started the fire.

As the days crept forward towards Easter and the date of the arrival of the Assize Judge, on circuit of the counties, Eleanor became desperate to find the railwayman. It was the only thing she could think of now, the only additional piece of help she could give Henry. The man, however, did not seem to be known in the local yards, and was certainly neither driver, stoker, porter nor guard.

She and Doris took to walking John in his perambulator along the streets near the burned-out factories, looking for the man, whose round head and small, sharp features were so vividly etched in Eleanor's memory. Even though the local newspapers had taken up the search with their headlines of 'Lycester Railway Worker Sought', there had been no response. It was not until they encountered Bert Glover outside their factory, and Eleanor repeated as much as she could recall of the man and his manner, that they gleaned any new hope.

'Why,' Bert began, frowning and thinking deeply, 'that could be the chap I've spoken to once or twice when I was nursing that old boiler.' His gaze went across to the boarded-up factory. 'Now then,' he chewed his nails in deep concentration, 'he wasn't a local railwayman.'

'But he knew me,' Eleanor protested.

'Yes!' Bert began to remember more, 'he lives locally, but he's based at Crewe. He's . . . he's . . . a ropeman, that's it! That's what he told me. He has to check that things like ropes and chains and tarpaulins off the trucks go back to their depot. He works all over the region. A bit of a free agent. He was telling me he often goes to a picture palace in the afternoons, then does his checking in the evenings when more of his ropes and things are in the sidings, and then, if he can get home, it's often on the last train.' He looked up in amazement. 'I never thought of it being him – never would have from the way the newspapers told it, don't suppose he did either, even if he was at home to read it. But I reckon I can find him for you now. I know he has a dog and takes it for walks on George Park. Leave it to me. I'll go up there now and start asking. I'll soon find him, and be glad to have something to do. When can we get in there, gammer, make a start?' He nodded to the factory. 'Gaffer will start up again, won't he?'

'If it's humanly possible,' Eleanor answered, as much touched by his linking of the old-fashioned titles of gaffer and gammer, as by his eagerness to help.

'*I've* been in, you know,' Bert confided. 'Took one or two of the men who could lay bricks and do carpentry. Nothing we couldn't tackle ourselves, if insurance would cover the materials. Then with some new machines, them new Excels is what we'd want, and a new boiler. . . .'

'Steady on, Bert, we've a long way to go before all that could begin to be done, and of course the insurance company won't settle until the outcome of Henry's trial.'

She felt their foreman would have appreciated just how far off such a day was, if he could have seen Henry that evening. Now in the remand block of the local prison, his incarceration seemed so much deeper and more difficult to deal with, so much more removed from freedom and normality.

Sometimes rebellion had glowed in his eyes when she had visited, and she had felt she must calm and steady his feelings, but this evening he was defensive, hardly raising his eyes to hers, seeming to keep even his thoughts removed from her.

'Do you feel all right?' she asked.

His glance came sharply to her face, and he grimaced at the inadequacy of the question. 'I feel . . .' he began, 'I feel as if I have fought in a second world war, and lost it,' and looking at her hands outstretched but forbidden, added, 'but even at the front it was never so lonely as now.'

'Henry . . . we're thinking of you all the time . . . we're doing everything we can.'

Nothing would give him heart. She told him of Bert's belief he could find their missing witness. He merely shook his head and said that nothing short of a cast-iron alibi would be of any help. She ignored his pessimism, and told him that Bert thought their own people could do the repair work.

'What for?' he asked.

'When we re-open,' she said quietly, but he did not reply.

She walked very slowly back to the Asher's home that evening, wending her way from the prison on the outskirts of the town past the motor service shops, springing up it seemed on every corner. A display of first Michelin, and then of Dunlop Magnum tyres, had been mounted in adjoining windows. Her steps faltered, and stopped, as she recollected a recent case in the newspapers where a tyre-track had led to a man's arrest for murder. Could Henry's fingerprints on the one wine bottle found whole at the scene of the fire, send him to prison – for life?

She stood before the shop, reading things about tyres of eight hundred and twenty millimetres that meant nothing to her, thoughts racing like trapped creatures hurling themselves senselessly at the merciless bars of their cage. Not again! She screamed inwardly. Not again! Surely she was not going to lose her man again, and couldn't this kind of loss be worse than death? Imprisoned *for life*. Wasn't that a living death for an ambitious man like Henry? It had all seemed so outlandish, so bizarre, but now she could see that it was possible he could be convicted in spite of his innocence. She understood his sudden lack of hope. She wondered if perhaps his counsel had told him even more than she knew of the dire factual evidence against him.

Her legs felt stiff as if she had stood looking into the shop of motor spares for hours rather than minutes, and it was with some effort that she forced herself on her way, knowing that if she was much later Doris would begin to wonder, and then there was John. She shook her head as she remembered the over-possessive mother she had been a few short months ago. Now she was grateful for anyone to offer to have her baby for a few hours. She sometimes felt John looked at her as if he could not quite understand all the changes in his surroundings and in his mother.

Her way lay past the burned out factories. She could

hardly bear to look at them this evening, and at first took no notice of the man who seemed to be lingering under the lamp near their factory gate, beyond noticing that he was small and slightly built. Her thoughts were entirely with Henry again. It was only as she was passing the man that she recognized the thinly aesthetic features of Roland Wright. She was so surprised she stopped, and as he would have walked on, she side-stepped in front of him aggressively, unable to let him go so easily. He gave a half shrug of distaste, a lift of his thin neck and chin above the white wing-collar, and would have bypassed her, but again she stepped in front of him, with what felt like righteous rage coming over her.

'I'm sure you'll be glad to know, Mr Wright, that we have traced our missing railwayman.' She exaggerated their progress, the remark leaping spontaneously to her lips. 'We have another witness!'

'Stand out of my way.' He attempted to pass her yet again, but he was obviously disconcerted. Eleanor felt her frustrations spilling over and was determined not to fail Henry through inaction as she felt she had Greg by failing to recognize his earliest symptoms.

'Oh, no you don't!' She placed herself before him yet again. They both became slightly breathless, like slavering dogs circling, looking to catch each other's throats. Unless he resorted to physical violence, he had in the end to stand and listen. '*We* know the truth of this matter, dont we *Mr* Wright,' she spat the words at him. 'Perhaps we're the only two at the moment, but soon, when your financial difficulties are known, everyone will see you for what you are.'

'It's your husband that's on trial, madam, not I.' His voice was high, wavering off the edge of control, his fingers plucking nervously and rapidly at the sides of his black overcoat. 'This matter is *sub judice*, and should not be discussed.' He turned, and began to walk quickly the opposite way. He was now going her way. She easily kept up with him.

'It's being discussed by every man you, or we, employed. They've guessed the truth. And with this new witness we shall prove it!' She let him go then, dropping behind, but finally shouting after him. 'You're a wicked man, Roland Wright, you should confess for the good of your soul – for you've precious little else left.'

She watched the hunched figure, scurrying away, before resuming her own walk back to Doris's. Now she went over in her mind far more telling remarks she could have made. She should have said their witness would tell of his previous attempt to set fire to his premises. But what use? Henry had said he needed more than rumours, the evidence had been so successfully rigged against him. He said what he needed was a miracle.

The encounter with Roland Wright had given her no satisfaction. She felt belittled and dirtied by it. Nothing, short of seeing the man pilloried would compensate for what he had done to Henry. He deserved no mercy. She recalled how she had wished her father dead, when she had heard him ill-treating her mother, and wondered if her own true personality was vicious and vindictive. She knew she felt years and years old, sort of withered spiritually, even her mouth felt as if it had taken on a permanent bitter twist.

As she let herself into the Asher's house, Doris came quickly to greet her, John in her arms. 'There's someone to see you,' she said.

'Me? Who is it?' With some apprehension she followed Doris into the sitting-room. A complete stranger rose to greet her. He was in his sixties, tall, well-groomed, a solicitor or barrister, she thought. Her heart thudded apprehensively, and for one ludicrous moment she wondered if it could be about her verbal attack on Roland Wright.

'I'm very pleased to meet you, Mrs Attersley. No, you don't know me, in fact neither does your husband, but I know of him.' Eleanor invited him to sit down again. 'I do not intend to take up your time. I know you have much on your mind. To tell things briefly, your husband saved my nephew's life when he was on the Western Front. It was my nephew's third day at Ypres, he was wounded and your husband fetched him in from no-man's land, right in front of the German lines and was badly wounded in the leg while doing so. Perhaps he has told you all this?'

Eleanor shook her head. 'No, nothing.'

'I decided then that if ever the opportunity came when I could help Henry Attersley, I would do so. Life does, I believe, provide the opportunity to return good for good, sooner or later. I own various properties in Lycester, and one has come empty. You and your husband are welcome to have this at a purely nominal rent, until your fortunes pick up again.' He handed Eleanor a piece of paper. 'That is an authority to my agent to give you the keys whenever you are ready to go and look at it.'

The man seemed gone almost before she had time to either collect her wits, or to thank him properly. She had to sit down, her overwhelming emotion regret. She wished she had not encountered Roland Wright, the incident seemed doubly soured because of this stranger's kindness.

'There are still a lot of good people in the world. At least you will have a home,' Doris said, and as if guessing her need for comfort and distraction, gently lowered John on to his mother's lap, adding, 'and we have still all that sewing to do.'

Soon, they were both tackling major alterations on a dark grey suit of Edgar's for Henry to wear at the trial, and there was little time left for any kind of introspection.

Their sewing also included the re-trimming of one of Doris's hats for Eleanor. She wore it on the very first morning of the Assizes, when she walked John to the city centre in time to see the judicial procession starting from the judge's chambers in the town hall, and processing to the cathedral for the civic service that always preceded the quarterly assize courts. There had been a late, light fall of snow the evening before and this seemed to give added splendour and significance to the pomp and circumstance of the red and black robes and grey wigs of the dignitaries, who moved slowly up the steps towards the cathedral. The grey gothic spire, the pointed windows and the yews and firs all seemed disconcertingly stake-like, impaling the stark whiteness. She felt chilled as the judge himself passed by, thin, his cheeks sunken almost cadaverous-like under his full-bottomed wig. His solemn eyes seemed to meet her's for a moment, and in them she thought she saw the impassive chill of law administered by the letter, by the book, without any recourse to such flimsy things as impressions or instincts. She shivered, the cold seeming to come from inside and spread outwards. For a moment the images blurred, all she saw were streaks of red on white, and she thought she would faint. Red on white, blood on handkerchiefs. A terrible omen? She fought the feeling of nausea, clutching the pram handle, and turning blindly out of the little crowd of sightseers. This would not do. It would be no use arriving at court that afternoon for the beginning of their case, only to pass out. She would be no help to Henry then.

The snow had gone completely by the time she and Edgar met their solicitor in the court ante-room. Amid the bustle and feeling of expectation in the wood-panelled room, which seemed to smell both of polish and authority, she felt curiously alone. She wondered how Henry looked in the suit. He had lost weight in prison and his hair was longer than she had ever seen it. She thought it made him look younger and more vulnerable. Policemen came and took up positions at the court doors. She was seated with the other witnesses. She heard the court being called to order, then the doors were closed, and they were all excluded until their turn came to go to the witness box.

The three days of the trial became fixed in her mind like a fierce, sharp, kaleidoscope of impression and emotion. Each day had its own special climax, its own newspaper headline. On the first day, Eleanor gave her evidence of finding the fire, and cross-questioned was unable to say what woke her, neither could she explain why the one unbroken wine bottle which had her and her husband's fingerprints on it, had contained petrol. She attempted to give her own interpretation of events, but was silenced by the judge.

The second day's news report told of Henry, pale but dignified in the dock, refusing to be riled by the harassments of the prosecution barrister as he lay before the court the evidence of the bottles, the short time in business, the heavy insurance, and how much Henry stood to gain. 'Here,' he said, 'was not a man committed to long arduous years of endeavour, here was an opportunist, out for quick gain, at whatever the cost.'

On the morning of the third day, Eleanor woke with a start, unsure where she was, her thoughts still with a dream that had been cruelly like the reality. Glover was in the witness box, cross-questioned about remarks he had been heard to make, concerning the best thing Henry Attersley could do with the whole place was send it up in flames. Despite the objections of Henry's counsel, another seed had been laid in the jury's minds. He too had tried to volunteer opinions about who had started the fire. Good as his intentions had been, even with her own inexperience of court proceedings, she knew Bert had only undermined the line of defence their counsel was trying to establish.

She lay for a moment longer in the stuffy, unnatural warmth of parlour-cum-bedroom, reluctant to begin this day in which she felt there must be a victim. The court case had been built up so dramatically on the news placards and in the papers, that there could surely be no happy ending. She thought again of Henry's total innocence, and felt anger giving her energy to respond to the challenge of this final day in court. If he was found guilty, she vowed she would shout out in court that Roland

Wright was the man who should be standing in the dock, and that she would spend the rest of her life proving it.

She had washed, tidied the room, changed and fed John by the time she heard Edgar and Doris stirring. Then she was startled by a knocking at the front door. She went to the heavy nets at the front window, but could see only the backs of several men waiting, attentive for the opening of the Ashers' front door. She heard Edgar come quickly downstairs and draw the bolts.

It had to be something to do with Henry. Had he brooded about the possibility of spending the rest of his life in prison, and done something stupid? She stood clasping the back of the sofa, unable to move. She heard someone coming to the parlour door, purposefully, but not too quickly, as if preparing an entrance, or words, suitable for her to accept. She bit her lip as the door swung inwards and a man came in, for a second she did not recognize him – because he was the last person she expected, the very last.

'Henry?' She questioned his reality.

He stepped forward as if to speak, then he too caught and held the back of a chair. 'I'm free,' he said, and stood shaking his head as if in denial of the words. She hurried over to him then, gripping his arms tightly, grasping and kneading the suit sleeves, as if like an emotion-torn parent finding a long-lost child, she must punish to release her emotion. Then her hands went to cup his cheeks, holding his face, her own eyes distraught with questions. 'I don't understand. What's happened?' she begged fearfully.

'It's all over. I'm free,' he repeated, and closed his eyes for a second. She saw how tired and drawn the face was she held between her hands. She traced the cheek and jaw bones lightly as if to heal and as he opened his eyes and looked at her steadily, there was a new assessment in them.

This is marriage, she thought, this, whatever the outcome, has been the test. This moment, more than any other, makes us man and wife.

'I should have believed you when you said truth will out,' he said catching her hands into his. 'Roland Wright summoned his solicitor to his home last night, made a full confession, and then, some hours later, shot himself.'

The long, low, exclamation that Eleanor breathed was such a mixture of emotions, such a combination of relief, incredulity and horror, that Henry shouted for Doris to come, to bring brandy.

Had she harried Roland Wright to his death, she wondered, as she clung to Henry's arm for support. Truly they needed each other as never before.

The newspaper headline of the third evening read: 'Startling Overnight Development'. Eleanor felt the words would be forever branded scar-deep on her soul.

14

The house, they were told by the agents, was in a terrace of large Victorian properties, built about thirty years before, overlooking a park, and near the last outward stop of the city tram service. Eleanor had been unable to bring herself to look at it while Henry was in prison, but now a new home seemed first priority.

Doris had suggested that she and Edgar would push John in his pram to the house, while Eleanor and Henry went on ahead by tram, so giving them a chance of first sight of the place by themselves.

Henry was still very subdued, wary almost, and full of mistrust. While she tried to dispel the feeling he had of being an 'old lag', she could not rid herself of the feeling of guilt. Had her verbal attack on Roland Wright been the last ounce to the weight of despair and guilt the man had carried? Was she responsible for his suicide? The trouble was that while the loss of the factory and flat were a common grief, their subsequent wounds were different. Now the twin crises of fire and trial were over, it would have been very easy for them to lose sympathy with each other in the profusion of niggling decisions that must urgently be made. In a week, they had made no progress beyond ascertaining that the insurance company would, it seemed, in its own ponderous time, pay out their claim. She knew that what was holding everything up was Henry's inability to see himself beginning all over again. His energy seemed utterly sapped. He had lost faith in himself and in life. She felt that if only they could begin to make a home again, it would be a first step back to normality.

The house seemed enormous after the factory flat, with front parlour, back parlour, kitchen and back kitchen. There was a large walled garden with neat cobbled paths and fluted blue-brick kerbs to beds of herbs, deep-blue grape-hyacinth and spears of later flowering lily-of-the-valley. Upstairs, there were huge bedrooms with high ceilings and above, smaller attic-rooms smelling of dust and full of motes swirling and shining in the sunlight. In two of the bedrooms, the previous occupier had left enormous wardrobes and in one, an ugly, limed-oak, bed.

'Well, anything's welcome, when you've nothing,' she commented.

'I'll have to go and see this man. Whatever the rent, I'm sure we can't afford a place like this.'

'He said a purely nominal rent,' she reminded him, 'and what alternative have we?'

'My aunt's willing for us to move in with her.'

'That's no good for the business though, is it?' she asked quietly.

'The business!' His tone dismissed the idea, but before more could be said they heard knocking at the front door. She went down to let Edgar and Doris in, and to pull in the pram.

When they had been over the house again, they assembled back in the bedroom where Doris sat on the wooden slats of the bedstead holding John. Eleanor had chatted on and on, trying to cover Henry's pessimism, and she had obviously succeeded, because Edgar cleared his throat rather portentously and said: 'We have a proposition to put to you. Doris and I wondered if you would consider letting us invest our money with you. Perhaps you might even consider letting me work with you, come in on the ground floor, as it were?'

'Invest your money!' Henry said, then laughed ironically. 'In what?'

'Your new business, of course, and don't get the wrong impression, we feel we would be getting into a very good thing, don't we Doris?'

'You have what a good many hosiery manufacturers would like,' Doris said, 'and that's a fresh start, and money to invest in the newest machines.'

'And men willing to start work tomorrow on the rebuilding,' Eleanor added. 'Our own men, just waiting for the word.'

'You're all mad.' Henry looked incredulously from one to the other. 'Even if I wanted to, I couldn't raise the capital again for materials and labour. Then it would be months before there was any income, *even* if I could win our customers back *again*. No. It's impossible.' He waved his hands indicating the walls around them. 'Let's face it, we can't even afford to rent a house.'

'Henry,' Doris began, her quiet serious manner immediately catching the attention of them all, 'my mother and father kept a small newsagent's and tobacconist's shop. All my life I was pushed into the backroom while they served behind that shop counter, all hours. The shop was rented, and when they died, and the bills paid, I had been left just over a hundred pounds, and the feeling that they had cheated themselves, and me, of living. I had come to think of myself as some kind of inferior being who must rush to do the bidding of all and sundry, as I had seen my parents doing in the shop. It was Edgar who restored my self-respect,' she reached out a hand for Edgar's 'and he is welcome to every penny I have to invest in the chance of a better future for us all.' There was an extra edge to her voice as she added, 'I'd rather lose what little we have, than have Edgar for ever scrambling to make a living on his own, as he is now. Don't be a *little* businessman, Henry. Take this chance, make this misfortune work *for* you, instead of against you.'

'We could raise about two hundred pounds, Henry,' Edgar added eagerly, 'and I do know about yarns, quite a bit about spinning, and an awful lot about buying on the wool markets. Before you had the fire, I told Doris I would give my eye-teeth for a chance to be in business with you. In fact I reckon *I* could have been more justly accused of burning the place out so I could have this chance.' He laughed, Doris and Eleanor smiled, but the jest fell on very stony ground as far as Henry was concerned.

'I wouldn't wish that fate on my worst enemy, and as for putting more money into that place. . . .' He shrugged as if he just could not bring himself to think of restarting.

'Well, think about it, old boy,' Edgar finished with forced heartiness.

It was a subdued little party that walked back to the city. Eleanor felt she should apologize for Henry's unenthusiastic reception of their friends' offer, but knew it would be tactless while her husband was with them. She also pondered that perhaps a mental hurt could need as much careful nursing and perhaps even longer convalescence than a physical illness.

When they were alone again, Henry sitting staring into the fire, Eleanor knelt before him and put her hands on his knees. 'We'd better go to see your aunt,' she said. 'We can't stop with Doris and Edgar indefinitely, good as they are.'

'Be patient with me. I'll go to the agents tomorrow, and if the owner of that house lives nearby, I'll see him first. I owe him some thanks anyway.' He placed his hands over her's, stretching his fingers so her hands and wrists were all encompassed. She was taken unawares by the warmth and tenderness the gesture expressed, and by a swift deep surge of emotion as he looked at her. She felt her lips part in sudden need of his arms about her. They had not slept together since the night of the fire, and their sofa-beds had not helped to re-establish their married life. She knew he recognized, and was surprised by her need, and there was the beginning of a tiny kindling between them. She ran her hands up his thighs a little. He sat a moment longer, then went to the door and placed a chair beneath the handle, wedging it fast.

'Henry!' she said with mock alarm. 'What are you doing?'

'It feels,' he said, putting out the gas light and finding his way slowly back to where she stood on the hearthrug, 'strangely like coming back to life.' He took her into his arms, then pulled her down on to the rug.

'This feels wicked somehow,' she said, trying to suppress a giggle.

'And it's really about as wicked as we've ever got, isn't it?' He laughed at himself, at her, 'and even this is legal.'

'But very sweet,' she whispered, as they made themselves comfortable, undressing as they knelt harbouring the warmth. Their love-making was given strangeness and mystery in the flickering light of the flames, as if they were in the security of an obscure cave at the beginning of time.

Later, without any warning, she wept. Wept for a warm hollow in a stretch of sand, wept for the trauma of fire and destruction, for a small book of seashells, a fur muff, and for that night's gentle deliverance. She tried to be very quiet, but Henry woke, and cradled her to him, pulling more blankets from his sofa to warm her, but not talking, or questioning, as if he knew these tears were beyond words to heal. They had been dammed up a long time and had to fall without check, or the hindrance of explanation.

After Henry had gone the next morning, Doris came somewhat apologetically to say that she felt they had no business to harry them to make decisions, and looked rather worriedly at Eleanor's tear-stained eyes.

'No, it's all right,' she hastened to reassure. 'I feel sure it was the first push in the right direction for Henry. He's gone to see about the house. It just needs things to go right now, and. . . .' She crossed the first two fingers of both hands. Doris repeated the gesture with emphasis.

When Henry did come back, he burst into the house like a man who could hardly contain his own energy. 'I don't know what came over me,' he said. 'I found the owner of the house, he's a leather tanner – ugh! the smell of that place – and before I knew where I was, I was telling him about us rebuilding, buying new machines, how we hoped to expand to spinning, then dyeing, finding new outlets at home and abroad. Half of it I hardly knew myself. I just opened my mouth and it all spilled out. I don't know who was more impressed – him or me!'

'What about the house?' Eleanor wanted to know. 'What did he say?'

'He said he knew anyone who showed the enterprise I had in saving his nephew, would not be downed by a fire, or wrongful arrest. He's arranging a dinner-party and inviting that nephew of his, and all of us.'

'The house, you didn't forget . . .' she tried again.

'*And*,' he went on triumphantly, waving away the question of the house, 'he's offered to stand as a guarantor if I apply for a bank loan. He's in a big way, Eleanor. Not one of your little businessmen, Doris!'

'Henry Attersley!' Eleanor exploded. 'What about the house?'

'Oh! We can have that.'

'Have it?'

'Yes, at a peppercorn rent for twelve months.'

'That's just a small nominal amount,' Doris said.

'That's it,' Henry agreed and gave her a smacking kiss

on her cheek. 'Go and put the kettle on, let's all have a celebration cup of tea. Let's toast the first son in the new Attersley's.' He picked John from his pram and whirled the astonished, gasping child around the room.

The breathless Attersleys was how Eleanor saw them all as, with the decision made, Henry launched them all into the rebuilding and reorganization. He went first to see his aunt, who not only renewed her support but promised various pieces of furniture for the house, and sent a further parcel of clothes she and Aggie Sansome had put together. 'It's not much,' she said, 'but when you've lost everything . . .' He also went to see Aggie and George, and returned with the news that he did not think Aggie was so well.

Then he put on the dark grey suit and began a hard and relentless round of consultation and negotiation with insurance assessors, builders' merchants, bank managers, knitting machine manufacturers and boiler makers. He used every contact he had formerly made, and his determination earned him respect and co-operation. He was neither shy nor abashed to go as a guest to opposing political clubs, one evening to meet Bert Glover to organize a working party to begin the interior reconstruction, the next evening to meet a go-ahead hosiery manufacturer who was willing to talk to him about the latest hosiery methods. 'I just don't tell one about the other,' he told Eleanor, Doris and Edgar. Their free evenings had become working councils of war, an opportunity to air ideas and to give reports of progress. Edgar was using his contacts as a yarn factor to mention the Attersley name whenever he could, sowing the seeds of what they hoped would be future business. Eleanor and Doris painstakingly made copies of a letter to all their former customers, apologizing for the delay with orders, but promising better service and better prices.

May saw the interior reconstruction complete, and the latest Excel knitting machines on site. 'Another fortnight should see us back in production,' Henry said. 'I think we should move into the house before then. We could go and fetch the furniture on Saturday.'

It was arranged that she and John should go for a visit to the Sansomes, staying overnight while he, George and the two Sansome boys returned to town with the lorry hired from the village garage. They would collect the furniture from his aunt's, and some they had bought in a local auction and stored at Edgar's, take it to the new house, stay overnight and return the lorry early on the Sunday morning.

The previous Christmas had been so taken up with work and worry at the factory, that their intended visit to the Sansomes had been put off, and it was nearly six months since Eleanor had last seen Aggie. She quickly realized that while physically there might appear little change, there was a great difference in the old lady's outlook. She had lost the cheerful aggression she had brought to the burden of her ill-health, and her speech was not quite so clear. Eleanor turned from contemplation of Aggie to find George's gaze on her. His eyes held hers and in them she read his complete acceptance of his burden, which could only become heavier and sadder as time passed.

'Come on, let's have a feel of him,' Aggie said holding out her arms for John. She placed the sturdy baby on Aggie's lap, who patted his ample knees with pleasure. John lay wide-eyed and very still, regarding her solemnly. 'You'll know me again, won't you me boy?'

John opened his eyes even wider, then turned his head to look at his mother. Eleanor smiled and nodded as if to reassure him he was all right, and with that he seemed to settle himself more permanently. 'He'll go to sleep,' Eleanor said.

'Let him then,' Aggie said making the little head more comfortable against her arm. She contemplated the little boy a moment longer, then asked, 'Will you tell him?'

Eleanor shook her head. 'No. I don't think he needs to know. It wouldn't help him.'

Later when the men had gone and John was asleep in Clarrie's old room, the two of them sat in the deep quiet of the May evening, the cottage door still open, for it was as warm as high summer, and Aggie was feeling the heat. The drone of the last bee could still be heard as it disturbed the fragrance from the pink hyacinths in the tiny flower-bed beneath the kitchen window, where later in the year George planted sweet, night-scented stocks, for Aggie's enjoyment.

'Happy?' Aggie asked, nodding her head, as if knowing the answer.

'Happy,' Eleanor echoed, after serious consideration. 'Yes, happy.' They talked for a long time, catching up with news of this and that, until Eleanor settled Aggie on her sofa for the night, and went to sleep in the brass-ended double bed, where George had for as long as she could remember kept a listening watch for Aggie on her solitary couch downstairs.

Eleanor too lay listening – to the settling of the house and the church clock chiming the quarters – and wondered how long George's vigil would last. For though she and Aggie had talked of Clarrie at great length that evening, it was George and his loving acceptance of his lot that touched her heart.

The evening papers carried the story of Attersley's re-opening on their front page, with a picture of Henry surrounded by his cap-waving workers. It was not without its effects. The next day Eleanor was in the office and received several telephone calls from city retailers with good wishes and orders. Henry said it was as much to do with the 'old boy' network as with the newspaper's story. Eleanor suspected that his liking for entertaining, and being entertained, prompted his remark more than anything else. But he was buoyant, effusive, and she just raised her eyebrows in an effort to debunk the idea.

'You'll see,' he said. 'It's not only what you know, it's who you mix with.'

She tutted, and waved him on his way to enjoy the whirl and clatter of his new machines, the warm smell of oil, the murmur of men's voices as they worked. It seemed to act like a kind of ozone to him, giving him an energy that few others felt in that unseasonal May of 1922.

Instruments in Holborn recorded a temperature of 88° in the shade and of 120° in the sun, and within one twenty-four hours, London ambulances took fourteen men and women to hospital suffering from sunstroke. In Westminster Court, the judge doffed his wig, and the city was said to be reminiscent of a hotel verandah in a South American town, as thousands of businessmen discarded their jackets and waistcoats. Children of all ages took to the various strips of water in municipal parks, and Doris devoted all her time to keeping John cool and happy while Eleanor was in the factory office.

Doris had begged to be allowed to look after the little boy, desperate not to lose contact with him now Eleanor and Henry had moved to their new home. 'It's like having a belated little brother to look after, something I always wanted.'

Eleanor knew they wanted children of their own, but as Doris had sadly said, they had just not come along.

It was Eleanor's one regret that taking an active role in the business meant she saw less of John, particularly in the early months of the restart, when not only was every penny ploughed back into the business, but so was every minute. She knew it had to be so for them to survive and progress, but there were days when she felt almost a twinge of jealousy as she saw her son go to Doris with such eagerness. She knew Doris spent her entire day pandering to his every need and whim, could see it in his impatient frustration when she was not able to run to him the moment he expressed a need.

There were compensations in their hard work. Her

own satisfaction lay in mastering the mysteries of double-entry book-keeping, where figures that had at first seemed to be credits, had turned, like traitors, into debits; and in her partnership with Henry. She felt sometimes as if their marriage had been some kind of rocket, ignited by misfortune, but to which she was still clinging precariously as it shot ever higher. She, who had been to such different heights before, was afraid of a fall, afraid that this fall might not, after all, be greater than the first. It had all been so unexpected. From the first she had anticipated a settled life with Henry, even a stolid kind of existence, and safety, not this hazarding of every little profit they made to expand, not this madcap feeling of love she thought only in keeping with the gay young things of the social scene.

Sometimes she half-rebelled against his cavalier arrangement of her time, but then she would recall his uninhibited joy in every hand's touch in a day's passing; in their love-making, pleasuring her sometimes so much she wondered that the world was ever the same afterwards. She often took covert looks at herself and Henry during a day's business to make sure no bright betraying ribbon of ecstasy clung to them, to embarrass their work-a-day selves. Enough to curl the edges of her ledgers, she often thought with secret glee.

Eleanor quickly became aware in those first four years how money, or the expectation of wealth, broadened one's outlook to a remarkable degree. Henry was quick to improve the furnishings of their home, and had an eye for a bargain at the sale-rooms. He took pains to return the hospitality he had received. Eleanor too began to enjoy the company of other business people, who extended their range of interests and pleasures. The war they felt had been a great leveller, particularly in the business world, and Henry was a man who had had an unusual initiation, and who could talk about it, and business generally, entertainingly and astutely, and still, to Eleanor's chagrin, tell the occasional *risqué* joke.

In no time at all, John was four-and-a-half years old, a sturdy young man, and then Doris startled them all one day by announcing that she was pregnant. 'The doctor says it might be because I stopped getting so stressful about it once I had John to look after.'

'It's worked out very well.' Henry slapped Edgar hard on his back. 'Here we are all established, with Doris expecting a baby and our young man about ready to go to school.' They had a little dinner party at Edgar's that night to celebrate. Doris looked radiant, reminding Eleanor of Sophie when she was expecting her fourth baby and getting ready to go off to America. A letter had come from the Irvings some months before, saying they were all well, but moving some thousand miles further west. Between the news of Lloyd and the children, Eleanor felt, or imagined, some reproach still for her speedy marriage after Greg's death. She had told them of John's arrival, but not the birth date, or his true father.

She felt curiously depressed as the four of them drank to the health of the coming baby, and when they arrived home brooded over what she felt was John's lost babyhood, a time she seemed to have barely glimpsed. Now he was to start school. Henry said they could and would manage the fees for a good private school just across the park, a school patronized by other city business people.

'What are you looking at?' Henry came to her as she stood at the window looking out into the darkness towards the park, where every afternoon mothers and nurses walked, some with younger children, to meet the slightly older ones from school.

'I wish we could have another child,' she said.

He did not answer at once, and she knew he could never quite forget the trauma of John's birth.

'I'm content, Eleanor, if there are to be no more, well . . .' he shrugged.

'I would have liked to have given *you* a child.' The emphasis was gentle.

'I have a child,' he said, 'and more important I have you. That's all I need, all I really want in life.'

She laughed at him then. 'And this?' She indicated the room they stood in with the Regency card table he had just bought at auction and rebaized himself.

'Just trimmings,' he said, grinning. 'Just trimmings.'

She knew it was true.

John came back from his first day at school carrying his first picture.

'Did you like it?' Henry asked.

'I liked the crayons,' John answered with enthusiasm, 'they're big and fat, and don't break.'

He held out his picture. 'That's Daddy,' he pointed to an expansive red figure, 'and that's you Mummy.' Mummy was red, yellow, blue and edged with black. For some reason, Eleanor found the crayoning disturbing. It was somehow too detailed, too perceptively done for such a young child's work.

'I'd say that was pretty good for one day at school,' Henry said.

'Give me a piggy-back, Daddy?'

'Yes, and a gallop around the park on Sunday for such a good drawing.'

'You like school, then?' Eleanor asked.

The little boy scowled down at her from Henry's shoulders, really thinking about that question. 'It was all right,' he said, 'but I don't think I shall bother to go again.'

Henry roared with laughter, as much at the consternation on Eleanor's face as at the remark.

She began increasingly to feel at a disadvantage with John. He and Henry seemed to have a far more natural and unrestrained relationship than she could achieve.

John developed quite a talent for drawing, and within a short time his love was obviously more for details than for the dramatic splendour of colour usual at his age. His infant school pictures were packed with tiny people, tiny animals, minute machines and grey clouds. Eleanor felt it all very unnatural, much to Henry's amusement, but occasionally she found herself thinking of her father, and caught herself looking for physical resemblances to Reuben in her son. It was said that traits and talents could skip a generation. Then she reminded herself that their son was being brought up in a home where kindness and love reigned, not, as Clarrie had once told her, where someone was being beaten all the time.

She found some extra relief from her anxieties in writing one of her detailed reports of John's progress to William. William, as ever, replied promptly, obviously taking much joy in news of his godson, and at once making exhaustive enquiries about schools where drawing and the arts were fostered.

15

Birthdays, Eleanor supposed, were times when it was natural to look back, and the eve of John's eleventh birthday, when another major change in their lives seemed imminent, gave her pause to wonder where time had gone.

Happy, busy years, minor downs, but many ups, which totalled, in the ten years since the fire, major progress. Henry, Edgar and Bert Glover were now directors of their private limited company, and ever active in the business marathon that spread the base of Attersley's ever wider, ever firmer. Exports to Canada had begun when Edgar had travelled there to visit his brother, who had emigrated as a very young man. Doris and their four daughters accompanied him. The children had, as Henry put it 'popped out as quick as peas from a pod, once Doris got the idea'.

Edgar had come home with reports of vastly inferior stockings in the shops, and with a list of wholesalers who would be interested in receiving samples. Feeling in the market was well disposed to an English manufacturer at that time, following the loss of confidence in America after the Wall Street crash of 1929. The Attersley exports had been nurtured and had grown, inch by determined inch.

The years of recession were a strange time when the poor were as hard pressed as ever to feed and shoe large families, and rents had to wait to be paid if half a bag of coal was to be bought. Yet with just a little spare money, there were bargains to be had. The middle classes made huge strides in achieving greater comfort, and Henry was supporting John's wish to go to a boarding school on the south coast, also recommended by William as having an excellent art master.

'It's only natural he should want to go,' Henry had argued. His friends at school are nearly all going. We should travel down and get the boy's name entered before it's too late.'

She wondered if it was not too late even now, for her ever really to know her own son. There was a reserve between them, a curious lack of candour, as if each withheld a major part of themselves from the other. Perhaps she loved him too much, wanted to share too much of his life? And John? Perhaps instinctively he knew he must climb out of her shadow. Was this why he was so keen to go away to school?

Only in his pictures did she feel he truly gave all of himself, and these often disturbed her. His drawings and paintings lined the walls of his playroom, and had the capacity to stop her short in her daily routine, to make her pause and look and wonder. He had just finished a painting of an old barn which stood on the far side of the park. Her eyes were drawn again and again to the black doorway, aware of the cavernous quality, of feeling able to fall through the picture into space or chaos. She felt her heart beating faster. 'This is stupid,' she muttered, picking up the painting from the desk and taking it to the window as if to dispel the impression with more daylight. The trees in leaf, the grass and the individual pebbles in the foreground, reminded her of the book of seashells Greg had painted. John had inherited his father's talent for detail, but he had also managed to conceal, or to reveal, a mystery in his tiny picture. She wondered if he sensed the lie in his own life, that Henry was not his father.

Henry came into the sitting-room as she still stood at the window. He came to her, slipping an arm around her waist in a way that told her she would always be young, fresh and desirable to him.

'One of John's?' He took the stiff drawing paper from her and looked at it carefully, adding slowly: 'He certainly has a talent.'

Eleanor looked again at the paper, 'And?' she queried.

'A vivid imagination, like his mother.' He looked at her solemnly. 'You worry too much about the boy, always have.'

'Then you see something sinister there too.'

'I see the boy has put himself into the work. You only have to watch him with his paints to know he does that – and I also see that he is a different child to the one you expected,' he regarded her kindly, quizzically.

'Sometimes I see my father with his black hair,' she breathed fearfully.

'Oh Eleanor!' Henry laughed. 'The boy can't help what he inherits. I see Greg in him when he stands tall and still, listening while adults talk and we think he's busy.'

'I hope, Henry,' her eyes brimmed with tears as she turned to him and encircled him with her arms, 'I hope, more than anything else that he learns your goodness and generosity.'

'You worry too much! You can't make the world fit him, like you did his clothes when he was small. He has to adapt, find what is best for himself. All we can do is show him the possibilities.'

'How did you ever become so wise?' she asked, half-joking.

'By listening to how the successful and happy got where they are today,' he answered seriously, 'and not being afraid to risk and speculate as they have done.'

'But that hasn't anything to do with what I am talking about,' she protested.

'Oh, yes! It has for me. I have to be at the top of the tree because you are with me. I've never been comfortable at the bottom. I want to show John the view from the top, the possibilities, Eleanor, the possibilities! I'm only just beginning to grow to be the kind of man I feel properly comfortable with.'

'Well, it's certainly not in keeping with your upbringing,' she said. Then feeling this sounded too derisive, added, 'and not mine, either.'

'No! but it's our *future*,' he asserted, '*and* I have another plan!'

'Henry! The school you mean?'

'No, no. Something else. I should not have mentioned it. It's too soon to talk about it yet.'

'You mean you want to wait until you have made up your own mind.'

'Until I've explored all the possibilities, yes.'

'Until it's too late to talk about it, you mean, when it's all arranged, when the furniture's on the lorry.'

'The furniture on the lorry' had become a stock phrase in their married language. The example they used for the decisions Henry made before telling Eleanor anything about them, but, as Henry alway retaliated, she always helped him put up the tailboard, to make each venture a success. She always threatened that one day he would go too far and outreach himself, and her patience.

This time there was no way she could guess at, or make him reveal what he had in mind, and to pay him back, she decided to take a more subtle revenge. They were entertaining that evening, and she had a new dress he had not seen, a pretty pink dress which she knew did something rather special for her tiny neat figure, and she had also bought pure silk, flesh-tinted stockings and pale beige, heeled shoes. She looked, and felt, amorous, and as she assessed the look of the dress, the hem-line nearly up to her knees, and the feel of the soft silk on her legs, she was a little shocked with herself, shocked that she could be the kind of woman who would attempt to lead a man on, even when the man was her husband. She heard Henry coming to the bedroom door.

'They'll soon be here,' he said as he opened the door.

'I'm coming,' she said hastily. 'I'm ready.' The door-bell rang as Henry came fully into the room. She saw a swift shock of unexpected desire sweep over him, leaving him for a moment speechless, then he said: 'That's new, isn't it?' and added, without pause and with a cautionary tone, 'You know, "Tiger" Warburton's coming.'

She could have laughed aloud. Tiger Warburton had a reputation as a bit of a one for the ladies. The dress was a success, and having started out down the path of acting the siren, she smouldered away very deliberately every time Henry looked her way during the evening. She looked at him through half-closed eyes and her hand brushed his as she refilled his glass, making him lose the thread of his conversation. Tiger, one of their managers since the inception of a spinning section, was equally enthralled, and Eleanor found herself having to be especially nice to his wife, a plain but mercifully placid woman, who obviously worshipped her husband and could see no wrong in anything he did or said. Eleanor felt Tiger must get away with quite a lot. He was certainly very open in his flattery, as also were the other two business associates who had come to dinner.

Towards the end of the evening, Eleanor saw a different look in her husband's eyes. Did anger kindle with the intensity of both his astonishment and his desire? Quite suddenly she felt like a very small girl, and, by the time their guests came to leave, had let the role of enchantress slip noticeably from her shoulders. Henry narrowed his eyes, and looked hard and calculatingly at her, as if warning that it was too late now for a change of roles.

When the front door was closed behind their guests, Henry leaned back on it and stood looking at her, at ease at last to take in the full effect of the dress and the silk stockings. She caught her breath, feeling he almost undressed her with his eyes, and moved to the bottom of the stairs.

'Will you check the fires?' she asked, already in full retreat towards the bedroom.

'That won't take me long,' he answered and she felt she could almost hear the chuckle in his voice.

She ran to their bedroom and pulled off the dress, wrapping herself quickly in the brightly flowered, black kimono he had brought back from one of his London trips. She had hardly lapped the belt over when he came into the room, having already taken off his coat and loosened his tie. She looked at him warily, wanting at once to be close against the crisp whiteness of his shirt, to feel the heat of his chest and arms through it, and at the same time to run away and hide from this passion she had kindled.

'Henry, I . . .' she began and then stepped slowly backwards as he came silently towards her. 'This is silly, Henry,' she appealed.

'Hoist with your own petard, is what I've heard it called,' he said, still advancing.

At the last moment she gave a gasp of excitement, slipped under his arm and ran from the room, glad that John was sound asleep, the cook downstairs in her basement flat and the maid in her attic-bedroom. She ran to the playroom where earlier she had studied the picture of the barn, where a large rocking-horse stood by one wall, a school desk and a globe like reproving ghosts in the middle. She pressed against the wooden horse, moonlight filtering through the window nets, biting her lip so as to suppress a nervous giggle. Really they were both too old for this kind of game. Then with a nervous little shiver, she anticipated that Henry would never be too old for just this kind of thing!

He certainly neither looked nor acted like a man nearing his fortieth year as he came into the room, quietly closing the door and pausing to let his eyes get used to the darkness.

'I know you're here,' he breathed, laughter bubbling beneath his whisper. 'You brazen hussy, you.'

Her own excitement and laughter escaped in a smothered sound, half a sneeze, half a laugh, and she saw his face turn immediately to where she stood. The next moment she was pressed against the wooden rump of the horse, Henry teasing her neck with his lips and tongue and tiny touch of his teeth on her ear lobe. She squirmed against him, laughing quietly still. His hands fell to her waist holding her closer to himself.

'Henry, I. . . .'

'Sssh! The talking was for downstairs.'

She found he was quite capable of undressing himself, and divesting her of all unnecessary garments, without any pause for planning. Just like his business activities, she thought wildly, and yet succeeding just the same.

He lifted her until she seemed to ride the wooden haunches of the horse, swaying back slightly, ever moving and responding like a well-tuned harp to the touch and skill of its player, until he lowered her slowly, at first, on to himself.

It was a long time before they could bear to become separate, and allow the room to drift back to its normal evening atmosphere, although the rocking-horse never would again.

'We'll go to see Holywell tomorrow,' he whispered later as they lay companionably together in their bed.

'Holywell?' she queried drowsily.

'Tomorrow,' he answered, as if in confirmation of a simple statement, and before falling asleep added, 'and wear that dress again.'

She had not understood at first when Henry insisted on setting off very early to drive just twenty miles out into the country. 'I want us to have plenty of time to look round, and I want you to see it as I first did, in the early morning, with the sun out.'

'Holywell,' she said, 'is it a religious thing? I've never heard of it.'

'It's not far from an old Saxon church, and I understand it was built on the site of the original manor, burnt down by outraged tenants at the time of the enclosures in the sixteen hundreds. So I supposed the two things have been put together to make its name. "Holywell Manor".'

'Oh! it's a building,' she said, 'I thought. . . .'

She stopped, not sure what had been in her mind, and became wary as Henry unexpectedly turned the car between two large gateposts which were largely obscured by massive growths of ivy. He stopped the car, and holding her hand led her along the remnants of a gravel drive. Rhododendrons and conifers competed for space and light beneath a fine row of horse chestnut trees, which were in a full pink flower. Henry drew her to a halt beneath one of the magnificent trees. 'Listen!' he said. Bird song, then the drone of bees busy in the blossom above their heads seemed to make the peace and quietness of the place more absolute. 'I miss the country,' he said, and listening they trod more quietly along the moss, which had spread from verge to driveway, setting the gravel like more precious stones in its greenness.

'It's a lovely spot,' she said, pointing to where the tower of a Norman church showed through a clump of firs.

'Holywell parish church, built over the ruins of the original Saxon one, when this small village, this countryside, was a thriving medieval market centre.'

'How do you know so much about it?' she asked.

'It's a strange thing but I've sort of collected bits of information over the years. I knew of the place when I was a boy; it was the place where the first huge flocks of sheep were enclosed around here. The beginning of our local woollen industry.' They walked up to the front of the manor as he talked. It reminded Eleanor of one of the large vicarages that the Victorians favoured, with steep, gothic-looking gable ends. There were magnificent elms, copper beeches and limes on the neglected lawns, but the house itself was shabby and forlorn-looking, with peeling paintwork and window panes dulled with grime and obscured by the bright new tendrils of Virginia creeper.

'What a shame,' she said. 'I suppose it was lovely once.'

'And could be again.' He went on to tell her of the owner who had lost his only son in the war, and who now lived in a nursing home on the south coast, quite near the school John wanted to go to, and who wished to be rid of the place 'almost at any price'. His pause was ominous, and she turned on him, suddenly, incredulously, realizing what this outing was all about.

'But it's too big!' She walked up to the front porch as if challenging the place, attempting to display it to him. 'It's too big! It's ridiculous.'

'This is where I want to spend the rest of my life,' he said quietly.

She walked up and down, agitated by the very idea, throwing disjointed remarks at him: 'Why haven't you mentioned this before? When did you come here? Have you even been inside? How did you meet the owner?' Henry did not answer and, as she stopped, the peace of the place seemed overwhelmingly on his side.

'I notice the one thing you don't say is that we can't afford it,' he remarked at last.

'No, because knowing you, you've already been into all that. Probably already raised the loan!' she retorted, almost savagely. 'Henry, won't you ever be satisfied?'

'Yes,' he replied quietly. 'This is what I want.'

'What do you want to be, one of the landed gentry? You!'

'Yes,' he replied with quiet emphasis, his face taking on the set, determined look she had come to know so well, 'even me. I want to live here, to bring the heart back to this house and this land, to ride, to join the local hunt, and to have my wife and boy accepted in the county.'

'Huh! Fine chance.' First the boarding-school hundreds of miles away for John, now this. It was too much. She marched back towards the car. Henry followed, got in, started up the engine, but instead of turning away, down the drive, drove slowly around the house to the back, where years of grass grew high between the slabs of a stable yard.

'The buildings are all sound,' Henry said as he pulled up again. 'Roof's waterproof. It's only a cosmetic job that the house itself needs in the first place.' He seemed pleased with the phrase, and repeated it, leaning back in the driving seat, hands behind his head, contemplating the property, dreaming. . . .

She was furious, why had he not confided in her before? Her mind seethed as she tried to order the feelings that told her Henry was wanting too much. How could she explain her dread, superstitious perhaps, that everything in life had a price (other than just money) to be paid for it, and that Holywell was something they could not afford. It was almost like *asking* fate to give them a tumble for their audacity.

'You'll be like, like . . . you'll fly too high,' she snapped. 'With the business I could understand, if we had to get bigger it all seemed logical, but. . . .'

'Icarus,' he supplied, as if he had not heard her latter remarks, and went on complacently, 'No, I think if the banks are willing to speculate, then it's a safe bet that we'll come to no harm. Land has to be a good investment.'

'We'll come to no harm because here's where I stop, and if you won't drive me home. . . .' She got out of the car and walked smartly away, to the front of the house, and down the drive.

She had walked far enough to begin to wonder what Henry was doing, even whether he had gone home another way, leaving her stranded some twenty miles from home. It annoyed her even more, that just at the second she allowed herself a backward glance, he came around a bend and saw her looking. He stopped by her, but when she ignored him and went on walking, he drove at walking pace alongside her, to the great amusement of a carload of young people going the other way. They shouted cheerfully and waved enthusiastically, but neither she nor Henry responded. One of them threw back the gibe: 'Oh dear! They must be married!' The laughter lingered in Eleanor's ears as the car roared out of sight.

He let her walk a little further, then said matter-of-factly: 'You might as well get in. I shan't leave you, and the nearer we get to town the more people we shall meet.' She slammed the door as hard as she could, having the momentary satisfaction of seeing Henry's face register disapproval, but he said no more – on any subject.

Dinner too was silent. Eleanor kept her gaze on her meal, involuntarily contrasting that evening with the night before, when she had worn the pink dress for the first time. They seemed like two different people. Henry even *looked* different, she thought, as she glanced up to return the cruet to the middle of the table. He even looked older. Had he really taken her refusal to go with him on the latest venture so much to heart?

Good heavens, she thought impatiently, she had borne with him through a lot!

She made little forked mounds of her mashed potatoes, and pushed them to the perimeter of the plate as she mentally listed the growth of the business. All of which she *had* agreed to work for. First the factory, then the private limited company. She consolidated a larger, firmer mound: the extension for the production of men's and boys' underwear. With a sigh, she contemplated the untidy remaining heap of potatoes, the unworked bit, and pushing her fork through them, left the meal.

She heard Henry go out after dinner, and then wandered restlessly around the house, uneasy because he had gone without any word of parting, or any explanation of where he was going, or when he would be back.

She went to their bedroom and stood looking out over the parks, as she remembered Henry had done the first time they had looked over this house, ten years before. That in itself did not seem possible, ten years: ten, swift years. 'Happy years?' She seemed to hear Aggie Sansome's voice, and see old Gunnie, nodding to her, urging her on. Their deaths had left the world a much poorer place, she thought, mentally qualifying happy, eventful years, years which she supposed had truly seen her grow from girl to woman. The girl had died with Greg, and the woman, as she saw it now, had begun and matured with Henry, gaining poise from his adoration, confidence from his devotion. Oh, how she loved the damned man! She admitted this with exasperation.

Perhaps he, in turn, had gained confidence as their marriage had blossomed, feeling he could leap any hurdle, revelling in every new gamble, strutting like the proverbial rooster at each success, refusing to accept setbacks. She remembered what had nearly been a very ugly scene with a bank manager when money had been too tight to launch the exports to Canada. Accompanying Henry to give him moral support, as she thought, she had been very upset at the verbal battle that had almost verged on the physical, in the manager's office. Coming out she had felt emotionally ravaged, and embarrassed by the covert glances from dark-suited clerks and the more openly curious customers, but glancing at Henry she realized he had enjoyed it all! He had radiated the look of the victor.

She tutted, and sighed and laughed. There was just no dealing with the man, he was . . . the only words that eventually seemed right were: part of her and she part of him, and without each other. . . .

Her gaze returned to the window, to the darkening park, and it was with something of a shock that she recognized Henry's figure. He was walking slowly, reflectively, around the perimeter path. There was something indecisive in his step as he came to the gate nearest the house, he hesitated but then passed on. Watching, she became aware that this time Henry was having to come to terms with quite a different set of circumstances. This time she was not on his side. This time he was trying to convince himself that he was wrong, that he must curtail his ambitions, and he was diminished, she could see that even from a distance. If their ways diverged even on a small matter they would each be less, and this was not a small thing. This was a house he wanted to live in for the rest of his days. She went, slowly at first, down the stairs, out and across into the park, turning the opposite way to Henry. They would meet on the far side.

16

With the employment of a formidable, but efficient, lady typist in the offices of Attersley's, and the responsibility and interest of renovating Holywell Manor taking up more of her time, Eleanor found her role dramatically altered. Almost in spite of herself, she found she had become an important member of the village community. Beginning with the people they employed to help with cleaning the house and clearing the grounds, she and Henry were treated with deference, and as they became better known, they were asked for advice and sought out for assistance with local projects.

They took up their regular church-going again. Eleanor became a member of the Mothers' Union and Henry was quickly enlisted on to the list of readers and sidesmen, the manor being handy for anyone wanting to leave messages about church matters.

Henry, who had ridden farm horses as a child and more spirited mounts while he was in the army, arrived home one evening just in time to stop Eleanor sending away a horse he had bought that morning at Lycester racecourse sales. Eleanor found herself having to lead the impatient animal around while Henry prepared a stable for it.

'Why couldn't you wait until things were ready first?' she grumbled, trying to keep her own feet from under the hooves as the pair of them circled.

'I saw the mare and really liked the look of her. She's a bargain.'

'I'm sure she is,' Eleanor commented drily as she passed the stable door on her next round.

'Keep going, love,' Henry encouraged. 'I've just got to go up to the farm for some straw.'

'Henry! You're not leaving me with this . . .' she tried to stop and see where he was, but the impetus of the horse kept her going. 'It's pulling my arms out of their sockets!' she shouted, threatening to let go if Henry put one foot outside the stable yard. For one panic-stricken moment she thought she was alone, then glimpsed Henry and John sitting on the wheelbarrow at the far end of the yard, both helpless with laughter.

The incident did not help endear her to horses, but Henry was soon riding every day before he went to the factory, and every evening, giving John lessons on a splendid, arch-necked, grey pony he bought. The local hunt were eager to have Henry as a member, part of the land attached to the manor being a traditional location for the first cubbing meet of each season.

She enjoyed being part of village life again, and treasured the walks she and Henry had in the evenings: times when many business decisions were made, after long discussion in the calm, quiet, time before bed; times when they were quiet together, the only sign of their passing, a bird clattering and complaining as they startled it from its roosting place; times for talk of world affairs; times of communion.

Henry flourished like a plant at last put into its proper environment. He loved Holywell and no amount of labour to restore it to beauty was too much, although from time to time his sudden enthusiasms were a little much for Eleanor.

'Eleanor! Look!' he had shouted to her as she set foot in the door after a shopping trip for chintz for drapes. 'Look! Beams!'

She had stood aghast at the sight of him, and her sitting-room. She had had the oak floor scrubbed and repolished, the paintwork washed and the windows cleaned ready for the new curtains. Everything was now covered in plaster-dust and the floor cluttered with the boarding he had ripped from the ceiling. He looked to her like some maniacal creature as he gestured to the filthy, nondescript-looking beams above his head. She would have much to say when she got over the first shock, but at that first discovery she turned from the room and shut him very firmly in, with his beams. Already, though, she was calculating that if there were beams in the sitting-room . . . it seemed she was going to have to be very patient before she started work on things like drapes.

For six months, as soon as any room in the house was cleaned, a film of powdery dust settled immediately. In that time, all the downstairs beams had been exposed and oiled, and when finally it was all finished, and not one minute before, Eleanor admitted to Henry that it was all worthwhile. The darkened beams had a beauty of their own and added grace and beauty to the seasons, whether it was as foil to the spring colours and flowers through the windows, or those Eleanor massed in vases through summer and autumn, or to make a picture-postcard setting for the decorations at Christmas.

John was always given a tour of the things Henry had accomplished as soon as he came home for the holidays. He invariably approved, and often helped Henry with the latest project, loving the house and the country; making detailed drawings of plants and animals; riding with Henry, and going to business with him. John had proved a hard-working pupil at his school, and was benefiting from the careful guidance of the talented art teacher there, just as his godfather, William, had predicted. It was planned that he should go on either to university or to a London art college, where William would be on hand if ever needed. Henry was as keen as anyone that the boy should have as many doors opened to him as possible, but made no secret of the fact that he hoped John would finally follow him into the business.

But as each term ended and John came home, Eleanor felt it was like greeting a different young man. He seemed to grow up so quickly. Sometimes she could see Greg so clearly in him when he worked at his easel in the garden of Holywell, or in his moments of introspection; at others it could be Greg's father, Bertram Hamson, she saw, particularly in his almost prudish attitude to an unreformable gardener Henry insisted on maintaining, who occasionally slept off a hangover in the tool-shed – and sometimes she fearfully glimpsed her own father, Reuben Lewis, in John's dark hair and fine pale skin. Henry privately insisted that it was her scrutiny that drove John ever to his company, rather than that of his mother.

'You're smothering him with care as you did when he was first born,' Henry insisted.

'I can't help caring . . .' she had begun curtly, then stopped as Henry drew her gently to him. 'No, I know that, and some day John will, too, but let him out from under that microscope of yours!'

The one time she felt she had real contact with her son was the day George Sansome telephoned from the village doctor's house to say that he had woken that morning to find Aggie dead on her sofa. Eleanor had felt stricken for George and for herself, and the seemingly distant fifteen-year-old had slipped his hand into hers. 'You loved Aggie,' he said.

'I did,' she answered, her eyes brimming with tears and impulsively she lifted his hand and kissed it.

He had not retreated from her then, and two days later

when she and Henry returned from the funeral, John had brought a tray of tea to their room with a cut-glass vase filled with the first violet buds from the Easter hedgerows.

'And you worry about the boy,' Henry said, bending to smell the tiny rain-sweet flowers.

The occasion and John's thoughtfulness had left her awash with tears and memories. What would Greg have thought of his son, she wondered. How strange it was that perhaps John had in the end been given the very same opportunities by Henry as his real father, or grandfather Hamson, might have provided.

It was John's christening she was to recall when later that same year the news came that Gunnie had died of peritonitis. Travelling to Honsfield, she learned that Gunnie had carried on in her shop to the last, thinking that as the violent pains she had been suffering had miraculously gone, she was better, unaware that her appendix had burst. Travelling home again by train, Eleanor had been reassured to think that Gunnie had died in harness, as she would have wanted, and consoled herself with happier memories of her and Aggie, and how well the illmatched pair had got on together at that christening party the Sansomes had given for John. In her bag, she had the few bits of jewellery Gunnie had left her – 'for old times' sake', her will had read.

Though John grew more and more to be his own man, occasionally she wondered if they were not all too happy. It seemed like tempting fate. Sometimes as the thirties slipped by, she stood in the quiet of the morning looking over the peaceful country and yet listening, when the wind blew from the right quarter, to an alien sound – the great infuriated roar of some new gas turbine engine for jet propulsion being tested by a man named Whittle some five miles away. It seemed to hold almost a threat in its enraged mechanical gusting.

Henry, having fought against the Germans, took very seriously the news of the growing aggression of the Nazi party in Germany. In 1930, 107 members were elected to the Reichstag, in 1932, 230. Hitler was appointed Chancellor of Germany in 1933 and Reichsführer in 1934. The following year the Nuremberg Laws deprived Jews of citizens' rights and their persecution began. While Germany restored full conscription contrary to the Treaty of Versailles, and signed an Anti-Comintern Pact with Japan, English young idealists went to fight in the Spanish Civil War. At home, the country was split by a more domestic matter – the continued devotion of Edward to the American divorcee Mrs Simpson. In 1936, he finally decided to give up the throne and married Mrs Simpson in 1937.

In the September John left school, the threat was more immediate, the reprieve earned by Chamberlain the year before with the declaration of 'peace in our time', had run out, and the parish church at Holywell was more full than usual for the Sunday morning service on 3 September 1939.

The hymn began, 'Oft in danger, oft in woe,/Onward, Christians, onward go', and while the congregation certainly finished the first verse, it was only because the words were so well known to them.

Eleanor saw her son's head turn to the aisle, following others, to watch Henry leaving his sidesman's pew at the rear of the church and carrying a note to the front. The vicar took it from him, but when Henry would have left his side, put out a hand and held his sleeve, as if in need of support. The organist stopped, and the verger, thinking something was wrong with the organ he was vigorously pumping air into, popped his head out from the back, then, seeing all eyes directed to the front, disappeared once more, only seconds later to emerge in full, mouth agape. The group of Sunday School children on the front two rows, also gazed around and wondered what had happened. Then all attention was with the Reverend Richmond who moved to the centre of the nave.

'I have to tell you that the Prime Minister, Mr Neville

Chamberlain, has just announced that we are at war with Germany.'

Henry's gaze sought his wife and son as the first seconds of war were held in silence. Then, startling everyone, one of the women choristers cried out aloud, 'Oh, no! Oh, God, no!' then covered her face with her hands and sobbed hysterically. There were sighs and exclamations from all around the church as she was helped from the choir stalls and out through the side door.

The vicar held up his hands again and addressed his congregation. 'I think we can do no better at this moment than to finish our hymn, before making special prayers for the safety of our country, our allies, and perhaps very particularly we will pray for the safety of our young men and for the courage of our young women, in the days of trial that lie ahead for us all.'

Of course, Eleanor thought irreverently, he would have such a speech all ready, but the catch in his voice when he mentioned the young people had been unrehearsed as was the raw agony of fear she felt for John. He's eighteen, her mind repeated over and over again, eighteen. Just the right age, the right age for war. What had they been called in the Great War, the war to end all wars, 'cannon fodder'. The outrageous thought of conscription, of the whole panoply of war to which they were now committed, made the intervening twenty years seem no more than a long, hot afternoon. Not again, not again, she too wanted to cry out.

The concerned group outside the church with their subdued conversation and their reluctance to leave their fellow parishioners seemed quite alien to Eleanor. She needed to be alone with her immediate family, to come to terms with this thing that had openly threatened since 1937, or even 1935, and was now reality. They were at war with Germany.

She was glad that for one rare Sunday they had no guests for lunch. Even so, during the meal the three of them seemed only able to discuss the war in general terms: how the call-up would affect the factories; the political lead-up to the war, Munich, the rape of Austria; the years of rearming by Germany.

'We have a lot of leeway to make up,' Henry said.

'I shall go straight into the Air Force, if neither of you object, and not wait for conscription,' John said.

'You fool.' The words came automatically and without emphasis, as Eleanor heard her son pledging himself as willing to die.

'I wouldn't rush into anything, if I were you,' Henry said, hastening to soften and yet still endorse her condemnation. 'Time enough to go if there's no alternative. We might be able to get you exempted for management at the factories, essential work to keep things going at home, that kind of line.'

'I wouldn't want that,' John answered quietly.

'No, of course not! You'll want to be one of the heroes, like the million who died last time!'

'It won't be like the last time, Mother, nothing like.'

'The dying, and the suffering and the grief, will be the same. People don't change, even if weapons do. Oh!' With a sudden exclamation of impatience with the follies of men she pushed away her meal, rose and left the room by way of the french windows. She heard Henry say: 'No, let her go.'

Once in the sunlight, she walked around the house the way Henry had driven her the very first time she had seen the place, through to the stables, the warmth of the September afternoon easing the physical tension. Her footsteps echoed loudly in the cobbled yard, the empty boxes. The weather was so good the horses were only brought in for an evening feed as yet, though they were just beginning to be prepared for the season's hunting.

She wandered into the tack room, full of the smell of leather, surveying the saddles on their trees, leathers hanging from the walls, then to the feed room, lifting the lids of bins, running her fingers through oats and bran, smoothing the shiny brown linseed in its smaller container, almost as if she were taking stock, busying her mind with something, or trying to hold on to something she felt slipping away fast. She watched her own hands, pale brown against the bright veneered mahogany slithers of linseed, the mature hands of a woman nearly forty. She stilled their useless occupation. A moment of truth, she thought quizzically.

If life has taught me anything, she thought, it must be that at these times one can either retreat and confine the area in which one may be further hurt to smaller and smaller limits, and have to become less oneself to live in that area, even to the point of wanting to extinguish oneself completely or, one has to grow big enough to encompass the loss and deal with the trouble. One has to learn to face the days without dreading what is still to come, without recoiling from one shock and forever anticipating the next. One has to tackle fears by gripping past victories and past survivals.

'So!' she straightened the lids on the feed bins, she would have to learn again to let go, to love and to let go. She glanced around as the sun was suddenly obscured from the doorway, and felt as if she had conjured her son with her thoughts.

'Mother.' The word hung lightly, almost experimentally, between them. 'I have to go, you know.'

'Yes. I do know.' Impulsively she lifted her arms to him, and he came and hugged her, kissing her cheek. 'Let's walk, shall we?' She led the way towards the walled kitchen garden.

'I think there is something else I should tell you,' John said, stopping near a bench surrounded by autumn-high growths of balm, mint and parsley. He sat down, scooped up a handful of loose gravel, and let it drip stone by stone slowly through his fingers, watching each stone fall, each find a new resting place.

'I've always wanted to please Dad, always felt I would do anything to make him happy, but,' he let the rest of the stones cascade from his hands, 'I think once I make the break, go away from home again, away from the factories and the business, I shall not want to come back.'

She remained silent, letting the full implication of what her son was saying sink home.

'Of course I suppose it depends what kind of war I have.'

Spoken with all the assured optimism of youth, she thought. Youth that could never envisage its own demise, age did at least give the grace to consider extinction of oneself.

'So the business thing was always to please your father,' she stated. Was that wise?'

'Perhaps it was expedient.' He looked at her and grinned disarmingly. 'I went and had a look at how the Chelsea set lived. I wasn't drawn to it. I preferred Holywell Manor – I'll always be grateful to you and Dad for life here – and I knew I would have plenty of leisure for painting. Don't look so surprised. I'm a realist, like you, not a romantic empire-builder like Dad, but . . .' he shrugged and stopped.

'But?' she prompted quickly, feeling she must not let barriers rise between them ever again.

'I've always felt that somehow I've let *you* down, fallen short of what you expected. Sometimes I've found you looking at me, as if you were searching for a different person.'

'Ah!' The sound escaped, low, privately, like the instinctive reaction to sudden pain – so the barriers were, after all, of her own making. She looked away, plucked at a leaf of balm, crushing and smelling the sharp lemon fragrance. When she looked at John again, she saw that she was confirming what he had previously only suspected, that she had been looking for someone else. This was not the time for deviation, yet the time for this truth was long past. Again there had to be a compromise.

'You were such a different child to what I expected, and yet just to say that, is quite ridiculous. I know *now* one shouldn't expect one's children to be anything but their own selves. I suppose,' she chose and said the words with infinite care, 'I was always looking for more of your father in you.'

'Father's rather unique though, isn't he?' John said with quiet reproof. 'That is exactly it really. I feel you are saying to me "Follow that!", and I know I can't.'

'No, you're wrong, so wrong. I think what I was trying to say to *myself* was, that even though this son is part of me, part of my love and my life, yet he is his own man. I think, if anything, I've always been a little in awe of you, even as a baby you had such definite ideas and wishes. So you see it would be very wrong of you to try to *follow* anyone. You must work for your own ends, your own ideals and ambitions.'

'So, after the war, you would help Father understand if I did not come back into the business?'

She nodded. 'I can take a far more active role in the business if it's what your father wants. I certainly know all the background!' They both laughed, for Henry's enjoyment of his working life was aired at most meal-times.

John stretched with an air of well-being and a satisfied sigh, as if this talk had solved all his problems. 'You'll look after this place too, won't you? Part of me will always be in these green acres. Oh! that sounds a bit Browningish, sorry!'

'If anyone should be sorry, I think it's me,' she answered. 'I should have *said* more often how much you meant to me, how much I loved you.'

'You've shown me well enough.' John's face was open, frank. 'It was just this wretched imagination of mine. I often lay awake at night trying to fathom what the secret was I thought you were keeping from me.'

She thought of the dark brooding doorways in many of his childhood pictures. Her breath came tight, but she shook her head at him as if in mock reproof. To reveal a secret too late might tear a whole life apart.

'I know,' he said, 'stupid, wasn't it? I'm glad we've had this talk. You know I had even decided to quiz Godfather William about it when I was next in town. Lay the ghost once and for all, as it were, before I get involved in this war thing.' His mouth was already open to laugh, when he saw the unguarded alarm flit across his mother's face. She quickly tried to look astonished but it was too late. She saw his anguish, his sad and tortured withdrawal, as again he came up against the secret that had so plagued his life.

Eleanor was dismayed, but not surprised, when William arrived in a state of some distress the following Friday.

'Where's Henry – still at the factory?' he asked, after they had embraced and he had sat down.

'It's John, isn't it?' she said, without answering his question. 'He's been to see you.'

'Yes. . . .' William rose again quickly and came to stand before her, his manner bringing the same swift alarm as the time he had come from Switzerland with the news that Greg's illness was terminal.

'He's guessed about Henry,' she said.

The look in William's eyes did not entirely match her statement. 'I didn't tell him anything, Eleanor, but. . .' he shook his head and turned away, sighed deeply. 'I wouldn't have believed it of John . . . what he did . . . I would have trusted him implicitly.'

'What do you mean? For goodness sake, William, tell me everything!'

He spread his hands as if to say he had very little alternative. 'John came to stay with me for a few days, as you probably know, before his posting came through to his training squadron. He seemed very abstracted when he arrived, and immediately after dinner began asking questions about you. It amounted to a cross-questioning, and he wouldn't be put off. Where had his father met you? Had I known you before you were married? All that kind of thing. Finally he confronted me, saying he did not think you were his real mother – that he believed his father had been married twice. . . .'

For a moment she lost the thread of what William was telling her. She felt as if she had been slapped violently on the cheek.

'He was convinced he was a child from a previous marriage. Of course I. . . .' He stopped as Eleanor slumped into a chair. He took her hands. 'Are you all right? There's more, I'm afraid.'

She looked up at him, her lips parting slightly as if in shock, but she felt no other revelation could hurt more than this. 'Go on,' she whispered.

'When I arrived home from the hospital last evening and went into my study, the place had been ransacked. At first I thought it was burglars, then I realized that the only things that had been pulled right out were from the drawer of my desk where I kept all my old diaries and notebooks. These had been gone through, and . . .' he turned away from her, bitter regret in his voice, as he said violently. 'Damn my passion for keeping notes and records of every bloody thing!'

It was the first time she had ever heard William swear. 'And. . .' she prompted him. She had to hear it all now.

'And the diary containing the reference to John's christening had been torn to shreds and hurled all around the room,' he paused. 'Make no mistake, Eleanor, the notes I had made would leave John in no doubt that Henry is not his father.'

'And he had thought it was the other way around,' she said wonderingly. 'How strange.' Even as she uttered the mild-sounding comment, she felt both hurt and an unreasoned resentment. When she remembered his birth so vividly, she was irrationally amazed that he should not *know* she was his mother.

Henry came home while she was still sitting trying to come to terms with this totally unexpected assumption of John's.

'I don't think I've ever known the boy destroy anything before,' Henry said, after listening to the story. He got up, went to the mantelpiece and selected a pipe. 'And where is he now?' he asked.

'This, I don't know,' William answered, 'and I'm worried. All his clothes, his new uniform, everything is still in his room at my flat, but he did not come back last night.'

Henry put the pipe back into the rack. 'He has to report for training next Wednesday, one of us should hear something of him before then. Pity he wasn't told the truth years ago. . . .'

'How could we!' Eleanor almost shouted at him. 'How could we? What would people have said! What would Bertram Hamson have done! What would other boys have called him!' She knew her real anger lay in Henry's immediate and unquestioning acceptance of John's misapprehension.

'Is this any less cruel for him?' Henry asked.

'This pilot training will take his mind off it,' William began.

'Oh! so we should rejoice there's a war!' she interrupted with anger. 'If he's shot down quickly, that should really distract him!'

'Eleanor!' It was Henry's turn to shout now, but she glared back at the two men, unrepentant. 'How can you know how this hurts?' she said.

'Isn't it more important how it hurts John?' Henry replied.

It was a very stilted dinner that evening, with William hurrying to catch the train back to town. The only thing all three agreed on, was that they would each keep the others informed as soon as there was any news of John.

William rang from London just after midnight to say that when he arrived home John's things were all gone, and there was a brief note. 'It just says: "Sorry for the intrusion and the mess. John." '.

Eleanor was to hear no more until Henry came home

from the factory unexpectedly on Monday lunchtime.

'John's been to the office. He was there when I first arrived this morning. Eleanor . . . he's in quite a state. He sat in my office looking like someone who's been bereaved, or like a child that's lost a puppy, or something . . . I don't know.'

Henry's distress seemed only to harden her own. 'Where is he now? Is he coming home?'

'I don't know about now,' Henry's voice was flat, expressionless, 'but he says he won't be coming back after the war – not to Holywell – nor to the business.'

'I think the business was in doubt anyway,' she began sharply, resenting that John should use this as an excuse to tell Henry he did not want to return to the business. It was not just.

'He's knocked the bottom out of my world, I can tell you,' Henry went on. 'If Attersley's is not for him, who is it for?'

'Well, for us, I suppose.' She refused to be dragged down to such extremes of despair. 'After all, it was the two of *us* who started it, not John.'

'But he was there, always in the backs of our minds.' Henry looked at her despairingly and shook his head. 'Maybe we should finish, sell up.'

'For goodness sake,' she was shocked, but refused to take his remark seriously. 'Henry Attersley without a business, it's like trying to think of Winston Churchill without a cigar! Anyway *this* shareholder doesn't want to sell up, and we're not going to disinherit John, are we, even if he does reject us. . . ?'

'Oh! he's done that all right!'

'For a time, perhaps,' she tried to reason.

'You haven't seen him!' Henry insisted.

'He had already told me he didn't think he would want to come back to the business.'

'And Holywell?' Henry asked, his voice not even.

She did not answer immediately, feeling she and Henry were walking round and round the problem, and each other, and had at no point touched. 'Surely,' she said at last, 'surely, eighteen years of love can't have gone just like that.'

She was to feel just that when, in the middle of the afternoon, after Henry had finally decided to go back to town, John's green MG sports car came fast up the drive, spluttering the gravel on to the lawns as he parked in front of the house. She felt almost apprehensive as she watched him from her bedroom window. She was sure he was aware of her, but he did not look up, and there was a certain unkemptness, a wildness even, about his appearance, his hair and his unbuttoned jacket hanging off his shoulders.

She heard him come upstairs and go to his room. She waited several minutes then went and tapped on his door, and entered. He stood with his back to her, and she saw he had sorted a small pile of books, which lay on his bed.

'I'm glad you've come home before you go off to start your training,' she began.

'Spare me the small talk. I've just come for a few books.' His tone was rough, rude and unforgiving.

'I'm sorry you found out,' she said, equally uncompromising.

'*Sorry* I found out!' He turned savagely, asking: 'Do you know how I feel? I feel *sorry* I was born!'

'John!' Her exclamation was as much response to his ravaged appearance as to his remark. She stepped forward, aching to embrace him and to comfort him, but he turned away savagely, rebuffing her.

'John,' she repeated more gently. 'You only know a few, stark facts. Let me tell you the full story.'

For a moment she thought he would listen, but then she saw distaste, almost hatred, cross the boy's face again. 'You have no right to look at me like that,' she said firmly. 'We've both loved you, done everything to make you happy, from the moment you were born.'

'I don't want to know!' he interrupted violently,

momentarily clapping his hands over his ears. 'For all these years,' he began again, as he rapidly threw his books into a small leather suitcase, 'the one person I felt loved me without reservations, without making judgements all the time, was my . . . was the man I thought was my father.' He snapped the case shut and faced his mother. 'You've taken him away from me now.' He turned to leave, and though she put a restraining hand on his arm, he brushed passed her, emotion now thickening his voice, 'If you had ever let me feel at ease with you, told me the truth, I could have . . . loved you enough to die for you.'

Long moments later, when the last sound of his departure had faded, she stood remembering that first great heartache of Greg's death, of being alone until Henry had come to her aid, saving not only her, but Greg's baby too.

'I lived for you,' she whispered to her departed son.

She felt so many things were coming to an end, and events allowed none of the leisurely approach that Britain had adopted at the beginning of the First World War. Winston Churchill, almost a solitary voice, had constantly warned against the German threat, asking how the future would judge a nation who, victorious against the same Germany through measureless sacrifice, could allow itself to throw away everything that had been so bitterly fought for. He had pointed to the 'manoeuvres' of over 3,000,000 German and Italian soldiers. There was no time for the rallying of noble volunteers as the last time, no immunity for those at home as before. Evacuation of children from the areas of key military targets was in full swing by that first day of the war, and conscription, by the new name of National Service, followed the recall of all territorials.

It was from a business contact, a traveller in yarns in the south, that they eventually heard that John had passed out as a pilot on 10 February 1940 and had been posted south to a fighter squadron on 13 March. The traveller's son, a mechanic on the same base, had mentioned John Attersley as being the best flyer in the latest draft, and casually enquired if the boy was any relation to Henry.

'I had hoped he might contact us before this. We could have gone to his passing-out parade,' Henry began, but then lapsed into silence as the chimes of Big Ben from the radio indicated it was time for the nine o'clock news. Listening to the evening news together in the sitting-room of Holywell had become a regular feature of their lives. Eleanor's eyes as always wandered to the framed watercolours of the countryside round about which John had painted. That evening they were sobered even more by the news of the fall of Finland.

'William telephoned this morning,' she said breaking the silence, 'he says I should write to John and tell him everything.'

'That's quite a task. It'll be a book!' Henry tried to make a joke of the idea, but then added seriously, 'But I wish you would.'

'I've already started,' she said.

Henry came to her, pulled her up into his arms and held her. 'I'm so glad,' he said. 'I can't bear losing all contact with him, like this.'

'Nor can I. I decided after William called that I would do this, and I will write to him regularly, as if nothing is amiss – which it isn't as far as we are concerned – and if he doesn't read them, or doesn't answer, well . . . I shall feel better *doing* something.' She was surprised and moved to see tears in Henry's eyes when she looked up at him. 'Oh! my dear.' She reached up and pulled his head to her shoulder. 'Henry, please don't, I can't bear it.' They stood in each other's arms and shed a few companionable tears together, before being able to discuss the form this first long letter should take.

As they talked, Eleanor decided she would keep a diary so as to remember all the news from the business and the happenings at Holywell so John need never completely lose touch.

From the same business contact, Henry learned that John was flying Spitfires and they knew he was involved in the Battle of Britain, the battle of the few against the many. Reports of the numbers of enemy aircraft shot down seemed to raise daily through that long hot summer, leaving Eleanor with the devastating vision of tiny Spitfire fighter-planes buzzing the might of German Dorniers, as she had seen on a spectacular piece of cinema newsreel. Then, at last, a letter came addressed to just Henry. The few words were very soberly weighed and evalauted both to each other, and in their own hearts.

Dear Father,

I find I have to think about the word before I write it but, as has been said, eighteen years is a long time.

I am fine, tired, but we all feel we are doing a worthwhile job.

John

Eleanor at least found herself pleased for Henry, but Henry was angry that there was no word addressed to her. The pattern was to remain the same, and Eleanor made herself content with it by being busy. She began to work regular hours in the business, but she also set herself a secret goal, willing herself towards the day when John would address her personally. It became a game of chance she played each time a letter came. Had she won or lost? Her heart beat faster each time she picked up the familiar envelope to see whose name was on it, and each time she consoled herself that John occasionally made comments which at least proved he read her letters.

Henry regularly exploited his business contact to glean extra news of John's squadron. Eleanor felt he was a little too persistent, and ran the risk of being taken in for questioning for spying! But in late October, he came beaming into his office, where she was sitting at her own desk, at her daily work of negotiating and processing government orders for woollen underwear, outerwear and socks for the armed forces. He leaned back on the closed door. 'Good news about John. I've just had a message. . . .'

'He's not coming home on leave!' She felt her heart begin to pound.

'No. It's better than that!'

'Better?' Her eyes searched his face, and her mind the possibilities. 'He's coming off operations?' The ache to see him surpassed by the wish for his safety.

'Yes, but better than that!'

'Henry! Please tell me!'

He came to her, and putting an arm around her waist, walked her to the window.

'John is being sent on a flying instructor's course, and then will be posted to Canada to help train their pilots.'

'Canada,' she breathed. The idea of the country brought visions of tall firs, lakes – and peace. 'He'll be out of the fighting. Oh! Thank God, thank God! But is it true? Where does he get all this information?'

'It's true, never fear. Our traveller's son has a friend in the Squadron Commander's office.' She did not answer, still half questioning, still only half daring to believe. Henry pulled out a small jeweller's box from his jacket pocket. 'I've been looking at this for weeks, wanting to buy it for you, but somehow it wasn't appropriate until I heard today's news. . . .' She opened the box he put into her hands. Inside lay a Royal Air Force regimental brooch, the bow on which the wings rested set with small exquisite diamonds.

'It's beautiful,' she breathed. 'Thank you, Henry. I shall wear it all the time.' She let him pin the brooch on to her costume lapel, then put her arms around his neck. 'Thank you so much – for everything.'

He kissed her with the same timeless, all-demanding passion which always took her by surprise. She drew away.

'What's the matter?' he asked.

She laughed a little shakily. 'If I'm not careful you'll be wanting to make love to me on the office floor.'

'Everyone will have gone home in a few minutes.'

She tutted at him, then put her fingers over the brooch. 'I love it,' she said.

'Come on, let's go home, you'll feel more relaxed there.' He caught her reproving look and grinned. 'We've not had anything to celebrate for a long time!'

As they travelled home, Eleanor leaned back in the corner of their Rover car and appraised her husband. She was not sure that in his late forties she did not find him more attractive than he had been as a younger man. His hair, now a distinguished dark grey, was allowed to grow a little longer these days, although his frame was as robust as ever, his face seemed leaner. He was much more the outdoor man too, more tanned as a result of riding and having to spend more of his time supervising the extra land he had bought around Holywell. She sat half-smiling, thinking of his farming activities. She was amused at the caution with which he viewed farming, displaying none of the adventure or verve he brought to his business. He held a deep respect for the imponderables of nature, seeming to distrust any activity which had to rely so heavily on the fickle weather.

Her eyes caught the multi-coloured glint of diamonds in the sun's low rays, and she pulled her costume coat together a little more so she could see the new brooch more clearly. If this news of John were true, this piece of jewellery would always be especially precious to her. She smiled thinking how, over the years, Henry had always managed to find the perfect gift to please her, even though, at the time she had *not always* thought it was what she wanted: the gramophone, the vacuum cleaner, the magnetic window cleaning device that had fallen off the outside of the flat window and broken the factory window below. . . .

Suddenly her day-dreaming ended, and she was wide-eyed, alarmed, as the car made a sudden sweeping curve to the left, and came to an abrupt stop in a wide, deserted field gateway.

'What is it? What's the matter? Have we hit something?'

'No.' He leaned over to her seat, put an arm around her shoulders and kissed her. 'I haven't been able to take my eyes off you all day, sitting there at your desk smiling with that stupid frilly bit of blouse poking out of your jacket.' He flicked the pink frill. 'I've been listening to you charming the birds off the trees, and watching the men rushing to open doors for you, pulling out chairs, *even* taking the receiver off its hook for you!'

'I could have my own office,' she said demurely.

'You'll stay where you are! In fact I'll make sure everyone knows *who* you are! I'll have a name board done for your desk. *Mrs* Eleanor Attersley.'

'Keep off!' she added.

'A good idea!' He leaned over again and kissed her, his lips warm and trembling with sudden gentleness. 'Let's just have a little stroll, shall we?' He got out of the car, led the way to the gate and sighed deeply as they both leaned over, experiencing the renewal of spirit from the quiet expanse of stubble fields, bordered by the double-stacked leaf masses of the great elms, rusty with autumn. 'I feel a weight's been lifted from my shoulders with this news of John.'

'It's like being reprieved,' she said. 'I'll just be glad when he's actually gone to Canada.' Even as she said the words, she had an odd premonition that Canada might come to mean more to John than just a country where he had to go to train pilots.

'He'll always come back to Holywell in the end,' Henry said suddenly, as if his thoughts were moving much in the same way. 'Always, no matter what. I know it deep down. He's listened too long to the songs the old place sings.'

'The songs?'

'Of course. Each quiet, beautiful place has songs, for those who listen quietly enough and long enough. My grandfather used to say he liked the songs of the summer evening fields the best – in the spring he was too busy with his lambs to listen. And John's listened at Holywell. I've seen him lying on his back on the lawn, watching the clouds go over, and listening, far more than either of us have ever had time to do, I guess.' He turned to her, and she thought the low evening light was suddenly unkind to him, deepening the lines. He looked tired, she thought, and when he said, 'Let's go home, shall we?' she nodded decisively and they walked back to the car, arms about each other, close like young lovers, 'playing tram-hosses', as he said.

She knew that to Henry she would always be young. It was as if in love's iris he kept a miniature of her, perpetually young, perpetually loved. It was not, she realized, the same for her. She felt she had never known Henry as a really young man: the Great War had wounded and matured him before she had properly seen him as an individual. She had thanked God for his age and for his limp when this war had started, and his ageing only seemed to make him more dear to her.

'I think I love you more each day, Henry, if that's possible.'

He looked at her steadfastly. 'I think perhaps we should be on our knees thanking God for each other, and for John. . . .'

'And remembering all the other sons, and people not so fortunate,' she added slowly.

Henry bought her a beautiful Sheraton writing-table and had it put near the window of the sitting-room, where she could write the diary and her letters to John. She wrote of Holywell, the business and of England – as far as the wartime censorship would allow. She told him how she had become involved with the work of the Women's Voluntary Services after the wife of one of Henry's titled hunting acquaintances had been approached by a London friend to form their county's first branch. Some of her WVS experiences were happy, even hilarious – the pie scheme for harvest workers, the sewing parties to camouflage the nets or the running of children's clothing exchanges. 'Children who grow quickly are a real problem with clothes rationing.' Other times when they were rebuffed when trying to find homes willing to accommodate evacuees, or when bus loads of tired and homeless people from bombing raids in Coventry arrived, the face of war on the home front was a little grimmer. But there were humorous moments even then. She wrote at length of the London family they thought would be permanent war guests at Holywell, but who had retreated from the horrors of the country, back to the blitz, as soon as they could. The woman had been found shaking with terror the first evening because she had *heard* a cow.

Great news was mingled with the small. She mentioned the loss of 3350 Canadians when Dieppe was raided, the German invasion of the Channel Islands, and the attempt by the Italian and German air forces to bomb the island of Malta out of existence. She went on to the winter Sunday evening she had been to church: 'I thought I had walked straight down the church path when, by the dim shuttered lights of a solitary car, I found I was within an inch of walking smack bang into the chruch wall!'

'Your father spends a lot of nights at the factory now, being responsible for the organization and supervision of the local fire-watchers in one large section of the city's factory area. It makes him look tired, and the night air certainly does his chest no good, but . . . it's the war! The local bakery has switched to the production of the 'national loaf', no more plaits and cottage loaves, it's all going to be like oblong bricks, (and dry at that!).

'D–Day. THE Day,' she wrote triumphantly on 6 June 1944. 'Our airborne troops have landed at the mouth of the Seine. The rescue of Europe has begun. Now we know what all the convoys throughout these summer nights have meant, and we know the reason for the huge formations of planes each towing two gliders, side by side, and looking most dangerously close. These pilots were practising for this huge drop of men. They say that 31,000 airmen have been over France during the day – no doubt some you have helped to train.' She knew from the tone of his letters to his father that while he was happy in Canada, a good half of him had wanted to be where the actual fighting was.

Once D-Day was over, the stream of pilots to be trained was stemmed and finally news came that John was to be posted back to England. He seemed, with undue haste, to write to say that he would in any case return to Canada as soon as his demobilization allowed.

Two weeks after Winston Churchill's victory speech to the nation on 8 May 1945, which followed Germany's unconditional surrender, Henry dropped the speech he was rereading, which was to be delivered to the Sixteenth Annual General Meeting of Attersley's Ltd', on to the sofa between them. 'What is it, Eleanor? What's happened to upset you so? You went very quiet after William telephoned last night. What is it?'

'I didn't want to tell you before your meeting,' she began, but now he had asked, she knew she would have to tell him. She also knew how he would feel, when she passed on the news William had telephoned with. 'John went to see William yesterday. . . .'

'John! He's home!' Henry interrupted.

'He . . . was.' She watched the same chill, the same first disbelief she had felt, pass over Henry's face. 'He came back to this country five days ago. His demob had apparently been pushed through quickly because he is to be employed by the Canadian government on special air-filming work. He . . . flew back to Canada yesterday.'

'Without coming to see us?'

'I could hardly believe it.' They were both very still, Eleanor unthinkingly straightening Henry's papers. Then their glances met, their eyes holding the same hurt. So great was their understanding of what the other felt, that there was no need for words, if indeed there were words to express their disappointment and desolation.

Eventually Henry rose and poured them both a drink. 'I suppose,' he said with a sigh, 'we shall just go on.' He picked up his papers. 'I shall say clever, heartening things tomorrow, about how, in spite of allocation of yarns, clothes rationing, fire-watching – and ungrateful sons – Attersley's Ltd marches profitably on.'

'Yes,' she agreed, her heart hard with disappointment, 'and we must look at some of the managers who have been with us through the war, and bear in mind those who *are* coming back, with a view to bringing new blood on to the board, and fairly quickly I should think.'

She was aware of Henry's sad interrogative glance as he agreed with her.

In the next six months Eleanor wrote to John just twice, she had not the heart to write more – or yet not to write at all. She and Henry became ever closer, more companionable than ever before, finding occasional relief in talking, being angry, or speculating about John.

'I suppose it doesn't matter how many, or how few children anyone has, in the end it is just the two of you again, just husband and wife,' Henry said after one such discussion.

'As long as *we're* together,' she agreed, 'that's the most important thing.'

'The most important thing in the world,' he agreed, clasping her hand with firm, warm tenderness.

Then came a letter from Canada addressed to them both. Eleanor held it in her hands, heart thumping. This was something special, or awful, she thought. She passed it to Henry, who opened it, and began to read aloud, 'Dear Both', then he stopped, silently taking in the contents. Then he looked up, handing over the letter. 'He's married, to a Canadian journalist. Apparently he fell for this girl and they had the opportunity to do a joint commission, articles and films on the forestry and fishing industries, so they just up and married, and are making the trip their honeymoon.'

'He says when they return if we would like to go and visit, they would be pleased to see us,' Eleanor read the end of the letter with disbelief. 'Go to see them. . . .'

'I'd rather have been invited to the wedding,' Henry said uncompromisingly. Suddenly overcome she turned away from him, quite unable to talk any more. 'Come on,' he said 'let's take that fat labrador for some exercise. By the time we come back, we'll know what we want to do.'

When they came back Henry sent two cables, one to John's Toronto apartment and one to the American-based film company he now worked for, both with instructions to forward. Both cables read the same:

CONGRATULATIONS. WHEN CAN WE COME AND MEET OUR DAUGHTER-IN-LAW?

They travelled to Toronto a month later, but the cable they sent advising John and Leone of their time of arrival was only delivered after they had found their own way to the apartment. They arrived on the elevator just as John was seeing off a business acquaintance, and not expecting to see them, he did not recognize them for a second or two. Then his face lit up. He shook Henry's hand heartily, and after a brief pause kissed Eleanor dutifully on the cheek.

'You're thinner,' she said, 'and you look much taller.'

'You,' he said quietly, 'look exactly the same.'

It was a start, but Eleanor saw in his eyes that she had not been forgiven, and indeed she felt he tolerated rather than enjoyed their visit.

Leone was beautiful, brilliant . . . and cold. 'The Snow Queen' Henry labelled her in private, and they returned to England full of foreboding for John's future happiness. The worst aspect of it had been to see the way John was so blindly obsessed. He hung on her every word, and sketched her incessantly.

Three years later, when John, subdued and seeming much older than his thirty-two years, had been to visit them twice, but Leone not at all because of professional commitments, there came the totally unexpected news that Leone was pregnant. 'This perhaps will be the answer, make her settle down,' Henry hoped.

Eleanor travelled to Toronto again as soon as her granddaughter, to be named Lois was born. She found her daughter-in-law interviewing nannies and planning to return to work, and a sweet-faced, fair-haired granddaughter. When Eleanor took the child into her arms, the tiny, still faintly sticky eyelids struggled to open, then seemed to try to focus. Looking down into the midnight blue eyes, dark with the knowledge of untellable sources, soon to be lost, it was as if each acknowledged the other as her own.

'Why, she's from Greg!' Eleanor thought wonderingly, raising her eyebrows at such a notion, and yet. . . . Yet she felt she must almost glow with love for this child, as she experienced a new union. All her instincts told her that this child completed her life circle, flawlessly.

She looked up to find John's eyes on her. She smiled at him and put the child into his arms.

17

Two years later it was with a sense first of shock, then of profound relief that Eleanor recognized John carrying the blonde-haired Lois as he climbed from the taxi at Holywell Manor.

She met him in the hallway and was stricken by his haggard appearance. The child too was tired and unkempt.

'Thank God you're here,' she said, kissing John's inclined cheek and taking the hot, sticky Lois into her arms.

'She's gone, Leone's gone,' John said, dropping exhausted into an armchair. 'Left us for good.'

'At last we know where we stand. When you get over the shock, it'll be a relief I should think.' Eleanor was deliberately businesslike, seeing the need of both for rest, not emotion.

'I'll never get over it,' John said quietly, 'whatever she is I. . . .'

Eleanor's lips parted in shock, realizing the full extent of his hurt, as John added quickly: 'She's living with another man. I found out ten days ago.'

John's distress, and Lois's fretful weariness, made coherent conversation impossible, and it was not until both had been fed, John re-established in his old room, and Eleanor sitting by Lois, holding the bemused child's hand in reassurance, that she had time to realize Lois's extraordinary resemblance to her true grandfather, Greg. The fair hair with the flick of a wave from the right of her forehead, and the courage in those dark, puzzled eyes.

'Where's my Daddy?' she had demanded persistently. Eleanor had carried her to John's room and shown her John sprawled on the bed in exhausted sleep. She had smiled conspiratorially at Eleanor. 'He's tired,' she whispered, and lowered her own head on to her grandmother's shoulder.

Henry came home to find Eleanor still holding the sleeping child's hand. He stood looking down at them both. 'Never mind,' he whispered, '*we* can see she is all right now.'

It was Henry who insisted John must obtain full legal guardianship of the child. 'We want no more heartbreaks, no more upset for the poor little mite. This is her home until you've something better for her.'

In a few short weeks Lois altered their lives, her bright hair bobbing here and there, her joyous cries of '*Here's* Gran and Pop!' made the thought of her ever leaving again, hard to dwell on. When Henry insisted on hiring a nanny and told Eleanor still to spend some time each week carrying on her business commitments, she knew it was sensible. Soon it was an established three mornings a week, and the rest of the time she spent at Holywell, joying in the house and gardens as she never had before. At last she planted her long planned alpine rock garden, Lois helping.

The one sadness for Eleanor was that John found it impossible to settle. He went back to Canada, and she was sure it was only to be nearby should Leone decide to return to him. Better fortune came with his job, and assured that his daughter was happy at Holywell, he took a prime post with a television network in Canada. His enthusiasm for his work was, they felt, the saving of him when twelve months later Leone took an overdose of sleeping tablets.

'The newspaper reports say it must have been accidental,' John wrote, 'but Leone was not so popular any more, and was losing assignments. I think she was sufficiently over-egotistical to regard this as the end.'

He came home more often after Leone's death. He started painting again, having set up a studio in a large third-storey room. One spring, for his birthday, Henry had it improved with extra skylights, ready for his next visit. Eleanor knew he hoped John would eventually stay and take an interest in the business, and she could not deny that John kept up to date with all the company's activities. She secretly hoped he would one day call her 'mother' and sound as if he was pleased!

She was aware, too, that her husband brooded about the future, wondering whether the business would be able to survive death duties should anything happen to him. 'I don't want to have worked all these years just to hand the biggest share over to the government,' he said. She knew he was bringing himself gradually to the decision that Attersley's must go public. His reluctance was that he might lose personal control, the guiding reins extending into more hands. He would be responsible to the impersonal, faceless shareholders who bought on the Stock Exchange.

One reason he was digging his heels in was, she thought, the perverse instinct he had to hold out against anything Bert Glover so persistently advised. She had tried to persuade Bert to let the matter rest a little, to give Henry time to come to terms with the idea, but Bert was difficult as always to quieten, and continually quoted accountants and stockbrokers. Henry, as persistently, refused to listen. She could never decide whether the life-long antipathy between them was because under the surface they were too alike, or too different. All they had in common was a spiky admiration for each other's skills.

As she could not imagine her life, or Attersley's, without Henry, her only concern was that he should reach a decision soon. They had already had many heated discussions on their evening walks. She had made the point that he knew the sensible answer, and was merely putting it off. He stalked ahead after that, and she stood and watched him go, thrashing at the wayside nettles with his walking-stick. For over a week he set off on his evening walk without asking her to go, and she had not attempted to follow, knowing that it was himself he had to convince, but she missed those hours together.

The following Monday, she had arranged to call at the factory with Lois after taking her to the cinema as a treat for her fifth birthday, so that Henry could take them home. They were later than they had anticipated and when they arrived at the factory, the gate-keeper was ready to lock up, and looking out for them. 'Mr Attersley said to take you up to the top floor. He's going round the new extension. Can't keep pace with them fully-fashioned nylons, can we, ma'am?'

'The demand seems to be increasing all the time, thank goodness,' Eleanor agreed, as he showed them to the lift.

'Can I work it, please?' Lois asked. 'I know how to do it.'

'We'll be all right, thank you,' she said to the gate-keeper and nodded to Lois, standing back as she closed the gates and pressed the button.

The new storey, built on to house more machines for the now vast nylon trade, smelled of paint and oil, a lighter, different smell altogether than the old wool knitting machines, she thought. Henry called to them from the far end of the department. Lois immediately began, what must have looked, a very long trek for her five-year-old legs, between the ranks of machines, which stood back-to-back in double rows. Each bank of machines had on a trial run of the hose half-completed, six dozen being knitted simultaneously along the sides of each walkway.

When Lois had almost reached Henry, he bobbed back out of sight, and she giggled and shouted, 'Grandpa', a stern reprimand in her voice. Never slow to take up her delight, Henry was quickly leading an hilarious game of hide-and-seek, and, as usual it was Eleanor who called a halt, for he had Lois screeching with excitement. After the traumas of 'Snow White and The Seven Dwarfs', and a large tub of ice-cream, she could well anticipate a feverish headache or an upset stomach.

She walked to where Henry stood, and was about to comment about the new department, when she saw a special light in his eyes as he showed Lois how the threads in the machines passed from spools to needles. 'There's the future,' he said straightening up, as Lois crouched fascinated to peer under the complexities of the knitting machines, 'that's what I've got to plan for.' He paused, then took a deep breath. 'I've decided, I'll call a special meeting of the directors for Friday.'

'Well, thank goodness for that, it's taken you long enough.'

'I know, I know,' he held up a pacifying hand, then extended it towards Lois. 'Come on, young lady.'

'Home?' Lois asked.

'Home,' Henry confirmed, nodding his contentment to Eleanor over the head of the child who grasped their hands.

Attersley & Company Limited, a public umbrella company for Attersley (Hosiery) Limited and Attersley (Men's & Boys' Wear) Limited, was floated six months later, and was very much over-subscribed, thanks to the history of steady growth and constant good figures they could publish.

The autumn of 1962 saw Henry Attersley a very contented man, particularly when he was approached to become master of foxhounds.

'I feel I've reached a pinnacle,' he told Eleanor one evening as he surveyed the garden from their bedroom window, the late roses in full colour, the trees still heavy with their summer's weight of leaves. 'My business is going exactly as I would want, my home life, you, Lois, Holywell. Now I just want John home, then I'd be glad to lean back for a bit . . . but life's pretty good.'

'Pretty good,' Eleanor confirmed, slipping an arm around his waist, and cuddling him.

'You only love me because I warm you,' he said pulling her round to him.

'Everyone should have at least one cuddle a day,' she

said, then laughed. 'I can remember one occasion when it definitely helped.'

'When?'

She paused for a moment, remembering. 'The first night after our wedding – at that hotel . . . do you remember that awful woman?'

'It was a different world,' he said reflectively, then looked at her with such tenderness, 'but the same girl.'

'You spoil me with your love, Henry, you always have.'

'Nothing's too good for you,' he said simply. 'Nothing.'

'Is this mutual admiration society ready for bed?' she asked.

'I've never needed asking *that* twice.'

'You never get any better,' she shook her head at him as he stood, finger raised like an impresario, waiting for two more words, 'thank goodness.' They went to their bed laughing at this favourite old piece of private patter, and with contented memories of greater passions, now spent.

Five weeks later, a sudden, early evening fall of snow created problems as Henry drove home. The roads had been wet earlier, then the temperature had dropped dramatically, then snow had fallen. He was four miles from home when the car skidded from his control and ended with two wheels in mid-air over a ditch. There was no alternative but to walk home, which in summertime would have been no particular ordeal, but the conditions were appalling and for every step forward, he seemed to slide two steps back. The wind was bitterly cold, and he was dressed for a ride home in a comfortable heated car, not for walking in arctic conditions.

The wind and cold air made him breathless, then when he was within sight of the lights of Holywell, the snow came again, a swirling blizzard of fine flakes. The shortness of breath became a tight, blinding pain across his chest. He felt desperately sick, and wet through with icy perspiration. He had to hang over a gate and rest, feeling the wind cutting through the fine wool of his overcoat and suit as if they did not exist.

When the pain and his breathing eased, he was so cold, and his blood-starved brain so bemused, he felt it would have been easier to stay where he was, sleep like they said arctic explorers did – but Eleanor would be wondering where he was. The thought roused him. The house lights swung dizzily before him as he forced one leg before the other. He fell forward on his front door, his hand grabbing the bell-pull as he slumped down.

Eleanor followed the doctor from the bedroom some four hours later. Henry was propped up in bed, sedated, sucking air shallowly through his mouth.

She gave Dr Browne a cup of coffee. He had become a friend since Lois had been with them, contracting the usual childhood illnesses.

'Sit down, my dear,' he said, handing back his cup. She sat, a chill that was not physical suddenly coming over her.

'What is it?'

'I'm afraid it is more than just the after-effects of a long, cold walk . . . there is some heart damage. Whether this struggle against the wind and snow has hastened it, or whether it would have happened anyway, we can't know, but I should like a specialist to see him – perhaps tomorrow afternoon if I can arrange it.'

Eleanor spent the night resting in an armchair by Henry's bedside, just once going into her granddaughter's room to watch the sleeping nine-year-old, thinking briefly of Greg and how short her time had been with him, and how many years had rolled by since then, and that it seemed that she and Henry had been together little longer, and she was fierce with the need for many more years.

She did not accept it was not to be, even when the specialist confirmed massive, irreparable heart damage, not really until pneumonia saw him in an oxygen tent set up over their bed.

She held his hand to the end, but there were no goodbyes and no return of consciousness as he slipped slowly away. Towards the end, the doctor removed the clear plastic tent, so there was nothing between them. Her eyes never left his face; she was with him, experiencing with him, and when she could not keep him, when his arms raised as if to ward off something, or someone, she stayed his hands and whispered to him. 'Don't fight it, Henry, don't make it harder.' Then his jaw relaxed in final surrender, her mind heard him say: 'Why are you looking down there? I'm up here.'

'Yes,' she silently answered, 'but I can't see you, Henry.'

It was the moment of separation, spirit from body, lover from loved one.

18

The bleakness of that separation was never completely to leave her. If Greg's death had left her bereft, this left her naked, vulnerable to a new bereavement whenever the memory was repeated, ever as sharp, ever as total.

After the formalities, it had been a relief to see Lois go back to school; the child had grieved too much – her eyes looked dark and hollow and she needed young company. John, who had arrived the day after Henry's death, wandered disconsolately, spending much time with her, but seeming involved in some private struggle about which he was reluctant to speak. She wondered if he was thinking of staying at Holywell permanently, but even when five weeks had gone by since Henry's funeral she felt unable to try to converse with him at any length, or to persuade him to stay. Perhaps, she thought, this was what was meant by losing one's will to live, certainly she had lost the energy to make any endeavour. Her life seemed like some wind-held thread which hovered precariously over an empty chasm. Her days were a haphazard darning up of time, a fragile web tended and persistently held on to by John, William, Edgar and Doris, by messages and letters from many friends and acquaintances.

John tried gamely to take the place of both of them in the business – as far as he was able. Often his role was mere messenger between the other managing directors and his mother, who, with the inheritance of Henry's interests, was controlling shareholder.

'They would all be pleased to see you back in harness,' John told her. 'They need a familiar face around the office, someone in absolute charge, particularly with these delicate wage negotiations going on. I think even father would be surprised how much he is missed.'

She remembered Henry's daily, good-humoured greetings to everyone, his cheerful capacity for work – the feeling that there was a captain at the helm when he was in his office – and was not surprised.

'I think you should go in,' John quietly persisted, 'Father would have wanted you to.'

What Father would have wanted . . . what Henry would have wanted. She felt the phrases were meaningless now that he had gone.

'Bert Glover asks after you all the time. He's really cut up about things, seems sort of lost, like an old bell that has lost its clapper. He has nothing to strike against any more.'

Then Bert and I have something in common, she thought, getting up and wandering out of the sitting-room, needing to be alone. Without being conscious of the direction she took, she found herself in the studio Henry had made for John. She was surprised to find it had been tidied up and there were folders and files she had not seen before, spread on the long bench. She wondered again if John was preparing to come home for good. If so she felt like telling him it was too late – too late for Henry – and she did not care what happened to herself now. In an uncharacteristic gesture of spying, she flipped open one of the box-files, and found herself recognizing her own handwriting. She looked closer, turned the corners of the pages to see her writing on every sheet, pushed her fingers to feel the depth of the pile of letters, then hastily closed the file. The dates she had glimpsed went back into the war. John, it seemed, had carefully kept every one of her letters. She left the room quickly, feeling suddenly and nervously the need to be out of doors, where she and Henry had solved so many of their problems.

She went out of the side door, through into the kitchen garden. The late February day was not cold, and she walked towards the seat under the protection of the wall. The basic herbs the garden boasted grew around the seat, and dead stalks of balm and shrivelled spires of the spearmint were protruding through the wooden slats. She never had made a real herb garden, collecting the rare and fragrant plants as she had always intended to do. Still feeling upset and tremulous after finding the letters, she began absent-mindedly breaking back the dead growth, tidying and clearing the way for new shoots, clearing the seat. It was with surprise that she recalled it had been with Greg she had planned the herb garden, not Henry.

She straightened and looked all around her – at the house, the spinney beyond the garden wall, to the church which defined another boundary. She thought of the lawns and paddocks flanking the front drive, all these she had watched Henry clear, plan and bring to life. She looked back to the small patch of herbs, at the dandelion which speared its leaves, ingratiating itself into a tiny bare patch. She bent quickly and dug at it with her fingernails. She would have it out!

'What are you doing?' John's voice startled her, but she did not look up.

'If this is where I shall end my days – I might as well have it as tidy as possible.' Her answer was abrupt as she fought and dug at the hard ground.

John knelt by her and his hand clasped hers, staying

the needlessly savage battle. It both startled her, and embodied her loss – the loss of the touch of a hand, the loss of every tenderness between man and woman. She looked up at her son, tears that had a yearning anger flooding her eyes.

'I'm not leaving again,' he said, 'my future's here with you and Lois. I . . . mother . . . I'm so sorry.'

His pain touched her, and she remembered what Henry had said about John having listened to the songs of Holywell. She put a hand on his arm, comforting, giving remission. 'He always knew you would come back,' she said.

Three days later she went into town and ran the gauntlet of sympathy (tears from the women office-workers) to Henry's office. She sat at his desk, where there was a pile of papers awaiting attention, and felt terribly alone. She didn't begin to make even a physical filling of the chair. There was a tap at the door, and to her bidding Bert Glover came in. He carried a further sheaf of papers towards the desk. She was shocked at his appearance. He looked ravaged and stammered his greeting. He looked an old man. Bert, of all people . . . .

'You and John taking over.' It was more a statement of his own urgent need than a question. 'It's what he'd want.'

'Yes,' she repeated his words slowly. 'It's what he'd want.' They looked at each other a moment longer, a moment filled with memories of cobbled yards, dray-horses, fire, disaster, hard work and success, and of the verbal battles between the two men, and now their mutual loss.

She held out her hand for the papers he carried and for an instant, she thought he was going to cry but instead he muttered: 'About time' and left her office. It seemed they would carry on the folklore of Attersley's, the chivvying, surface-irritability of Bert Glover versus the rest of the management.

It was some time later, when she was almost halfway through the neglected paperwork, that she remembered how she had scrubbed out her father's cottage after Greg's death. She had not changed so much over the years, like her mother there was still the capacity to do 'a bootlace job'.

Also in Hamlyn Paperbacks

Brenda Clarke

ALL THROUGH THE DAY

At the dawn of the century pride and money clash . . . and deep-rooted passions last for generations.

A feud between two wealthy families rages across the wildly beautiful countryside of Dartmoor.

The Reads are respectable Nonconformist shopkeepers; the Hunnicutts dark and stormy High Church landowners. But love – and greed – constantly cross the battle lines, adding new disputes to the old hostility. Until Emily Culverhayes, who marries first a Read and then a Hunnicutt, finds herself at the centre of a terrifying web of powerful emotions, intrigue and murder.

Also in Hamlyn Paperbacks

Angela Thirkell

WILD STRAWBERRIES

A delightful classic of the Thirties

David Leslie is utterly irresistible . . . or so he seems to Mary Preston, who is spending an enchanted summer with his rich, eccentric family.

For David dances divinely, plays and sings all the latest jazz hits, and is planning to produce a best-selling novel.

Also he has promised to take Mary to a place in town where they serve wild strawberries.

So life seems totally idyllic. Until David brings a rival along to the restaurant – a horrid young woman who has been to college and does something in broadcasting.

Then the ruffled feathers fly . . .

'A novel of laughter with just enough sincere emotion . . . I have never recommended a novel about which I felt so certain that everybody would enjoy every page of it' – Sir Compton Mackenzie